W9-AZT-396

The
BLIND FAITH
HOTEL

# *The* BLIND FAITH HOTEL

PAMELA TODD

MARGARET K. MCELDERRY BOOKS
NEW YORK LONDON TORONTO SYDNEY

Margaret K. McElderry Books
An imprint of Simon & Schuster Children's Publishing Division
1230 Avenue of the Americas, New York, New York 10020

Book design by Krista Vossen
The text for this book is set in Fournier.
Manufactured in the United States of America
2 4 6 8 10 9 7 5 3 1
Library of Congress Cataloging-in-Publication Data
Todd, Pamela.
The blind faith hotel / Pamela Todd.—1st ed.
p. cm.
Summary: When her parents separate and she and her siblings move with their mother from the Northwest coast to a Midwest prairie farmhouse, fourteen-year-old Zoe, miserably unhappy to be away from the ocean and her father, begins to develop a deep attachment to her new surroundings, when, after a shoplifting episode, she is assigned to work at a nature preserve.
ISBN-13: 978-1-4169-5494-1 (hardcover)
ISBN-10: 1-4169-5494-5 (hardcover)
[1. Family problems—Fiction. 2. Prairies—Fiction. 3. Nature—Fiction. 4. Interpersonal relations—Fiction. 5. Coming of age—Fiction.] I. Title.
PZ7.T56685Bl 2008
[Fic]—dc22
2007043912

*For all things wild and beautiful. May they endure.*

*There are so many people whose stories are woven into this one. I am grateful for the opportunity to say thanks to Michael Gifford, with deepest gratitude for his devotion to all things wild, and for generously sharing his journeys; the Ragdale Foundation for a window on the prairie; Toni Hunter for giving me a glimpse of her world; Jo Ellen Siddens for her contagious love of nature and expert knowledge; Audrey Brown and Lynn Gifford for a lifetime of modeling grace and faith; Donn, Justin, Jessica, Katie, and Megan, the loves of my life; Elizabeth Berg, Veronica Chapa, Nancy Horan, Michele Weldon, Joan and Russ Fee, Patti Cone, Judy Dooley, David Jakubiak, Janet Nolan, Sallie Wolf, and Esther Hershenhorn, whose writing enriches all of mine; Bruce Modahl, Phyllis Kersten, and Jill Baumgaertner for reading and offering insight; Maureen Sauvain for listening and caring; Erin Malone for enthusiastic shepherding of this book; Karen Wojtyla for her deep editorial wisdom; Bara MacNeill for her keen eye; Sarah Payne for her assistance; and to the memory of my grandparents, Emma and George Brown and Marie and Robert Warnimont, my aunt Ethelyn Ledoux, and my father, George Lawrence Brown Jr., with understanding and peace.*

"Not at every moment of our lives, Heaven knows, but at certain rare moments of greenness and stillness, we are shepherded by the knowledge that though all is far from right with any world you and I know anything about, all is right deep down. All will be right at last."

—Frederick Buechner, *The Clown in the Belfry*

# CHAPTER 1

The last time Zoe saw her father, he was out on the water, drifting away.

The last time. Was it? Things were uncertain. She could never be sure.

This is what she knew for a fact: She'd been lying awake, staring out her window at the moonless dark, when her father came to tell her it was time to go. She pulled on a fleece jacket over the T-shirt and sweatpants she'd worn to bed and went down the hall to throw cold water on her face. They were waiting for her, all of them, outside in the car with the motor running, white smoke rising like a ghost in the blue-black sky.

They drove the curving road along the bay in silence. Her mother and father were in the front seat of their old red Subaru station wagon. Zoe sat in the middle in back, where she always sat, with her seventeen-year-old sister, Nelia, and six-year-old brother, Oliver, on either side of her. She looked past them, peering through the mist-soaked windows at the blurry world, trying to drown out her thoughts by listening to the creak and moan of the windshield wipers. The lights from the cars that passed them on the road were like eyes that searched the darkness.

When they reached the terminal, they turned off and took their place behind a line of cars waiting at the ticket booth. It was too foggy to see the boat coming in, but they could hear its mournful horn sounding as they drove down the hill to the dock.

The man in the booth leaned out the window, grinning behind a thick gray beard, as their station wagon pulled up. “Going back up to Alaska, Daniel?”

Zoe’s father pulled out his wallet and handed the man a stack of bills. “Yep. Bundle of crabs up there this year, Jim.”

“Well, I hope you get your share before they close the season down.” Jim counted the bills, snapping them down on the counter. “Just one, then?”

“Just one,” her father said, “unless you kids want to come along and freeze your tails off too.” He tossed the words over his shoulder, but did not look back at them.

Jim slapped a ticket into Zoe’s father’s rough palm. Jim glanced over at Zoe’s mother. “Annie, you call if you need any help.”

She turned her face to him and nodded. Her smile was as fragile as blown glass.

“You don’t deserve her. You know that, don’t you?”

“I know it, Jim.” Her father put the car into gear.

“You kids mind your mother, you hear?” the man called out to the solemn faces in the backseat.

Zoe’s father parked the car, and they walked to the end of the ramp with their father and a line of other foot passengers waiting to board, hoods pulled up over their heads, their shoulders hunched against the damp chill. Waiting: This was the part Zoe knew how to do, the part played over and over by the one left behind. "Good-bye" was the first word she'd learned. For as long as she could remember, her father would leave their home in the San Juan Islands several times each year and make the long journey up to Alaska to catch crabs or halibut or salmon.

They never knew for certain when he would come back. If the fishing was poor, the boats might stay out for months at a time, until they'd earned their wages. A good catch, and he would be home sooner, happy, laughing, and with plenty of money to spend on them.

But this time was different. This time, when he finally came back, his face tanned and polished as a stone, tired, lonesome, and ready to sleep, they would be gone.

They stood together on the pier, seagulls wailing and diving down around them. Oliver ran after the birds, and Zoe reached out to pull him back to the safe center.

"Watch out," Zoe said, reeling him in. "You're too near the edge."

Oliver swooped in the other direction as soon as she let go of him.

Her father wrapped an arm around Zoe and she leaned into him, trying to memorize his face. It was an old habit, something she fell into every time he left, as though she could keep him safe by burning his image into her mind. He had a boy's face, wind-burned and weathered like all the fishermen, but with an easy smile and keen blue eyes. He was slight, but with surprising strength in the muscled arm that held her. When she was little, she thought he was a giant who could do anything. Now she saw that he was a man of ordinary height, his face lined with worry.

Nelia sat down on a wooden bench, facing the water, hugging herself. It was so cold you could see her breath puffing out under the hood of her blue Windbreaker. Their mother stood off to the side.

The ferrymen waved the last of the cars into position on the back of the boat, then made a final call for passengers. Oliver sailed over, and his father encircled him with a rough hug. "Be good, Liver," he said.

Oliver threw his arms around his father's neck and held on until he had to be gently pried loose.

"I don't want you to go." His voice wobbled at the edge of tears.

"Got a job to do, Ollie. Some big ole granddaddy crabs out there are just waiting to crawl into my net." Their father made his hands into pincers and pretended to nip off Oliver's nose.

"You could change your mind," Zoe said. She squared her body at him. "You could come with us."

Her father's eyes hooked hers. "Don't make this harder than it has to be, Zo."

She turned her face away and stared out at the water.

Her mother stepped between them and took hold of Ollie's hand. "She's not the one making this hard, Daniel." Ollie leaned away from her, reaching his other arm out toward his father, but he couldn't span the distance between them.

"It's my fault, isn't it, Annie? It's always me," her father said. "Well, I'm not the one who's taking off and not coming back."

"I'm not going to stand by and let them be hurt by you."

"And you don't think there's a world of hurt in what you're doing to them?" He kicked at an empty bottle, sending it rolling and twisting away. "Damn it, Annie. I'm their father."

Her mother's face tightened.

"Stop!" Nelia got up from the bench as though someone had yanked her. "I can't stand you two doing this any longer."

Zoe glanced nervously at the ferry crouched under the gray sky and the dwindling line of passengers. She didn't want her father to go. But she wanted the pain to leave. She wanted to go back and start over, and she wanted all of this to end. She didn't know what she wanted anymore.

They were closing the gates and getting ready to pull up the ropes. Zoe thought her mother was going to say something, but instead she took Ollie's hand, wheeled around, and walked toward the row of cars on the other side of the terminal.

Nelia sighed and pulled the zipper on her coat up tighter. She went over and kissed her father on the cheek. "I'll miss you," she said. Then she turned and walked back toward the car, leaving only Zoe and her father, standing like sentinels on the line between the past and the future.

"Zoe?" Her father said her name as though there were a question attached to it. But she did not answer him. She stared at the ground, unable to lift her eyes for the weight they carried.

She could feel her father looking at her. They were connected like that. He was the one person who would always listen to her, the one she could go to with all of her questions. Some people gave you answers the way doctors passed out suckers, just to keep you quiet. But her father wasn't like that. She knew she could ask him anything.

Anything. Even the question that was wearing away at the inside of her skull: "Why are you letting her take us away from you?"

"Hey, McKenna." One of the ferrymen called down to them from the deck as he hauled in the ropes. "You going to Alaska or not?" The horn sounded again.

her kissed her on the forehead. Then he picked up bag at his feet and slung it over his shoulder. "I love . That's yours to keep. No matter what."

e wanted to say, "I love you, too. Don't die. Come back to us." She wanted to say, "You don't love us. Not really. Not enough." But she said nothing.

Her father walked slowly up the ramp and onto the boat. Zoe remembered something. She bolted for the parking lot, fumbled with the car door, and reached into the backseat for the sign she had made the night before.

Then she ran, breathless, nearly slipping on the wet slats, all the way to the end of the pier. The boat was pulling away. She stood in the mist, holding her hand-lettered sign up, hoping her father could see it. There was a deafening noise as the engines fired up, churning the water and spitting sludge.

Zoe stood alone on the dock, watching the space grow between them. Her father was on the top deck now looking back at her. She saw him lean out over the rail, cup his hand over his mouth, and call something out to her, but she couldn't hear him because of the rumbling of the boat and the wind.

"Wait." She heard Oliver's voice, and looked back to see him scrambling toward the end of the pier. His eyes were set on the ferry. He would have run right off the edge of the dock if a workman in an orange reflector vest hadn't reached out with one arm to block him, and now he struggled to get loose.

Zoe dropped the sign and threw her arms around Ollie. The workman looked down at them. His eyes were full of pity, and she resented it.

"What's the matter, Ollie?"

He was crying and had to sputter out the words. "Booda's gone."

"No, he's not, Ollie. He's in the way back. I saw him there."

"I put him in Daddy's bag. So he wouldn't be lonely."

"No, Ollie."

"I want him."

The air was so thick, Zoe felt as though she were choking on it. "It's too late," she said.

"Make the boat come back."

"We'll get you another bear."

"I only love Booda." He buried his face in Zoe's shoulder, and she held him close.

Nelia and her mother came striding across the pier.

Zoe turned on Nelia. "You were supposed to watch him."

"I don't see why you're making such a big deal out of it. He's all right, isn't he?"

"Like you would care."

"Shut up, Zoe."

"You shut up."

Her mother bent down and held Ollie by the shoulders. "What's wrong?" she asked.

Ollie tried to answer her, but his words were smothered by sobs.

"It's Booda," Zoe said over the top of her brother's head. "Ollie put him in Dad's bag."

"Oh, Oliver," their mother sighed.

They stood together at the end of the pier, watching the disappearing boat. Ollie's weeping faded into a quiet sniffling. He wiped his moist, red face on his sleeve. Their mother put an arm around him and guided him back toward the car.

Zoe went over to pick up her sign and hugged it to her chest.

Nelia tipped the sign back so she could read it. "You spelled it wrong," she said.

"What?" Zoe looked at the letters on the front of her sign. The black ink was running in the rain.

"Bon voyage," Nelia said. "It's b-o-n, not b-o-n-e."

Nelia thought she knew everything.

# CHAPTER 2

The movers came early the next morning while Oliver was still in his pajamas sitting on the cold wooden floor, watching cartoons and eating cornflakes out of a paper bowl. Zoe was in the kitchen, wrapping dishes in the "Help Wanted" section of the *Seattle Post-Intelligencer*, something she'd promised her mother she'd do all week and had never done. She was making a big deal of it, slamming cabinets and crumpling paper as she crammed everything into a box they had found behind the Safeway. It was bad enough that they had to move so far away. Why should she be the one doing all the work? It was like being forced to dig your own grave.

The television chattered in the background, interrupted every now and then by a cascade of giggles. Oliver's laugh was like water. It soothed her somehow, made her feel like things weren't falling apart after all.

The rumble of a truck in front and the slamming of doors drew her out to the living room. She stared through the picture window, still holding a wrapped mug. There were two men standing on the front porch, both in navy blue work shirts. One was tall, with red hair fading to gray. The other was short, stocky, and dark. Zoe twisted the lock on the door and opened it.

"Yes," she said.

The big man smiled, and his mustache went along for the ride. It was shaped like a whisk broom and was a surprising shade of orange, much brighter than the close-cropped hair on his head.

"Gooooood mornin', sunshine. You must be Nelia."

"Zoe."

He shook his head and rested his big hands on his hips. "My mistake. Your mom told us all about you. Zoe; you're the twelve-year-old."

"Fif*teen*," said Zoe. Almost. She was fourteen. But why tell him? He didn't want to know her.

"That so? Well, nice to meet you. I'm Al. That there's Ray." He pointed a thumb back over his shoulder at the short man behind him, who smiled at her, took off his hat, and smoothed his dark, poorly cut hair. There were damp circles under his arms. He was wearing one of those thick black belts around his waist, support hose for the back. She didn't like either one of the men.

"We come to help you move some things into that U-Haul out there."

Zoe stone-faced them. She was good at playing dumb.

"We're friends of your mom's."

"Friends?" Zoe said.

"From down at the café," he explained. "Flounder Bay," he added, when she said nothing. "On Commercial Avenue."

"I *know* where my mom works."

The big man stared down at her. He had huge freckled arms, bursting from the short sleeves of his shirt. There was wiry red hair crawling all over his thick neck and barrel chest.

She didn't want to let them in. They didn't belong. Her mother had had no right to tell them to come. Zoe stood in the doorway, a seawall in a storm, trying to hold back the wave of the future.

"My mom's not here," she lied.

"Maybe we should wait outside . . . until she comes back," the short man said.

At least *he* had some manners. Zoe watched the big man's eyes look past her into the living room.

"Al?" She heard her mother's voice and turned to see her coming out of the hallway from the bedroom. "I thought that was you and Ray. C'mon in. I see you've met Zoe."

"Yes indeed," Al said.

Zoe had to unwrap a pair of mugs so her mother could pour stale coffee left over from breakfast. Al and Ray seemed to thrive on the stuff. They hunched at the counter in the kitchen, hefty bottoms spilling over the backs of their stools, and downed several bitter black cups and made small talk with her mother, while Zoe watched them all out of the corner of her eye. After they drank the coffee down to the dregs, they set to work, storming through each room, pillaging and plundering, sweeping up everything in their path.

Zoe's mother paced back and forth through the house, choosing what made it into the lifeboat and what got pitched overboard. "Yes, this. No, that. Maybe, but wait until the end and see if we have room."

In between, she barked orders. "Ollie, turn the television down. I can't hear myself think. Where's Nelia? I sent her into town hours ago. Zoe, is that cabinet empty yet?"

She checked boxes and furniture off a list on a yellow legal pad as Al and Ray lumbered by with tables and dressers strapped to a hand truck. She was a great maker of lists of things that never got accomplished. You could tell she was taking pleasure in finally getting something done, even if it *was* dismantling their lives.

Her blond hair was held back with a clip, and she was wearing blue jeans and one of Zoe's father's plaid shirts, with the sleeves rolled up. She was one of those women who looked like she could have been pretty if she had taken the time to work at it a little. She wore makeup, which she usually did only if she was leaving the house, but it had been spoiled by the smudges of newsprint all over her face.

Zoe looked like her father—blue eyes, tawny skin, and hair the color of mink. She smelled just like him too, her mother told her, like wind and salt. She was short, but lean and strong. People often took her for a swimmer or a dancer. But the truth was, her body had been shaped by climbing rocks, wading through rivers, and paddling kayaks. She hated being inside.

Nelia looked exactly like her mother: same small features, fair skin, and blond hair, but there was a spark of something in Nelia that made her beautiful, and in her mother it was a light that had gone out. Zoe's mother and father had gotten married in the chapel at Fishermen's Terminal on her mother's eighteenth birthday. So she wasn't that old, but she seemed tired and wrung out. And there was a sadness about her, even now, especially now, as she stood in front of each piece of furniture, deciding its fate, or bent down to seal the boxes and write their futures in black Magic Marker.

She stopped now and then to stare out a window or rest against the wall and close her eyes. Sometimes she would pick up something and turn it over in her hands, as though she were trying to remember something about it. She got quieter as the morning wore on; even ordering people around seemed like too much effort for her. Zoe might have felt sorry for her if she hadn't been the one who was ruining all of their lives.

Zoe looked away from her mother at the vacant, stained walls. "I'm going to make lunch," she said, her voice echoing in the hollow room. She wasn't trying to be nice. She just couldn't stand to watch.

All that was left in the refrigerator was a lonely jar of strawberry jam with dried-up crust around the cap and some forlorn vegetables pushed to the back of the crisper and forgotten. It made Zoe want to cry just to look at them, foods that were like the last people picked in gym class or the girls who were never asked to dance.

She flopped some limp celery onto the counter, along with the jam, a half-eaten jar of peanut butter, a loaf of bread, and a package of cupcakes her father had bought before he left. Her mother would always send Zoe or Nelia to the store with one of her famous lists and tell them they could buy only what was on it. And even then the items had to be on sale. But her father went up and down the aisles with them, throwing things into the cart, not even looking at the prices or worrying about whether they already had one at home.

When she was younger, Zoe often felt sorry for herself on those days when everyone else's parent showed up for an open house or a science fair at her school, and she had to go alone because her father was fishing and her mother was working nights. She was always the one who was assigned another parent and child to stroll the halls with her; she was a spare sock in a drawer full of pairs.

But when her father was home, he did everything with her. He took Zoe down to the boatyard while her mother worked on Saturdays, and he let her help sand the decks and shine the brass fittings on his boat. He took her hiking in the mountains, taught her how to tie knots that wouldn't come undone, and gave her spending money if she helped repair his nets. When they'd lived in Seattle, he had taught Zoe and some of her friends of the moment to knit.

"Come back tomorrow," he had called to them as they left. "I'll teach you how to purl." Then he'd told Zoe, "Heck, I'm even man enough to crochet."

He called himself "the new mom in town." Once he had answered the door wearing a lacy apron. The salesman had asked for the lady of the house. "You're looking at her, mister," he'd said with a wicked grin.

People loved her father. He was a walking party. He made everything fun. And he had courage. That was the thing about him. He wasn't afraid.

Zoe was digging the last bit of peanut butter out of the jar when Nelia walked in. She'd been in town, returning the house keys to their landlady.

"Took you long enough."

"I stopped at Tyler's. You didn't expect me to leave without saying good-bye, did you?"

"You were out with him last night. Couldn't you have said good-bye then?"

"Actually, I was out with Mason. We took his boat out to see the sunset off Deception Pass."

"What if Tyler finds out?"

"We're leaving anyway. What's for lunch?"

Zoe offered her a piece of celery, which drooped as she held it out to her.

Nelia pushed it away with a disgusted look on her face. "No, thanks. I don't eat anything without a backbone." She lifted the lid on the container of sandwiches and closed it again, then sniffed the air, wrinkling her nose and looking perplexed. "What's that smell?"

Zoe tilted her head to the side. "Al and Ray."

Nelia walked off toward the bathroom. Zoe could hear someone rummaging through the boxes in the hallway, followed by a sound like air coming out of a tire. Then her mother's voice: "Nelia, what are you doing with that Lysol spray?"

Ollie came into the kitchen and then left, pouting, when Zoe told him he couldn't have a cupcake. He looked lonely and confused, a lost boy. She was putting their lunch into the cooler when she heard him screaming and ran into the living room. Al was standing in the corner, red-faced with effort. He had the television in his arms and he was listing to one side, nearly falling over, trying to shake Ollie off his leg.

"Let go," Al puffed. "I'm gonna drop it."

"It's mine," Ollie howled. His face was wet with tears and his mouth was jagged. He was sitting on Al's foot and had both arms wrapped around his leg, while the big man staggered backward.

"Stop it, Ollie!" Zoe peeled his fingers off one at a time and dragged him screaming back toward the doorway. She fell down, and Oliver collapsed on top of her, sitting in a heap in her lap, his face buried in her T-shirt, crying.

Al let the TV drop to the floor with a bang and lifted up his pant leg. There was a red gash on his hairy shin. "That kid bit me," he said.

Zoe glared at him. "What did you expect?"

Al's big face was drenched in sweat. "So, this is what I get for trying to help."

Oliver quivered in Zoe's arms. He was just a little kid. How could anyone expect him to understand what was going on? He probably thought Al was the robber everyone always warned you about, the one who would break into the house if you answered the phone and forgot to lie and tell him your mother was in the shower, when the truth was she was working at the café and wouldn't be back for hours, so there was plenty of time to kill everyone in the house.

"I want Daddy," Oliver cried. "I want him to come back."

Zoe's mother burst through the open front door. "*Now* what happened?" she asked, half question, half accusation.

"He sunk his teeth into me," Al groused.

Oliver glowered at him, David facing down Goliath. "My daddy's going to spank you when he gets back." He got to his feet and ran from Zoe's lap to his mother's legs. "When is he coming?"

His mother bent down to hold him. "We'll have to see, Ollie."

"When he's caught enough fish?"

"I don't know, Ollie." Her shoulders sagged with the weight of him. "I don't know."

"Why don't you?"

"There are things we have to work out."

"Why?" he sobbed. He threw his head back and bawled the same word over and over until the whole house was filled with it: "Why? Why?"

"Ollie, please stop crying."

"N*oooo*."

"Please, Ollie." She took hold of his shoulders. "Please!"

Ollie arched his back and spread his arms wide, something wounded and broken, spiraling down in a free fall. "Why isn't he coming back?" he wailed.

His mother adjusted her grip, struggling to keep him from slipping away. "I told you, there are things to work out," she said, her voice heavy with despair. "He's got some demons to fight."

Oliver stopped wailing. He plugged his mouth with his finger and chewed on it, his breath coming in short gasps that shook his whole body. "I fight demons," he said.

An uneasy silence settled in the room. There was rain coming in through the open doorway. It was always raining, always gray and stormy. Outside, the U-Haul waited on the drenched street. Al had slipped out the door, and was standing next to the station wagon, showing Ray his scars.

Zoe looked at her mother. She had her cheek pressed down onto Oliver's head, her body absorbing the waves of quiet sobs that rose and fell in him. "You should have told him the truth," Zoe said.

Her mother looked at her wearily. "And what exactly is the truth?"

"You don't love him. That's why you're leaving. You don't love any of us." Zoe turned her back on her mother and walked away.

When they had finished lugging the suitcases out to the car, Zoe went back inside one last time. She walked down the hallway and stood in the doorway of her room. There were light spots, like ghosts, on the floor where the rugs and furniture had been. And there was a dark blank square on the yellow wall with a Scotch tape mark above it where her favorite poster had hung, a picture of an Alpine meadow, avalanche lilies and Indian paintbrush, at the top of Mt. Rainier. You had to get there at just the right time to see the flowers. At such high altitudes the season was short, one small chance to bloom and then it was over.

Zoe tried to remember what her room had looked like when they'd arrived, but she couldn't. For the first time, it occurred to her that someone else had lived in that room before she had, and they had left no mark. Someone would come and paint over their lives in this house too. It would be as though they had never been there, never even existed.

Her mother came up behind her, her footsteps echoing in the empty room. She put a hand lightly on her back, but Zoe shrugged it off.

"I know you won't believe me," she said, "but I wish it didn't have to be this way."

"You don't mean that. If you did, you wouldn't leave Dad. He needs us. Can't you see that? Something terrible could happen to him without us. You don't know what will happen."

"No, I don't. I don't know what will happen to him. But I know I have to take care of you, and this is the only way I know how. We have a chance for another life, and I have to take it, as much for your sake and Nelia and Oliver's as for mine."

"That's a lie," Zoe lashed out at her, tears flooding down finally, tears that she knew would never stop. "This isn't for me. This isn't what I want."

Zoe held the back door of the Subaru open, waiting for Ollie to squeeze in beside the cooler and the bags of clothes that wouldn't fit in the way back. She took one last look at the house, a clapboard yellow cottage that sat in the middle of a row of other houses that faced the bay, lined up shoulder to shoulder like mismatched soldiers, each slightly different in color and style.

They had lived so many places, all along the coast from Bellingham to Seattle. The hangdog places they usually rented looked like no one really cared about them. They had rings around the toilet bowls that wouldn't come off, cracked plaster, and things that no one ever fixed. But this house seemed like a place you could be happy. This house had the look of permanence about it.

There was a view of the water from the bedroom on the second floor. The house was within walking distance of Snapper Steinman's grocery store. And there was a garden in front, with rhododendrons and rosebushes, enclosed by a white picket fence. She and her mother had planted tulip bulbs there in the fall.

But they would never see them come up. That was the thing about leaving. Your dreams were another thing that didn't fit into the car.

When they drove away, Nelia was in the front seat where her father should have been. Oliver reluctantly stopped squirming so Zoe could buckle his seat belt. By the time she turned around again, their house had disappeared. Just like that. Even the things that are solid and dependable in your life can go away in an instant.

They stopped at the marina on the way out of town to drop off two duffle bags of their father's clothes. Their mother went inside, while Nelia pulled the bags out and set them on the ground next to the car. It seemed like so little for a grown man to accumulate in his life.

"I feel like we should be leaving him more," Zoe said.

"Like what," Nelia asked. "A child maybe?"

"You're mean to the bone, aren't you?"

"It's what you were thinking, wasn't it? I don't like this any more than you do, Zoe. But you can't go on forever fighting a losing battle."

Zoe looked out at the boats rocking in their slips. "We shouldn't be leaving. We belong here."

Nelia shrugged. "Not anymore," she said. "We've got a new neighborhood: reality. If I were you, I'd move in and get used to it."

Zoe was the only one who turned around as they drove out of town. Oliver had fallen asleep. Nelia had her headphones on and was leaning against the headrest. Her mother had her eyes riveted on the road ahead. The last thing Zoe saw was the estuary. There were two herons fishing there, standing like statues, endlessly patient, waiting to spear something. She often watched them circling near the cliffs in Washington Park. One took to the air as the car drove by, beating its huge wings, neck curled and long legs dragging behind it. She tracked it for a long time, thinking it might loop back, but it just kept stroking northward and finally faded into the slate sky.

# CHAPTER 3

They were supposed to follow a schedule that told them who got to sit in the front seat. Their mother had written it down on her yellow legal pad, designing it, she claimed, around everyone's unique needs and personalities. Nelia would have the first part of the day because she was surly in the mornings—even more than usual. After lunch Nelia was supposed to switch places with Zoe, who by that time wouldn't be able to stand another minute cramped in the backseat with Ollie using her legs as a racetrack for matchbox cars. If they were still driving after supper, Ollie would move up, so he wouldn't whimper as much about Dad and Booda not being there.

The systems Zoe's mother came up with were always breaking down. She drove them crazy with her attempts to create order in some little corner of their lives. Once, she had bought them different-colored underwear to make it simpler to sort the laundry. She had alphabetized all the cereal boxes, and organized the medicine chest by category of disease. "Colds here, stomach flu there, insect bites and sunburn in the back: It only makes sense." That's what she always said. It didn't seem to matter to her that things always went to pieces again. It was the act of trying to put them together that soothed her somehow.

The seat schedule was doomed before it ever got started, because everyone but their mother thought it made no sense at all. Nelia thought the schedule should have been designed around birth order, which meant that she would get the front seat all of the time. She claimed it was hers by divine right. The prime real estate belonged to the oldest in the family.

Zoe thought the schedule should have been designed around talents. She was the only one who should sit in the front because, unlike Nelia, Zoe could read a map.

Nelia, being a realist, freely admitted that Zoe should be the navigator. It only made sense. "But why can't you just sit in the back and yell directions from there?"

It was Zoe's father who had taught her how to find her way in the world. He'd showed her how to read the tide charts and the well-worn folio of maps he kept stashed in the cabin of his boat. She learned how to read the symbols that helped you steer clear of hidden shoals and dangerous currents and how to tell one island from another by the shape of its inlets and bays and its place in the overall pattern. It was a matter of survival. Weather changes. Fog floats in. The shoreline fades in and out. And sometimes things happen that you don't expect. You had to know how to keep out of trouble, how not to get lost.

He knew how to use radar in the fog and a GPS to track his course. But he taught Zoe that you couldn't rely on them completely. Machines break, boats go down, and instruments go with them.

"You have to know the old ways," he told her. "Things any animal knows, but we've forgotten. It's the old ways that'll keep you alive out there someday, Zoe. You mind that."

There was a feeling to it. Some people were born with the knack of it. But even if you weren't, you could learn some of it. Pay attention. Notice which way the waves are breaking, how the water's colored, which way the birds are flying, where the sun and moon rise and set.

"And don't think you know it because someone else told you, Zoe." Her father told her time and time again. "If you can't feel it in your own bones, by God, it's not true."

Her mother put all her faith in maps. She always kept a Rand McNally road atlas with a black vinyl binding in the glove compartment of the Subaru. Each page was a map of a different state.

Before her mother had even told them about the move, Zoe had sometimes woken up in the middle of the night and caught a glimpse of her sitting at the dining room table, bent over the atlas, enclosed by the triangle of light that fell from the lamp above her head. Now Zoe understood why. Her mother had been marking the route they would take back East with a yellow line, which snaked from one side of each page to the other.

The excuse her mother had given for moving them halfway across the country, was this: She was going to make a bed-and-breakfast out of the run-down house she'd inherited in Selena, the town back in the Midwest where she'd grown up. That way they'd not only have a place to live, but they'd also have some money coming in. She was tired of working long hours for low pay to make other people's dreams come true. She wanted her own dream. *Her* dream.

It wasn't going to work, of course.

"Who's going to want to stay at this bed-and-breakfast, anyway?" Nelia asked. "Dysfunctional families like ours? It's hard enough for us to live with each other. What makes you think strangers will want to live with us?"

They knew everything there was to know about leaving. The method was always the same. Only the reasons were different.

They had moved from Coupeville to Forks when Zoe's father had gotten an off-season job at the lumber mill, and they'd moved to Seattle when the job had dried up. They packed up and went to Bellingham because Zoe's mother found a waitress job with good tips, then they moved to Anacortes. When they fell behind on their rent payments, the owner of the café where their mother worked offered to let them live in the rental house she owned at a reduced rate, at least until they got back on their feet or a new tenant turned up. Unfortunately the tenant showed up before their feet did, and they had to move again.

There had always been a good reason for leaving. But this time it didn't feel like they were leaving. It felt like they were running away.

"I'm hungry," Oliver said.

"Fifty-seven," Zoe said. She was counting the number of times Ollie asked if they could stop.

"We just ate," his mother said.

"You mean the sandwiches Zoe made before we left? That

was a sad excuse for a meal," Nelia said. It was her turn to sit in the back. It made her regress.

"I'd like to see you do better," Zoe snapped.

"Where are we?" Nelia asked. She had been in the backseat too long and was getting testy.

"Fifty miles from Spokane," her mother said.

Nelia fanned herself with one hand. "Zoe, open your window. I'm suffocating. I have a low tolerance for heat."

"Then why did you just put on my sweatshirt, without even asking?"

"I have a low tolerance for cold, too. Actually I can't stand anything that's not exactly the way I like it."

"I'm comfortable," Zoe said.

"Then come back here and see if you're still comfortable." She was leaning over the front seat, her head resting on her hands, like a whiny child.

"If we're going to enjoy this drive," their mother said, "we'll have to think about other people's needs besides our own. Riding in a car is like living in a small community."

Nelia folded her arms across her chest and sank back in her seat, watching Eastern Washington roll by outside the window. "A community of the damned," she mumbled.

By the time they reached Idaho and decided to stop for the night, there were NO VACANCY signs on all the motels. One more thing that hadn't made it onto her mother's yellow legal pad: Seat assignments, yes; motel reservations, no. They stopped for gas, and the woman at the cash register suggested a place that was a few miles off the interstate.

"It's a little down at the mouth," she said, "but it's clean enough all right."

Oliver stopped rummaging through the candy bar display and tugged on Zoe's shirt. "What's 'down at the mouth' mean?" he asked.

"It means fleabag," she said.

STARLIGHT MOTEL, T - UCKERS WELCOME, the sign in front of the motel read. The *r* was dark, and so was the NO VACANCY sign. But it was hard to tell whether it was the truth or just another burnt-out bulb.

Nelia, Oliver, and Zoe struggled, stiff-limbed, from the car, following their mother into the lobby. The man at the front desk looked like he had a beach ball under his white T-shirt. He was on the telephone, talking to someone he knew, and ignored them several minutes before deciding, apparently, that they weren't going to go away. "Hold up, Mike. Gotta tend to these customers." He set down the receiver.

Zoe couldn't take her eyes off the hair growing out of his ears.

"So, lemme see. What've we got here?" He rubbed his stubbly face that hadn't seen a razor in several days. "How many adults, and how many children?"

"Three children and one adult," her mother said.

"You travelin' alone with all them kids?"

"Yes," she answered.

"My dad's going to catch up with us later," Zoe added. It seemed important to tell him this.

"That so?" The man pecked at the computer keys. "Yer lucky. I got one room left . . . a single with a double bed."

"There are four of us," her mother said.

"One's all I got," he said.

"Maybe two of you can sleep on the floor in your sleeping bags. That might be fun," their mother said.

Zoe frowned. "Let's go somewhere else."

The man hiked up his pants. He looked mildly irritated. "I reckon all the somewhere elses was all filled up," he said. "Got that Elks convention in town. If you don't want the room, that's fine by me." He reached for a stack of papers and turned to go into the back.

Zoe's mother called out to him. "We'll take it," she said.

"Is there a pool?" Zoe asked, trying to salvage something.

"Pool's closed, missy."

"Will it be open in the morning?"

"Nope, closed for the season. Had some trouble with them filters."

"What about the game room?"

"That don't ever close," he said. "There's a Ping-Pong table, you and yer brother can take a crack at. Here's the ball and paddle," he said. He reached under the counter and handed it to Zoe.

"Don't you need two paddles?" she asked.

"One's all I got."

In the middle of the night Zoe woke up, panting. Her eyes darted around the room. There was an unfamiliar light coming in through the broken drapes. Outside the window there was a truck parked with its motor running.

She closed her eyes again and the nightmare came back. Her father was lying flat on his back a few feet beneath the surface of the water, his arms splayed out like someone who'd fallen from a great height. His clear blue eyes were wide open, staring up at her. He was sinking down and away. And here was the thing: No one could see him except her.

She wanted to help him, but there was something pressing down on her shoulders, a force that kept her frozen in place. She could see his mouth moving under the water like a fish, round then flat, round then flat. Slowly the haze of sleep parted and she realized why his mouth was moving that way. He was calling her name.

# CHAPTER 4

They made it through Montana on Wednesday and began the trek across North Dakota on Thursday morning in better spirits, after sleeping in a decent motel. But by the time they reached Fargo five hours later, they had all settled into a kind of trance brought on by the long highway that cut through the grasslands.

By evening they had crossed into Minnesota. Their mother had a kind of grim determination about finishing the drive now. But it was becoming clear that the job was wearing on her.

Zoe felt like they were in a prison, with the walls and ceiling closing in. She tried to sleep, but she kept getting jostled just as she was drifting off. "Stop kicking the seat, Oliver." Her back ached and her neck was stiff.

"I'm not kicking you."

Nelia rolled her eyes. "I'll switch seats with you, Zoe."

"No!"

"Zoe, why are you making things difficult?" her mother snapped.

"If I'm such a problem, why don't you just pull over and dump me like you do with everyone else."

"That's enough, Zoe," her mother said. She rubbed her hands back and forth on the steering wheel. "Can't you see how difficult this is for me?"

"Oh, I forgot. This is all about you."

"Stop. . . . Just STOP!"

The car weaved from side to side. Zoe's insides lurched. She turned and stared out the back window. The road behind them was being swallowed up as fast as they drove over it. There was darkness ahead of them and darkness behind them.

Oliver began to cry. "I want to go home."

"We don't have a home." Zoe shifted in her seat.

"Stop trying to upset everyone, Zoe." Her mother's voice was heavy with exasperation. "We *have* a home, Ollie. All we have to do is get there. We've made it this far. And we're not going to let any*thing* or any*one* stand in our way." She took her eyes off the road and looked directly at Zoe so long that Zoe was afraid she might forget to look back.

Zoe folded her arms and slouched against the door, like something wild backed into a corner. Oliver curled into a ball under Nelia's arm. Their mother hunched over the steering wheel, peering into the darkness ahead of them.

It began to rain, a slow tapping on the roof and doors. At first the rain comforted Zoe. It reminded her of home, where there was so much rain that it felt sometimes as though they lived in the ocean, rather than near it.

They pushed forward into the storm. The rain became a loud, drumming torrent, and the world outside the windows disappeared behind a wall of water pouring down on every side. The whole world was weeping. All the tears that would not come out of Zoe's eyes pounded on the roof and doors.

Her mother turned the windshield wipers up to high, and the *swish, swish* became a *slap, slap, slap*, which was still not enough to stop the world from dissolving in the flood.

A gust of wind caught the car broadside, nudging it into the other lane. A van sped past, so close that Zoe could hear the hiss of wheels on the wet pavement. Their mother struggled to keep the car from being blown off course, with the weight of the U-Haul tugging at them, throwing them off balance.

"What's wrong?" Nelia asked.

"It's just the rain."

They passed several cars that had pulled over to wait it out.

"Are you going to stop?"

"Eventually."

"What difference does it make when we get there?" Zoe asked.

Her mother didn't answer. She leaned forward, gripping the steering wheel harder. Zoe could see her knuckles glowing white each time a car came up behind them. She flicked on her turn signal and edged into the right lane. It was raining so hard that they could barely see the red taillights up ahead. Every now and then a big truck lumbered past them, drenching the windshield with a tidal wave of rain that shot off its rear wheels.

They passed a pickup that had gone off into a ditch. Zoe craned her neck to see if there was anyone still inside. There was a sudden, unexpected thump as their station wagon's tires caught the side of the road. She felt the world tip. Her mother whipped the steering wheel back, careening toward the far left lane.

Out of the darkness, a big black hulk bore down on them, white lights burning in the front, eyes that seared hers. Her mother panicked and rolled the steering wheel back toward the side of the road. The car was skidding. Zoe stopped breathing, surprised at how effortless it was for the car to skate over the surface, careening sideways. It was so much easier than pushing ahead. They slipped toward the shoulder, gracefully, as in a dance. She knew the car would have to stop, but she felt nothing—not even fear—until the jolt of the U-Haul rocking back and forth and the shock of the tires bumping off the road, where the car came to rest cockeyed, tilting off the pavement.

There was no sound except for their breathing and the steady slap of the windshield wipers and the drumming of the rain. Zoe's arm was over the seat and Oliver clung to it so fiercely that his fingers dug into her skin, but he did not cry.

Through the blur of water on the windows, Zoe saw that the semi behind them had pulled over. A man got out and walked toward their car.

Her mother rolled down the window.

"You all right?" he asked.

Zoe couldn't tell if he was angry or frightened for them.

Her mother nodded.

The man leaned in and stared at the shaken passengers. His coat was drenched and there was water dripping off his hood and running down his face.

"It's none of my business, lady. But if these were my kids, I'd want them off the road tonight."

They watched the trucker make his way back down the shoulder through the storm and climb up into the cab.

"What are you going to do?" Nelia asked.

Her mother was silent.

"If Dad was . . . ," Zoe said.

"Dad is not here. Do you understand? It's just us," her

mother said, her voice shaking. "This is all we've got." She rubbed at the fog on the windshield, turned the defroster up, and waited for a clear shot to get back on the road.

Zoe looked at the hunched shapes in the darkness of the car. Nelia, who could love her one day and hate her the next, Ollie, who was little more than a baby, and her mother, who thought she could fix what was broken beyond repair. This is all we've got.

But what if all you've got is not enough?

# CHAPTER 5

There was no town or gas station marked at the next exit, but there was a sign barely visible at the top of the ramp. It had an arrow at the bottom and an arc of letters over the top.

Zoe's mother leaned forward, staring through the fogged windshield. She read the sign out loud, then sighed and leaned back in her seat. "Peaceful Haven. Thank God. At least we can get some rest."

"It doesn't say it's a motel." Nelia peered over Zoe's shoulder at the dripping sign illuminated by their headlights. "It could be a church."

"I don't care what it is. We're sleeping there."

"Go ahead, then. Don't listen to me." She folded her arms across her chest. "Maybe we can ask for a room with a pew."

Their mother swung the car onto the two-lane highway in the direction of the arrow, and they drove out of the rain as though they were passing through a curtain. The growl of thunder and jagged spikes of lightning faded into the distance, like memories of trouble when your luck has finally turned.

The road wound through some woods and fields, leading

them farther and farther back into the hills. "Are you sure you went the right way?" Zoe asked her mother. It didn't *feel* right.

"Positive." She was leaning forward, scanning the roadside for something promising.

The houses were spaced far apart. Every now and then there was a barn with a pole lamp that lifted their spirits, like a lighthouse. They went several miles more without seeing a town or a motel.

Zoe chewed her nail and stared at the empty road. "Maybe we should go back. It seems like we should be there by now."

Her mother stiffened. "Why do you have to question everything? We've gone this far. It can't be that much farther."

A half mile down the road, her mother pointed at something shiny nailed to the side of a large overhanging tree just off the road. "You see? I told you we shouldn't give up." She slowed down, then swung her arm over the seat and backed the car up so she could aim the headlights at the sign. One side of it was curled. They couldn't make out what it said.

Her mother pulled over and got out of the car, shivering in the cold and wet night air. She stumbled as her foot sank down into a ditch that had been hidden by the tall grass along the roadside. But she caught herself. Then she managed to climb over a barbed wire fence by holding it down with her foot. She straightened the sign out, then opened the car door and slid behind the wheel.

"We're on the right track," she said. "It's the next left."

They turned onto a rutted road, so narrow that branches slapped at the windows and scraped the side of the car. She tried to steer around the potholes. Sometimes she would hit one, so there would be a loud thunk like a shotgun blast from under the car.

The car lumbered along until they reached a clearing. The road bent sharply to the right, then ended in front of a large wrought iron gate, where her mother stopped and turned off the engine. The words "Peaceful Haven" were woven into the top of the curlicued arch.

Zoe peered beyond the black iron fence at the white shapes shimmering in the headlights. "This is a cemetery."

Her mother closed her eyes and dropped her forehead onto the steering wheel.

Nelia shook her head. "Want me to see if they have any vacancies?"

Oliver had been sleeping in the back. He bolted upright when the car stopped. "Are we home?"

"It's all right, Ollie," Nelia said, softening. She put her arm around him, and he leaned into the hollow under her shoulder and planted his thumb in his mouth.

"We're not there yet," her mother said quietly. "Go back to sleep."

"How is that going to fix anything?" Zoe turned on her mother. "If we go to sleep, then we won't ask questions? Is that what you're thinking?"

Her mother let out a deep sigh. "You were right, Zoe. Does that make you happy?" She turned the key in the ignition.

"Are we going home now?" Ollie asked.

"We're going to whatever comes next."

"Is that supposed to make us feel better?" Nelia asked.

"Could you please, *please*, just . . ." Her mother never finished the sentence. Instead, she put the car in reverse and pressed down hard on the gas pedal. The engine roared and the wheels spun wildly, sending up a spray of wet mud. The car didn't move. Her eyes darted. She swallowed hard and put the car in forward, inching up a little. "Come on, come on," she said. She moved the gear shift to reverse and let the car slip backward. It teetered on the edge of the hole it was digging for itself; the U-Haul rocked side to side. Then the tires slid back down even deeper into the muck.

Her mother got out and walked from one side of the car to the other, looking at the hopeless situation she had created for them. Finally, she went around and opened the door.

"What are you doing?" Zoe asked.

"I'm getting the tent," her mother said. She leaned over them, reaching into the way back, and rummaged around, throwing stuffed animals, pillows, and blankets every which way.

"What?"

She took the Coleman lantern out of the back and walked around in circles, swinging the light until she found a grassy area on the other side of the gravel road. "I guess this will have to do."

"I don't believe this," Nelia said. "We're sleeping next to a cemetery that our mother has mistaken for a small out-of-the-way motel."

Their mother returned to the car and began hefting backpacks and suitcases into a pile on the cold, wet grass, until she uncovered the blue stuffed bag with the tent gear inside. They sat staring blankly at her as she walked across the road, lugging the bag, and stepped into the circle of lantern light. She flipped the bag upside down and shook the tent out onto the ground.

"We're driving across the country with a madwoman," Nelia said. "Next she'll be sending us for kindling so she can roast marshmallows."

Zoe got out and looked at the tires sunk in the ooze. She stood behind the open car door, as though it would shield her from something, and called to her mother. "We can't sleep here with a field of corpses across the road. Nelia and I will push the car out."

"Speak for yourself," Nelia muttered.

"Shut up, Nelia."

Her mother squatted down and sorted out the tent poles. "Even if you could, which is doubtful, there's no way I can get back behind that wheel and drive again until I've had some rest."

Nelia stepped out of the backseat on the other side. The car stood with its doors wide open. "We're spending the night here? The whole night?"

"Unless a tow truck happens by."

Zoe looked at her sister over the roof of the car. "What about Nelia? We can push and she can drive."

"Nelia only has a permit and she hasn't driven since she had that little accident with the drivers' ed car, remember?"

"That was completely not my fault," Nelia said.

"It doesn't matter whose fault it was," her mother said. She squatted down and began snapping tent poles together like they were Tinkertoys. "The point is there's not a single person here fit to back down that blasted road, let alone make it to the expressway and then on to the next exit, where there may not be a motel, anyway. We're safer here than we would be driving."

"It *does* matter whose fault it is," Zoe shouted. "This is *your* fault. All of it. You never listen to anyone." She dropped back into her seat and slammed the car door.

Oliver started crying. "I wanna go home."

Nelia got back in and tried to comfort him, but he just kept crying and kicking his legs until she dug into her backpack for the half of a chocolate bar she'd saved from their last stop. He gobbled it down, smearing a good portion of it on his face, where it mixed with his tears.

They watched their mother flip the ground cloth in the air as though she were making a bed. It luffed in the wind, then blew backward, wrapping around her legs so she had to peel it off and pin it to the ground with one foot while she reached over to grab some rocks to hold it in place.

"We can't just sit here and watch this," Nelia said.

It was silent, except for the sound of Oliver's sniffling. Their mother unrolled the tent and spread it out on the ground. The wind kept lifting it into the air, so she sat in the center and tried to thread the poles through the little loops in the top.

"You'd better go help Mom, Zoe."

"Why me?"

"Because you know how to set up the tent."

"She made this mess. Let her figure out how to get out of it."

"We're in the mess with her, Zoe, in case you haven't noticed."

Nelia yanked open the car door. "Okay, okay. I'll help. You watch Ollie."

"Leave her alone. Maybe she'll come to her senses."

Nelia ignored her. She stalked across the road and stood with her hands on her hips.

Ollie finished the chocolate and began asking for his daddy. Zoe got into the backseat next to him and broke open a bag of corn chips. They sat together in the backseat, watching the drama outside, as if they were at a drive-in movie.

Her mother managed to get all the poles threaded into the

loops. Then she motioned for Nelia to stand across from her and lift. They tried to get the tent to stand up, but every time they got one side up, the other collapsed. Each attempt was followed by another round of shouting and blaming. Then they would try the same thing all over again.

Zoe shook her head. It was never going to work because they had the poles mixed up. Her mother stood up and stared at the deflated tent, a defeated look on her face. Nelia knelt down on a corner of the ground cloth.

Zoe weakened. She rolled the window down and stuck her head out. "You have to use the long poles for the tent," she said. "The short ones are for the rain fly."

"I know what I'm doing, Zoe," her mother said. "This isn't the first time I've gone camping."

"Fine. Keep struggling. I won't say another word."

Nelia walked over and picked up the long poles. Then she knelt down on the grass and started pulling out the short ones. Her mother went around the other side and began feeding the long poles through the loops. They tried lifting it, but the tent flopped over sideways.

"Dad braces it with a log," Zoe called out.

Her mother looked at her.

"I was talking to Nelia," Zoe said. "I'm not speaking to you."

Nelia went to pick up a fallen limb. This time the tent rose in the air, as though a string were pulling it from the top. They set up the cross poles, and in minutes the flattened mound of fabric and net became a big blue dome, which they covered with the yellow rain fly, and staked down.

By the time her mother came back to the car for the sleeping bags, Ollie had fallen asleep, traces of chocolate and corn chips still on his lips. Zoe had her arm around him and he was snoring into her sleeve.

"I'll take him," her mother said. She struggled to lift him, but he was too big for her to carry, so she had to hold his hand and help him stumble, half-asleep, out of the car.

"I'm fr*eee*zing!" Ollie whined.

"Are you coming?" her mother asked, turning toward Zoe.

"No."

"You can't just stay in the car by yourself."

"Why can't I?"

"Because . . ." Her mother threw up her hands. "I'm too tired to fight with you anymore, Zoe. Sleep there if you want, but I'm stretching out in the tent. Otherwise I'd need a crowbar to straighten my legs in the morning." She handed her a spare flashlight. "Honk if you need help."

Zoe watched the light of the lantern swing away and disappear inside the tent. The night was cold, and the windows fogged over so she had to wipe them off to see. Everything around her—the trees, the gravel road, even her skin—seemed to be glowing with a faint bluish white light, coming from the moon that was drifting in and out of the clouds.

She climbed into the front, moved the seat back, and spread out a sleeping bag on the floor. Then she unzipped it and hunkered down inside; tight quarters, even for someone as small as she was, but it meant she'd be looking up at the sky. And the closeness of it made her feel safe.

When she was in Washington, out on the boat with her father, she had always slept in the little enclosed triangle at the bow of the boat, as far forward as she could. Zoe was the only one who liked learning about the night sky, so she knew things that Oliver and Nelia didn't. Celestial navigation: how to read the map of the sky. If you knew where you were compared to the stars, you could never be lost.

Sometimes at night, her father would cut the engine and let the boat drift. It was quiet, except for the sound of the wind and the slap of waves on the boat, and it was so dark that you could hardly tell where the sea ended and the sky began.

"You see the Big Dipper up there?" he would say to her, taking her finger and tracing the outline of it. "Make a line from the bottom of the cup, and it will lead you to the North Star, Polaris." He had composed a very bad song for her—"My Sweet Compass Rose"—and often sang it, loudly and off key.

From her tight little berth on the floor of the car, Zoe looked at the sky and felt her body relax, like the opening of a clenched fist. She was not afraid, not really. She couldn't see the graves from that position. She knew they were there, but you could forget a thing like that. You could put it out of your mind.

They were in a clearing, surrounded by a ring of bare, black trees, and over it all was an ocean of stars behind the scattered clouds. She sat up and traced the constellations on the windshield with her finger. She knew the easy ones, like the Seven Sisters, but her father knew many more. Winter nights in Alaska were long, the darkness was deep, and the stars, he said, were as thick as mosquitoes are in Minnesota. "You'll know them too, by the time you're as old as me. I'll teach you."

She felt like she was home again, rocking in the boat. Her father would be out on the water now, watching the night sky, somewhere in the Gulf Islands. He was winding his way north to Alaska, through the islands scattered up and down Canada's west coast. Zoe had been only as far north as Desolation Sound. But she could imagine what the other islands were like from her father's stories: big headlands, dark and looming in the night, mountains that reached all the way down to the water. He would be out among those islands now, looking up at the stars and remembering them. They were connected that way.

She scanned the sky until she found the Dipper, then held her hand up and made a right angle with her finger and thumb. The line of her thumb pointed to the North Star. Zoe could feel her father's hand on hers, like a phantom limb.

She could find her way alone. She was good at it. But she wanted her father back. It made her feel childish, but it was true. Why had he left her alone to figure things out?

There was a rapping on the window. Zoe sat up. Her mother's face floated outside. She unlocked the door.

"You scared me."

Her mother slid in next to her and closed the door against the cold. "Have you been crying?"

Zoe turned away. "What do you want?"

"I forgot to tell you something."

"What?"

"I'm sorry, Zoe."

Zoe tried to speak, but her voice gave way. Her mother put her arm around Zoe and pulled her close. Even in the dim light, she could see the aching fear and sadness that were hidden in her mother's face. Zoe could see Nelia and Ollie inside the dome tent, moving about like shadow puppets in the lantern light. The clouds had covered up the moon again. And the darkness had swallowed up everything else.

# CHAPTER 6

The house looked like it was being eaten by a pack of trees. It was the last one on the main road—the only road, really—that ran through the center of Selena. It had taken so long to get the car unstuck that the sun was beginning to set by the time they finally got there.

"Better late than never," their mother said.

That was one opinion. The so-called town consisted of a scattering of houses and stores, two bars, a post office, and a boarded-up station next to a pair of railroad tracks. The house their mother had grown up in was the last one on the left side, right at the place where the town dwindled away to nothing. The house was just before the sign that said YOU ARE LEAVING SELENA. HOPE YOU ENJOYED YOUR STAY, and just after the one that said, RESUME 55 M.P.H. Apparently when people left Selena, they left in a hurry.

The Subaru pulled into what was once a driveway, going as far as the weeds would allow, and then they sat there, all of them openmouthed, bewildered by the spectacle of it. Zoe couldn't see anything at first, but gradually she began to pick out a window here and a door there. The house appeared to be in a long-running battle, with nature winning two to one. The roof was missing more than a few shingles. The porch sagged as though it were about to give up and let gravity take its course. Huge evergreens loomed over the second floor, and overgrown bushes closed in on its flanks. Behind it all, the orange globe of the sun hung like a fireball about to drop down and finish the whole mess off.

Zoe had the sense of having arrived too late for something, although she didn't know quite what. It was a shipwreck of a house, something washed up in the shallows near an unknown shore, where no one knew or cared about it, all the inhabitants long dead or lost at sea, never to return. Most of the paint had peeled off, leaving it a dull ashen gray. And there were saplings growing up everywhere, even in the gutters.

"Good God." Nelia sighed.

"It just needs a little work," their mother said.

Nelia, Zoe, and Ollie got out and stood in a line, leaning against the car, as though they were afraid it might otherwise disappear when their backs were turned. Their mother paced back and forth, looking for a clear path in and not finding one. Finally she waded into the tall brown grass, lifting her knees high in the air like someone walking into deep water. Nelia took Ollie's hand and followed, walking on the path their mother had flattened down for them.

Zoe stood where she was, watching Ollie's head bob forward. She felt strangely distant from them, as though she were only a witness to the disaster, someone standing on shore watching with that familiar sense of horror and futility. She felt she should run for help, but she wasn't sure where to go or what to ask for.

"Let's see if one of these keys the lawyer sent will actually open the lock," their mother called out. She climbed the steps.

Zoe followed the path they'd trampled toward the house and stood behind Nelia and Ollie as they watched their mother fumble with the door. "We drove all the way from Washington for this?" Zoe said.

"Beats the heck out of Peaceful Haven," Nelia muttered.

"I want to go back to the car," Ollie said. He leaned away, pulling on Nelia's arm.

"Maybe the keys won't work," Zoe said, trying to lift her own spirits.

Nelia hugged Ollie in closer. "She'd probably tell us to drop down through one of the holes in the roof."

"Got it," their mother said. The door swung open and she stood on the porch, one hand extended graciously into the house. No one moved or spoke. "What are you waiting for?"

"Other options?" Nelia said.

Inside, the house looked less like a shipwreck and more like the collapsed face of an old beauty. "A Victorian, a painted lady," was how their mother had described the house when she'd first told them about it. Minus the paint, she should have added.

You could see that it had once been a grand house: the dark paneled walls, the pocket doors, the curved staircase, and the stained-glass windows fired by the setting sun. But its beauty had been ruined by time and neglect. There was dirt and clutter everywhere. The walls sagged, the stairs creaked, and the windows stared at them like dull, vacant eyes. It smelled like dampness and decay. And there was that same feeling hanging in the air, of waiting for something that came too late.

The unpainted lady had a past she would rather not discuss.

Their mother walked through the hallway and into the dining room. "It's probably not what you were expecting exactly, is it?"

Zoe ran a finger over the grimy woodwork. The question didn't seem to require an answer. Her mother was just talking to reassure herself.

"It's not perfect, I know."

"Not perfect?" Nelia said, her voice rising.

"Okay, far from perfect."

"Far from lots of things."

Her mother let the comment pass. "The structure's sound. It just needs a little cosmetic work. That's what happens when you have renters. They don't take care of things the way they would if it were their own."

"We've always lived in rented houses," Zoe said.

"Well . . . yes . . . ," her mother said.

Ollie was shadowing his mother as she moved from room to room, and rubbing his head, the way he always did when he was worried about something. "It's too dark in here," he said.

Nelia flipped the switch and nothing happened.

"The electricity should be on," her mother said. "I'll have to go down into the basement and see if I can find the fuse. One of you want to come along and hold the light for me?"

"I'll go," Zoe said.

Nelia took hold of Ollie's hand. "We'll go try that tire swing on for size, right, Liver?"

"It's too cold to play outside," Ollie said.

"Stop being so practical," Nelia admonished him. "You're barely six years old."

Her mother handed Zoe the flashlight. "It's down this hall."

She followed her mother into the gloom, trying to keep her mother's back in sight as Zoe felt her way along, shining the light in front of her. Even then, she stumbled a few times. It was strange to watch her mother confidently weaving in and out of doors and furniture with only the invisible strands of memory to guide her. Awful as it was, the house was as familiar to her mother as it was strange to everyone else. She walked along the wall until her hand fell on a knob. Then she turned it and pulled the door wide. Blackness opened up in front of them. "Here's what we're looking for." She stepped down onto the basement stairs.

Zoe aimed a beam of light at the wooden steps, worn in the middle from years of use. The air that drifted up from below had a stale, musty smell. When she reached the bottom of the stairs, her mother walked over to a metal box attached to the stone foundation wall, and flipped some switches. "Anything come on up there?"

"No."

There was another series of clicks in the darkness. "Now?"

"Nothing."

Her mother stepped away from the light and Zoe lost track of her for a minute. She was quiet for so long that Zoe considered going in after her. "Mom?" she called out.

Her mother's face appeared in the flashlight beam, directly in front of her. "How do you feel about dinner by candlelight?"

They went outside to carry in the suitcases. Nelia was leaning back on the porch steps.

"Where's Ollie?" her mother asked.

Nelia nodded toward the car.

"Doesn't he like the tire swing?"

"Not as much as he likes the car."

Ollie was sitting in the front seat making motor noises and jiggling the steering wheel.

Their mother opened the door and leaned in. "We're not driving anymore, Ollie. This is our last stop."

"I know," he said.

"Don't you want to come inside with us?"

Ollie shook his head. "I wanna sleep in the car."

He flopped himself over into the backseat and curled up in a ball. "I like it here," he said. "It's where I live."

"This should be interesting," Nelia said.

Ollie's empty stomach finally drove him into the house. They sat down at the dining room table, after washing the thick dust off of it, covering it with the reverse side of a sheet, and hanging their camp lantern from the chandelier.

"What's for supper?" Zoe called toward the kitchen.

Her mother walked into the room and set down a paper plate full of sandwiches.

"Looks like cooler cuisine," Nelia said.

"Do I like it?" Ollie asked.

"It's your favorite."

It didn't matter that it wasn't. He fell asleep in the middle of supper, his cheek resting on top of the table and his arms dangling underneath, as though someone had shot him in the back. Nelia carried him to the couch in front of the fire their mother had lit in the living room fireplace, and covered him with his old, frayed yellow blanket. But he woke up again and started whining for his bear. Zoe made the mistake of reminding him that Booda had taken a trip with Daddy.

"I want him back, now," Ollie howled. His face twisted into

a wet, red knot of pain. "When is Daddy coming home? I want him. I need him back."

He wouldn't stop crying until Zoe threw another sheet over the dining room table to make a tent, so they could pretend they were camping again. She laid two sleeping bags out underneath, and Nelia crawled in with them, after claiming she'd seen a millipede the size of a small dog coming out of the bathroom.

Zoe lay awake for a long time. It was quiet, except for the snap and sizzle of the embers dying in the fireplace. Ollie's little body shook with sniffling sobs every now and then, even after he finally drifted off.

"Are you sleeping?" Zoe whispered, nudging Nelia.

"Not anymore," she said.

"What do you think of our . . . this place?" She was going to say "house," but thought better of it.

"It's far from perfect," she said.

"We're never going to be happy here."

"I wouldn't lose any sleep over that," Nelia said. "Just hold your breath and we'll be somewhere else."

"That's not what Mom says."

"You'd be a lot happier if you'd just accept that you're living with a traveling theater company. Every few months you take down the tent, pack the trunk, get out of town before the reviews are posted, and run the show over again in a new location."

"You mean a circus?"

"If the shoe fits."

"Why did she have to bring us *here*?"

"This is her home. That's why."

"Home isn't a place. It's where your family is. And her family is all dead. Except for us . . . so far."

"Maybe that's why she had to come back."

"What do you mean?"

"I don't know. I'm just talking." Nelia pulled the covers up over her shoulder and turned her face away. "Go to sleep."

When Zoe woke up, it was pitch black. Heart in her throat; that was how it always was, every time they moved. It had happened so often that it felt like a recurring nightmare: the half-dazed confusion, the cold sweat, the groggy attempt to pull some memory back from her brain that would explain where she was and how she'd gotten there. Sometimes it was like that night after night, for weeks on end. Even though her body ached for sleep, she would fight to stay awake, just so it wouldn't happen again.

She could hear Oliver's breathing, even and deep, from the floor next to her. Nelia's hair floated in waves across the pillow on her other side. Zoe pulled back the sheet that dangled next to her face and peered out: faded wallpaper, a chipped ceiling dotted with water stains, the smell of mold mixed with smoke, like a fire inside a cave.

She rolled over and turned her face to the floor, breathing in the comforting scent of the pillow she had retrieved from the car. Images came flooding back: the long journey, the disappointment. So that was it. They had washed up. They were home.

Zoe slipped out from under the covers. She was still wearing the jeans and pale blue sweatshirt she'd had on the night before. She remembered feeling too tired to open the suitcase she had lugged in, which was now lying closed in the corner, reproaching her. Oliver was lying on his back with his mouth open. He didn't stir when Zoe reached under him and pulled out last night's dirty socks, which had fallen off her feet during the night. She climbed over him, hunched down on all fours so she wouldn't hit her head on the table, and managed to push herself out without waking him.

In the moonlight that filtered in through the windows, she could see faded photographs of people who meant nothing to her. She felt their eyes on her and walked carefully past them, away from her mother who was sleeping on the couch in the living room, through a kitchen full of skittering noises and animal smells. When she finally reached the the back door, she yanked it open and breathed in the night air as though she were dying for lack of it.

She pulled the hood up over her head and shoved her hands into the pouch of her sweatshirt. It was snowing. Big wet flakes jostled in the wind like reluctant dancers, wearily twisting and falling, before resting in piles on the black earth.

Snow, and it was nearly April. It figured. By now the tulip farms in the Skagit Valley would be carpeted with green leaves and spiky buds, but not in this place; not here. A white coat was building up on the bare tree limbs and bushes. The seed heads of last year's grasses and flowers had little round caps of snow, all placed jauntily on the northernmost side.

Zoe walked to the tree line to the west, and then retraced her steps all the way back to the marsh in the east. Find the four directions. That was what she had been taught, and taught well. Get the lay of things.

She had found out the hard way what happened when you didn't, the time she and her father had taken the boat over to camp on Orcas Island. The compass broke down on the way home. They had good maps and the weather was clear.

But halfway back, they were wrapped in a dense fog.

Zoe's father was below and she was at the wheel when the boat drifted into a cloud that closed around them like a trap. She peered into the blankness. It was all the same, every direction. She could no longer tell where they had come from or where they were going.

She called out to her father and he climbed up, but he made no move to help her.

"When was your last sighting?"

"I wasn't paying attention. Decatur. Fauntleroy Point, maybe."

"Where are you headed now?"

"South, I think."

"What's your distance? What's your drift?"

"I don't *know*. That's what I'm trying to tell you."

"You've got maps, don't you? You know where you came from and how fast you were going. Use dead reckoning."

Out of the fog a shoreline suddenly appeared in front of them. "James Island," Zoe said.

"Are you sure?"

"No, I'm not. Why are you asking me?"

A horn bleated at them and she spun around, but couldn't see anything but the gray curtain of fog.

"The ferry," she said.

"Damn right. Which direction is it coming from?"

"That way: east."

"It's half past twelve. That's gotta be the Sidney ferry coming in from the west."

The horn bleated again. She started sobbing. "I don't know what to do. Why can't you just tell me?"

Her father took the wheel and flung it around, opening the

throttle. The boat reeled as it turned sharply to the left. Zoe grabbed for the railing and missed it, falling as her father spun the wheel back and righted the boat. The ferry loomed out of the fog, a nightmarish vision, over Zoe's shoulder, so close she was afraid it would capsize them as it churned past, rocking their boat violently with its wake.

"Look at me, Zoe."

His blue eyes were the only thing she could see ringed by the fog—white smoke, a cold burn like dry ice. The boat swung back and forth. She thought she was going to be sick.

"I can't always tell you, because you need to know yourself."

"I thought I knew," she said.

"You *thought*. But there's something deeper than that."

"I don't understand. I don't know what you mean."

"What I'm saying . . . mind this, Zoe . . . is that there'll come a time when you'll have to find your way alone. You can't always count on others to save you. Don't pretend for a minute that it's not so."

When she reached the edge of the field to the north, Zoe turned back. She saw the tracks she had made in the snow-frosted mud, a thin line of footsteps leading to where their battered house hunched among the trees. Her tracks would disappear. You couldn't always count on trails, either.

She tilted her face up to the full moon, letting the feel of the landscape imprint itself on her body. The road was south, the marsh was east, and the woods were west. She closed her eyes and raised her arms, like the hands of a compass, feeling for the pull of the earth. That's what gravity was, after all: the earth pulling us back to itself.

One day it would be time for her to leave. She knew this the way she knew that there had been no motel; the way she knew that they would founder, cast adrift, and wind up regretting the whole trip. She would know when it was time to go, and she would find her own way. Even at night, she would know this. Even on a cloudy day when you couldn't see the sun.

# CHAPTER 7

"Wasn't that a stop sign back there?" Zoe asked.

Nelia's head swiveled, owl-like, and the car swerved with it. "That red thing?"

Her mother gripped the dashboard. "Nelia! Keep your eyes on the road."

"I was just turning around to see if Zoe was right. I don't have eyes in the back of my head, you know."

"That's what the rearview mirror is for." Her mother sat on the edge of her seat, her whole body tense from the effort of keeping one eye on the speedometer, one eye out for things that Nelia missed, and one foot on the brake pedal that she didn't have. "Maybe you should wait awhile before you take the driver's test again, Nelia."

"I just need to practice a little first, that's all. And for your information, Zoe, that red thing was a mailbox." Nelia's eyes appeared in the mirror, narrowing as they caught hers with their piercing gaze. "Next time tell me before you see—"

"There's one," Zoe said.

"Now, *that's* a stop sign." Nelia slowed down to a coast and rolled through it. "I'll stop twice the next time."

They had been to the grocery, the hardware store, and both schools to register for classes, and now they were headed to the post office in Selena. Nelia pointed the nose of the car at the parking lot, made a pass at the driveway, and missed, ending up with two wheels on the curb. She gunned the engine and throttled back out onto the steet.

"Nelia, you didn't—," her mother said. The last part of her sentence was drowned in the squeal of brakes. The car behind them swerved too late, stopping with its bumper smack against theirs. The driver got out of the car and approached the passenger side, just as their mother opened the door. She was a tall woman with frizzy, sandy hair and a red coat that flapped open like a cape. Zoe thought at first that she was going to take a swing at her mother, but instead she threw her arms around her neck.

"Annie Lawson! I knew it. I knew it."

Her mother craned her neck to get a look at her. "Weezy?"

"Mary Wines told me you were coming back. She's at the township now. You know how they are. Know all about everybody's business: foreclosures, civil suits, property transfers." She stood back, grinning. "You haven't changed. Not one bit since you were Bean Queen. Remember?"

"You don't forget a thing like that."

"That float and that goofy soybean bouquet they gave you! Why couldn't they just spring for a few roses? That's what I'd like to know." She bent over and looked in the car at Zoe, Nelia, and Oliver. "Oh, Lord, I don't believe it. These must be your kids."

"Zoe and Oliver," her mother said, pointing at the backseat. "That's Nelia in the driver's seat, the one who ran into you."

Weezy stepped back and surveyed the wedded bumpers. "No damage done, angel. Nelia, you look exactly like your mother at that age, you know that? Drive like her too."

"Weezy, don't tell her that."

"Well, they might as well know it. Sooner or later someone will tell them the truth. Your mother and I were the town troublemakers. She was bad and I was worse." She turned to Zoe. "And I'll bet you look like your father. Is your dad back at the house?"

"Alaska," Zoe said.

"That's right. He's a fisherman. Mary mentioned that. So when's he coming back?"

There was a painful silence. Weezy looked from one face to another, waiting for someone to break it.

"We're separated," her mother said, finally.

Weezy shook her head. "Me and my big mouth; we're a real pair, aren't we?"

"It's all right. I probably didn't mention it to Mary when I applied for the building permit."

"You're not tearing your old place down, are you?"

"Absolutely not. I'm planning to fix it up and open it as a guesthouse."

Weezy's face brightened. "Well, why not. Your grandpa used to love telling people how his great-aunt and -uncle rented rooms and pasture to cattlemen driving their cows to the stockyards in Chicago. It broke my heart to see that place run into the ground like that. I know. It's none of my business. But the renters! One was worse than the other. Not that it's your fault, since it was in a trust all those years after he died. A guesthouse?"

"A bed-and-breakfast."

"Well, hey, we'd better get these cars unstuck so you can get back to work. Annie, are you going to need any help fixing that house up?"

"Is the Dalai Lama Buddhist?"

"My cousin does home remodeling."

"Your cousin Billy?"

"That's right, charming Billy. I'll send him by."

Weezy walked around to her car and opened the driver's side door. "A bed-and-breakfast. You know I'm still a darn good cook."

Her mother smiled. "I'll give you a call. Maybe we can work something out."

Weezy put her car in reverse, and the bumpers unlocked with a metallic scraping that set Zoe's teeth on edge.

Nelia watched as she drove away. "Now, there's a woman who doesn't know where she ends and someone else begins."

Her mother walked around to the other side of the car. "This is a little town, Nelia. Everyone knows your life story."

"Yours is turning out to have a few surprise twists," Nelia said. "Bean Queen. I never knew we were descended from royalty."

"There were only fifty girls in the sophomore class. It wasn't much of a race."

Nelia studied her mother's face. "Go on. You can admit it. I imagine you were really beautiful back then. I mean, not that you aren't still."

Her mother smiled. "I *know* what you mean, Nelia. Why don't you let me drive. I'm not very good at being a passenger."

"You don't trust me, do you?"

"Actually"—her mother hesitated before deciding that this was a situation that called for the unvarnished truth—"no, I don't."

The house was sinking. That was the first unpleasant surprise Billy brought them. They were sitting at the round oak table in the kitchen, with estimates spread out like place mats in front of them, while Ollie raced matchbox cars over their feet.

Billy leaned over and stuck his head under the table. "Can I borrow one of those cars, son?" The word "son" dangled in the air, making Zoe's shoulder blades tighten.

Ollie handed up a tiny red corvette, and Billy set the car down in front of him and folded his meaty hands. The little car started rolling toward the other end of the table, picking up speed as it went, until it rocketed off the edge into Ollie's cupped hands. "The back of the house is holding, but the front is pulling down and away," Billy said. "The place is cockeyed."

Zoe rolled her eyes. Her mother gave her a look.

"What's causing it?"

"Water. This whole farm is riddled with underground springs. And they run deep. You know that swamp way back there behind the wheat field and the woods? They set fire to it when my dad was a boy. Thought it was just a lot of brush, but it turned out it was a peat bog. They never could get the fire out. It just kept smoldering and going down deeper until it burned its way all the way to groundwater and a swamp rose up."

"I know that place," Zoe's mother said. "You used to catch frogs there and drop them down my back."

Billy looked at her sideways. He had a tan and ruddy face, crinkled with laugh lines—someone who had spent a good deal of his life outdoors. "Now, that was self-defense, and you know it," he said. "You and Weezy, always tagging after me every time I brought a girl home. It was hard enough to get a girl to look at me."

Zoe's mother smiled. "We used to hide in the barn when you took Denise Stouffer up to the hay loft, hoping we'd get a chance to see you two make out. I bet you never knew that."

"Know it? I wanted to tie you both up, but Denise wouldn't let me."

"Whatever happened to her?"

"I married her."

"Guess we didn't spoil things after all. You'll bring her around sometime, won't you?"

Billy leaned back in his seat. "She passed away two years ago."

"No!"

"Lymphoma. We fought it a long time: chemo, radiation. But I guess they found it too late. We had some great years together. That's what you have to look back on."

"No kids?"

"We wanted them. It just didn't happen."

"I'm so sorry."

"Well, you pick up and go on. You know about that."

Zoe's mother looked down at her hands.

Billy tipped his chair back, pressed his hands into his muscled thighs, and glanced around the room. "Don't get me wrong. Your house is worth saving. Course you could tear it down. But you'll have to find someone else to help you if that's what you want. I'd rather fix the old than build new. Some people don't see it that way. But that's who I am. And the good news is, it's sinking slowly. This house has been going down a long time."

"So maybe we don't have to do anything about it for now?"

"That depends on whether or not you're in it for the long haul."

"What if we are?"

"Then you might as well get it done. Jack up the front, shore up the foundation . . ."

"Like a car?" Nelia said.

"Bigger jack," Billy said. That sideways look again. Was he kidding?

"Where are we going to be when all this happens?" Nelia asked.

"Waiting for the roof to fall on our heads," Zoe said.

He gave her a wry smile. "I'll hold it up long enough for you to get out the door."

"Billy Hercules," Zoe muttered, so only Nelia could hear.

"What was that?"

"Nothing."

"Then there's the siding, new woodwork, electrical . . . It's all here in the estimate." He pulled a sheaf of papers off his clipboard and slid them across the table.

Zoe's mother sat silently flipping through the papers in front of her. "I didn't know how much work it needed, Billy. I inherited some money with the house, but it looks like it won't be enough to fix it. And I don't have much money put aside beyond that except what we'll need to live on, until I get the bed-and-breakfast going. Of course, I could sell off some of the land. . . ."

"I wouldn't want you to have to do that. This place meant a lot to your grandpa. We go way back, Annie."

"The thing is, Billy . . ." She stopped herself. "I keep thinking of you when we were little kids."

His eyes crinkled. "They call me Big Bill now. But you can still call me Billy."

"I appreciate it. I truly do. But it seems like too much."

He picked up his black sports cap and yanked it by the brim over his close-cropped hair. "You can pay me what you can now to get the subs off my back, and pay the rest of it when you're able. I know you're good for it," he said.

"I don't want to take advantage of you, Billy."

"You know, your grandpa lent my dad money so I could go to trade school and learn carpentry. He was a good man, Annie. I'd just be paying back an old debt."

Nelia watched out the window as her mother walked Billy to the red pickup parked in front of the house. "He's really built," she said. "Looks like he works out."

"He's twenty years older than you," Zoe said.

"I can appreciate antiques, even if I don't want to furnish my house with them."

"Well, I don't like him. And we shouldn't be borrowing money from him," Zoe said.

"Why? It's not like we're never going to pay him."

"It's not good to owe people things." She walked over and stood next to Nelia at the window. "Big Bill," Zoe said, and shook her head.

"Kind of an unfortunate name for a contractor, don't you think?" Nelia said.

# CHAPTER 8

Billy and his crew moved in the next morning before the family even had the shades open. They stormed in just after sunrise and hacked and pounded their way all the way to dusk, tearing off shingles and rotting wood. Dumpsters, sawhorses, and aluminum ladders sprouted like dandelions all over the yard. The house filled up with the clank of crowbars and the gamey scent of men.

Zoe's mother began spending much of her time leaning over drawings of what she wanted the house to look like someday, with charming Billy next to her, scratching down changes. She cleaned the house with a vengeance when the workmen left every afternoon, but there was still dust in their eyes, dust in their food, and if you blew your nose, dust came out.

When she wasn't planning or cleaning, she was asking pointless questions. "Which white do you like better: ivory, parchment, or moon glow?" She was staring at an assortment of seemingly identical paint samples spread out on the remains of the kitchen counter.

"What's the difference? White is white," Zoe told her, just to get her off her back.

Her mother smiled gently at her and went back to sorting through the samples. It had become almost impossible to pick a fight with her. She was turning into someone Zoe didn't recognize. She seemed to get happier, the worse things got. And what Zoe hated most of all was the way she looked when Billy was in the house, how her face lightened, and how she laughed at things he said that weren't funny.

"I don't see how you can be so happy when everything is falling apart," Zoe said.

Her mother swept the white and whiter paint samples into a pile. "Sometimes things have to fall apart so they can come together in a new way."

Zoe slunk down farther in her chair and stared out the window at a workman wheeling away a load of shingles and tar paper. "Sometimes things just keep falling apart."

Nelia began pacing the house with a peculiar alertness. She took a sudden interest in the mysteries of the kitchen, turning the coffeemaker upside down and asking Zoe to show her how to work it.

"What do you want coffee for?" Zoe asked. "Aren't the buzz saws enough to wake you up?"

"It isn't for me. It's for the workmen."

"We're already paying them. Do we have to feed them and do their laundry, too?"

It didn't take long for Zoe to discover the reason for Nelia's unexpected generosity. His name was Garrett, a tall handsome boy with hazel eyes, a shock of thick black hair, a permanent tan, and a smile that would melt pack ice. He was related to Billy by blood, a nephew on his brother's side.

Garrett had a taste for good-natured mischief that got him into trouble on a regular basis: taking the screws off all the doorknobs so they came off in your hand or hanging the doors backward so they swung out instead of in. Billy fired him at least once a week.

He was always showing off for Nelia, racing his motorcycle engine underneath her window in the morning and sneaking off behind Billy's back to give her wild rides up and down the gravel road. Oliver followed him around like a puppy. Zoe tried for days to resist his bad-boy appeal, but he eventually found her soft spot too.

"Aren't you ever going to be done wrecking this place?" she asked him one day as he was ripping woodwork off one of the windows.

Garrett wiped the dust off his face with the back of his arm and grinned. "I suppose *you* could do better."

"It wouldn't take much."

He walked over and put a hand on her shoulder. "Meet me downstairs before Uncle Bill gets here tomorrow morning," he whispered. "I'll let you have a crack at it."

The next morning he was waiting for her in the dining room with a pair of huge leather gloves, a yellow hard hat, safety goggles, and a white dust mask he slipped over her nose and mouth. Then he handed her a sledgehammer.

"Your mom wants that wall to come down," he said. "Open things up a bit. Not too much backswing, now. That hammer's—"

He didn't finish the sentence because she was already in the middle of a violent strike and he had to jump out of the way to escape it. The hammer arced and missed the wall altogether, then hit the floor, leaving a large gash in the wood.

"It looks bad," Nelia said. She and Ollie were sitting in the living room on a sawhorse, watching like spectators at a baseball game.

"Don't worry about it," Garrett said. "We'll put a chair over it."

"Garrett, maybe you ought to take the hammer now."

"Give her a chance, Nelia. This is her first demolition."

"Her *first* demolition?"

"Keep your eye on the ball. Right here," Garrett said, pointing at a flower on the faded wallpaper.

It was an ugly flower, pink with yellow-tipped stamens sticking out of the center. It deserved to die. Zoe pulled the hammer back in slow motion and snapped it forward. There was a delicious sound of cracking plaster as the flower dissolved into rubble. White dust rose all around her.

"I hate that wallpaper," she said. Zoe scraped her feet on the remains of the wall, like a bull getting ready to charge.

"Hit it again," Garrett called out.

She picked out another flower to aim at and swung hard. A tremor went through her body from the impact, as the hammer sliced into the wall, opening up a hole. She swung again and a whole field of flowers crumbled to the ground.

Ollie and Nelia whooped and hollered with malicious glee, hooking arms with each other and dancing around the room. Having a license for destruction put everyone in a good mood. Zoe had never felt such pleasure. She wanted to smash everything in the house.

"I want to break something," Ollie shouted.

"All right, sport," Garrett said. "But you gotta dress for the game." He had him all rigged up in goggles, hat, and mask and was handing him a small claw hammer when Billy walked into the room, his face hot with anger. That was the last they saw of Garrett for three days.

Nelia, Zoe, and Ollie didn't have school for nearly three weeks. They'd arrived a week before spring break and their mother had decided not to enroll them in school until the vacation was over. So they had nothing better to do all day than watch their lives go from bad to worse. The destruction was unending. Men hung from holes in the ceiling, stuck out from under sinks, and crawled all over scaffolding on the outside of the house like ants on roadkill. Carpets came up. Woodwork came down. Noise and chaos broke out everywhere.

Ollie had to be watched constantly. The backyard was littered with piles of debris: pieces of walls, paneling, doors, dirty pipes, boards with nails sticking out, all of which Ollie found irresistible.

He thought the parade of men with tools was endlessly entertaining. They had set up a temporary office in the garage, where they hung their scuffed hard hats, spread plans out on plywood tables, and drank hot bitter coffee out of silver thermoses. He was always hanging around there, watching the workmen, following them, and generally getting in their way. The conversations he had with them were all the same.

"Is that a hammer? I like hammers. Do you have a saw in there?"

"Better not put your hand in the toolbox, son."

"I have a toolbox. That's a screwdriver."

"Yep. Don't touch that."

"You need this thing?"

"Put the drill down, son."

"Is this the button that turns it on?"

"Put it down, I said!"

Ollie was not discouraged. He worshipped them. People with tool belts were like superheroes to him. He started wearing Garrett's goggles and mask all day long, with a carpenter's apron tied around his neck like a cape. He called himself Hammer Man and ran all over the yard, fighting invisible evildoers. If you called him Ollie, he wouldn't even answer.

At night, when everyone had gone home, the house looked like the scene of a battle that both sides had lost. If Zoe woke up at two a.m., as she often did, she yanked open the windows and let the cold air in, just so she could breathe. Sometimes, lying in the darkness, she would hear geese flying overhead unseen, fools or optimists, maybe both. The weather was cold and the trees leafless. If someone didn't tell you it was almost April, you might think the world was poised on the brink of winter.

There were other migrants passing through in the hours before morning, more every day. Birds often flew through the night. It was safer that way. You wouldn't know that unless you were awake yourself and out in the open, feeling like they did that darkness was the only real shelter. She felt connected to them, these restless things, longing for a true home.

Soon she was leaving the house every night, going down the back steps into the kitchen, through the gutted rooms and out, stepping softly, careful not to wake anyone. One morning when she went out before dawn, there was a dense fog on the ground. She heard the keening cry of a seagull and looked up to see a lone bird wheeling in the mist. It had probably just wandered off course, and wouldn't stay. But it satisfied some deep need in her just the same, the longing to touch something that had touched what she loved.

As she walked out to the field through the fog, it felt like she might come out the other side and find she was at the shoreline again. She almost expected to smell salt, and feel the waves licking her feet. It was always foggy back home this time of year. Sunday mornings when her father was in port, she would go down to the dock with him to fish alongside the men in their knit caps and hooded sweatshirts, steaming mugs in their gloved hands, looking out with watery eyes at the endless ocean.

They always teased her, these red-faced bearded men, sitting on their coolers with their poles stretched across the dock.

"Watch that line," they'd tell her as she walked past. "You're too small to keep. We'd have to throw you back."

But she didn't mind it. It meant she was one of them. She belonged there. She was Daniel McKenna's daughter, and everybody knew it. "Selkie girl," they called her. "She's got that wildness in her, just like you, Daniel. You'll have to tie an anchor to her if you want to keep her."

She'd wander the docks looking for harbor seals, or just stare down into the water, waiting for her father to call her to bring the net and scoop up smelt. He was always complaining that the fish were disappearing.

"When I was young, you could dip your hand in the water and pull a salmon up. But they're all gone now. There's not a one of them back East, and they'd disappear here, too, if it weren't for the quotas. All that's left are the tame ones. Farms, Zoe, can you beat that? Like frickin' cows, they are. Next thing you know they'll have 'em grazin' in pastures on Whidbey over there.

"There's no room for anything wild in the world. All the

things that are free keep getting pushed to the edge. People won't be happy until they kill them all."

It was the edge places that Zoe felt at home in; the places other people passed over, the spaces in between, where things happened in silence and secrecy. That was another reason she went out in the early morning darkness. She needed wildness, craved it, the way other people craved love. Because it made her feel connected to something, made her feel understood.

She kept pushing farther out, looking for something, she didn't know what, until finally, out in the borderland, in the early hours of the morning, she stumbled on a hawk.

The first time she saw it, it was swooping down out of a tree, its wings pressed close to its body, like a diver, in a free fall. The huge bird swept past over her right shoulder, so close she could have reached out to touch it. It looked as though it might keep going down until it drilled straight through to the center of the earth. But at the last minute its huge wings opened like a dark cape and it began to rise, mounting into the air. Her heart pounded. Her eyes climbed up to the sky, following it. She realized, with a mix of terror and excitement, that it was chasing something.

The hawk beat forward, colliding with another bird in midair. For a moment they looked like lovers, locked in an embrace, as they tumbled to the ground. But they struggled as they fell, wings tangled, talons grasping, as they disappeared in the trees just beyond Zoe's line of sight.

She started running toward the place where they had fallen, pulled by some strange fascination. At first she couldn't find them, but as she squatted at the edge of the woods and waited, she caught a movement out of the corner of her eye and saw the hawk on the ground, standing atop a mound of feathers.

Was the other bird struggling under the grip of those awful talons? One wing fluttered hopelessly, jutting out at an odd angle from the bird's body. Maybe it was just a reflex.

She crept forward through the underbrush, and the hawk opened its wings and beat the air, as if to warn her. It tried to fly off, its victim locked tightly in its talons. But it was too much of a burden to carry. The huge bird kept losing its grip and dropping back down.

For one eternal second it stood its ground, staring at her fiercely from atop the hump of feathers as she inched slowly forward. They were almost at the same level, eyeball to eyeball, those red animal eyes burning with defiance.

With some ancient knowing, the hawk sensed what she wanted. It wasn't giving up without a fight. Zoe crept closer. The air split with a fierce squawking. Instinctively Zoe stood up and raised her arms skyward, stretching up to her full height. The hawk beat into the air, leaving the carcass behind, a temporary surrender.

A raspy sound echoed through the woods. She could feel the hawk's eyes on her as she walked over and picked the battered body up off the ground and held it in her cupped hands. It was so light; such a little thing to contain a life. How could it be so easily broken?

She had never seen anything this newly dead. It wasn't moving, but it was still warm, its feathers soft and yielding as she spread its intricate wing out wide. Its head dangled over the edge of her palm, the soundless beak open and the unseeing eyes still moist and full of a kind of dim light. She half-expected it to wake up again, to look at her in astonishment, lift its wings and fly off, as though it were all a bad dream.

The hawk was still *kakk*ing in the trees somewhere. Zoe was surprised to realize she did not hate it. It was the hawk, after all, whose awful beauty had first drawn her there.

Zoe laid the dead bird gently back on the ground. "Go ahead. Take it," she said out loud. She should be getting back, she told herself. Her mother would be getting up soon, realize she was gone, and ask a lot of questions she didn't want to answer.

Zoe went back to the house, slipped through the door, climbed the stairs to her bedroom, and crawled under the covers before anyone even knew she was gone. The sheets were cold against her skin; her body that was still warm, her limbs that still moved, her breath that came and went without thanks or notice. What a terrible joy it was to be alive, and what a fearsome thing to know what death was like.

She had come close to dying last summer when she and her father had taken Ollie camping at Mackenzie Lake in the Cascade Mountains. Her father was busy setting up the tent and asked her to watch Ollie, warning Zoe to keep him away from the water. But she hadn't.

They were standing on a rock ledge, flinging stones into the lake to see if they would skip, when Ollie decided to pitch in the car keys she had put down. He thought they would float, like the boat keys with the red and white fishing line bobber on the ring. The water was turquoise, so clear Zoe could see to the bottom, and so cold that even in summer there were rafts of ice floating across it.

She could see the keys lying on the white pebbles, deep underwater, glistening. It was so frigid that even seaweed couldn't grow there. Zoe could have told her father. He would have figured out how to get them. But she was ashamed that she'd let it happen.

Zoe shivered as she stripped down to her bathing suit and laid her clothes on the ledge. "Get back by that rock and don't you dare take one step closer to the water no matter what," she told Ollie. "*No matter what.*"

She leaned into the air above the lake, toes clinging to the cold stone. Then she moved back a step, her weight shifting from one foot to the other. She knew how to swim, but she had always been more comfortable on the water than in it. Swimming was what you did to keep your head up high enough to get air while you struggled to get back out.

Ollie was standing with his head down and his finger in his mouth. "I didn't do it on purpose," he said.

*"Don't you move, Ollie!"* she shouted.

Zoe walked backward several strides. She stared at the snowcapped peaks that surrounded the lake and the miniature icebergs floating in the center. Then she took a deep breath and let go, running full speed off the edge of the rock, into the air and plunging into the brilliant, biting water.

Cold stabbed her in the chest. Eyes wide open and aching, she fumbled with her hands on the sharp pebbles until she found the keys and closed her fist around them. Then she pushed off with her feet against the bottom. She tried to kick, but her limbs were already numb and barely moved. Fear gripped her. You could die in water like this. Three minutes was enough to kill a grown man.

Zoe clawed at the water with arms that felt like iron posts, desperately pulling herself toward the light at the top. Head throbbing, lungs bursting, she broke the surface of the water.

She gulped for breath and tried to will her whole body out of the water and back onto dry land.

She grabbed for the ledge, but her strength had been sapped by the cold, and she slipped off again. She opened her mouth, but no sound came out. The water closed over her face. She was sinking.

Zoe felt a hand grip her wrist and pull against the silken weight of the water that dragged her down. Her face broke through the water into light and air, and she saw her father's eyes, tense with fear and effort. He pulled her out of the water and up onto the ledge, and she lay there panting. Her father took his sweatshirt off and covered her with it.

"Ice," she mumbled.

He leaned his ear down close to her mouth. "What's that, girl?"

"Ice . . . " She shuddered, as she tried to form the words with lips too numb to move. ". . . cream . . . headache."

Oliver danced about on the rocks, flinging his arms into the air. "I SCREAM!" he shouted at the deep blue sky. "I SCREAM!"

Her father hugged her to his chest. Was he crying? Was he angry? She couldn't remember, and it didn't matter. What mattered was that she had needed him and he was there. She had almost been lost and he had saved her.

# CHAPTER 9

Her mother was already cleaning up when Zoe came down late for breakfast the next morning. She stepped around the old pipes that were piled in the corner waiting to be hauled out, sat down at the table, and poured some orange juice from the carton. "You could have told me," she said.

Her mother dropped a stack of paper plates into a garbage bag and turned to look at her. "What?"

"Nelia said you got a phone call about Dad."

"It's not as though I was trying to keep it from you, Zoe," she said. "You were asleep. I didn't want to wake you. Trish Albain called. She said the boat had mechanical problems. They went back for a part and left again."

Zoe clunked the glass down onto the table and stared at her mother. "Dad was back in Dutch Harbor? Why didn't he call us?"

"He tried, but the phone must have been out. That's why he asked Trish to get in touch with us. You know how it's been with all this mess. Maybe one of the wires was loose. Anyway, it's working now."

"What are you going to do about it?"

"About what?" Her mother set the bag down and wiped her hands on her jeans.

"About Dad going back out again."

"He'll be all right, Zoe."

"That's not what you said to him before we left."

"I can't control what he chooses. If this is what he wants . . ."

Zoe stood up, scraping her chair back. "I know what you think, because I heard you say it. Maybe you can lie to Nelia and Ollie, but not me."

"Zoe, sit down and talk to me."

Her hand tightened around the chair back. "No. I don't want to listen to you. I just want you to tell him to come back."

"Even if I thought that would change anything, I couldn't reach him now."

"Yes, you could. Radio the supply ship. Make up some reason. Tell him he has to come back right away because . . ."

"What?"

"We need him."

"Zoe, please . . ."

"If anything happens, it will be your fault." Zoe slammed the door open, drowning out the sound of her mother's voice. She shouldered past Billy coming up the walk, and started running toward the field, not stopping until she was so far out that she couldn't see the house.

Why did her mother always think she was right about everything? Why did she turn her back on the people she loved? She knew what could happen. There were so many things you couldn't control: freak waves and bad weather and things that were just plain stupid, like going out on a boat with Wes Albain.

Twenty-six men had died last season. Including Zoe's uncle Jack. Her father had gotten his little brother Jack a job aboard the boat he worked on—Albain's boat, the *Juneau*. Jack had been lost when the *Juneau* went down, and Zoe's father had nearly died with him. The truth was, there was a part of him that *had* died.

Her father had stayed in port after the *Juneau* had gone down, going to work at the boatyard, then at the processing plant, and hating every minute of it. Then one night he'd come home full of whiskey and announced that Albain had a new boat. Her father was going to meet him in Dutch Harbor. There was no talking him out of it.

Zoe was on the stairs in the darkness, listening to her parents argue, when she was supposed to be asleep. She could hear the panic rising in her mother's voice at the sound of Albain's name.

"You told me yourself, Daniel. If it hadn't been for Albain cutting corners, breaking safety regulations . . ."

"Well, I'm no prize myself, now am I, Annie?" her father had said. There was silence except for the endlessly ticking clock. "Albain is the only one who will have me."

Zoe had stepped out of the shadows then, and he'd turned on her, eyes burning. "Go back to bed, Zoe. You hear me? Go back to bed."

He was lying. She would have told him that if he'd only listened. There wasn't a captain in the fleet who wouldn't want her father aboard when push came to shove. It was something deeper that was driving him.

Her father had been the relief pilot when the *Juneau* had capsized in a storm, taking the life of his brother and three others. It might have been Wes Albain's boat that went down, but it was her father who'd been at the wheel.

❖

When they'd arrived, the house had looked simply old, feeble and neglected. Now it looked like an animal with its skin torn off. Outside, the workmen had ripped away the rotted siding, so that all that remained was a wooden skeleton, held together by oozing plaster, with dusty windows staring out at you like hollow eye sockets. The overall sense was of something missing, things that were not quite right and never would be.

Inside they had hacked away plaster, leaving a patchwork of studs and piles of debris. And if that wasn't enough, the whole house was encircled by a bright orange plastic snow fence and yellow tape that said POLICE LINE, DO NOT CROSS, which Billy had picked up at a flea market. It looked like the scene of some violent, incomprehensible crime.

Neighbors started dropping by, hanging over the fence in their plaid flannel shirts and orange caps, asking pointed questions and giving advice. Some of them knew Zoe's mother from way back. Others had known her great-grandfather. Every one of them knew Billy.

Zoe tried to avoid them. She took Ollie for long walks each day to get him out of everyone's hair. He drove her crazy at times, pestering her with endless questions and getting her into trouble for things she didn't do. But she had always had an unreasoning love for him. He had been born just about the time that Nelia had moved on to junior high, leaving Zoe behind like an outgrown doll. Ollie was Zoe's consolation prize.

It bothered her, the way he was always hanging onto Billy's leg, and begging to let him help. And the worst part was, he had started calling him Uncle Bill.

"Stop saying that," Zoe told him.

"Garrett calls him that."

"Well, you're not Garrett. And Billy's not your uncle, so lay off."

"Mom told me I could," Ollie insisted.

"Mom isn't always right."

Their walks often ended at the river that wound through the woods at the edge of their property.

"People like us—like you and me, Zoe—the water's always calling us," her father had told her. "You'll see that someday. You can leave it, but you can't get it out of you. We're like shells on the beach. Sooner or later, the water comes and yanks you back."

She had never been far enough away from the water before to know if he was right. The only air she had ever breathed had had the taste and smell of ocean in it, air so full of moisture you could drink it.

But now things were different. When she went to the river, she felt like she was going home. She could sit at the edge of it for hours, arms wrapped around her knees, watching the light dance on the water, listening to its murmur. Her feet seemed to find their way there, even when she didn't plan it.

One morning she took Oliver with her. It was still early, and there was a mist hovering over the water. Oliver squatted by the shore, dropping leaves into the water one by one to float down the river and sail away.

"Where does the river end?" he asked her.

Zoe shaded her eyes from the sun. "It doesn't. It just keeps going until it empties into a bigger river."

"Where does that one end, then?"

"It empties into another river."

"Then what?"

"Another river."

"Then what?"

"I don't know. It empties into the ocean. Stop bothering me, will you?"

"Where does the ocean end?"

She thought about all the rivers—bloodlines—crossing the continent, flowing down to the ocean from the Continental Divide. And what her father had told her about the oceans all coming together off the Cape of Good Hope.

"It doesn't end anywhere. It just spills out into another ocean."

"Then it has to come back."

"No, Ollie, the water doesn't come back."

"It has to."

"No, it doesn't."

Ollie scowled at her. "If it just keeps going and going and going, it will get too full and spill . . . like the sink does when you leave the water running."

Zoe couldn't help laughing, which made Ollie so angry that he kicked some stones into the water.

"Okay, you're right. I guess it goes up into the air and turns into a big cloud that floats up here and rains back down into the river again."

"That's a dumb idea. You don't know anything."

"Suit yourself," Zoe said.

Oliver walked along the shoreline away from her.

"What are you doing, Oliver?"

"Waiting for my leaf to come back."

It was while they were walking home from the river that Zoe spotted the hawk again. There was one lone tree at the edge of their land, an enormous, spreading giant with limbs that reached all the way to the ground. The hawk swooped past them as they walked near it, flying low to the ground and then pulling its wings in close and rising suddenly like an arrow shot toward the top of the tree. She got a better look at it this time, its large cross-shaped body, bull head, and brown and white striped underbelly.

Ollie was the first to notice there was something odd about it. "It's got something in its mouth," he said.

*Now what have you killed?* That was the first thing that went through Zoe's mind.

Her little brother took off running toward the tree, and Zoe went after him.

"Leave it alone, Ollie."

"I want to see it."

The hawk landed on a high branch and then flew off again. When they got closer, they could see a dark shape on the branch.

"What's that pile of sticks up there?" Ollie asked.

"Well, what do you know," Zoe said. "It's building a house."

# CHAPTER 10

Cooper's hawk. The bird had a name and that was it. *William* Cooper, whoever he was. He couldn't have been the first person to see the hawk, but he was apparently the first one arrogant enough to slap his name on it. She imagined someone with knobby knees, sticking out of khaki shorts, a beak nose jutting out from under the broad tan hat he wore to protect his pasty face from the sun, as he followed trails of bird scat.

Actually, that was who Zoe was becoming. Whenever she could get away from the house before her mother stuck her with a chore, she went out to the fields, looking for the hawk. If it wasn't anywhere in sight, she would take the opportunity to nose around for odd bones, stray feathers, and shattered eggs under its roost tree. The tree had a name too. It was a bur oak. She had found all this out by rummaging around through boxes and old trunks in the attic until she uncovered a mildewed book with brittle yellow pages, *Flora and Fauna of the Great Lakes Region*, by Virginia Whitefield Dorcester. Even though the book had been written in the 1950s, Virginia and William had blended together in Zoe's mind so that now, when she read the book, she imagined a woman in a long white ruffled dress and parasol trailing after Cooper. "William, wait for me. My boot is stuck in the muck. William, I can't find the twins, Flora and Fauna."

When the workmen weren't pounding on the floor below or the roof above, the attic made a safe hideaway, a place Zoe could see without being seen. It was long and dark, with steep sloped ceilings that followed the roof. Its corners were jammed with old suitcases, broken lamps, shelves of chipped and mismatched china, boxes of letters and postcards, and dressers full of crocheted doilies and linens embroidered by someone who'd had too much time on her hands. It reminded her of Ye Olde Curiosity Shop on the waterfront in Seattle, where she had once bought a jar containing a frog with two heads; a museum of the unwanted, the discarded, and the strange.

One rainy afternoon she'd rifled through a box of photos in the attic, taking a few out and holding them up to the light that filtered through the smudged attic windows. A man in work clothes, her grandfather possibly, sitting on the back of a wagon. A teenage boy in jeans and a broad-brimmed hat squatting down with his arm around a moon-faced calf. A young woman standing next to a car with a flat tire, her hands raised as if to say, "What can you do?" It didn't surprise her that she didn't recognize any of the faces. Her mother's family was a closed book. If there were stories to tell, she never told them, even about her own life.

Zoe's father's family was made up of travelers and adventurers, restless people who lived on the edges and didn't quite fit in. Her great-grandfather had left his home on the west coast of Ireland and sailed to New York, then wandered until he'd hit water again and found a wife from a family of Norwegian fishermen.

Island people, her father called them. "The whole world used to be one big ocean, and some of us never forgot. We've been trying to get back to the water ever since we sprouted legs and crawled out."

She had heard the story of her father's ancestors so many times that she felt she'd lived through each century herself. On the docks mending the nets, or rocking on the boat in the darkness, he'd summon their spirits up with stories so real she thought she could see the spirits hovering in the mist. His grandfather's brother Joe, who'd gone overboard near Kalaloch and showed up two weeks later, paddling the Clearwater River with two Quinault Indians in a canoe. His uncle Casey, who was the best long-liner the fleet had ever seen, and Old Paddy, who'd forecast storms with his wooden leg.

"We can't sit still, not a one of us. Like it or not, that's who we are: people with one foot here and one foot lifted to take the next step."

Zoe's mother talked about her family only in passing. Every now and then she would make a comment like, "You remind me of Aunt Edna when you do that."

"Who's Edna?" they would always say.

"I've told you about her, haven't I?" But she never had.

"I just assumed they were all boring," Nelia said. "And that's why she never talks about them."

But there was another possibility that occurred to Zoe now, as she sifted through the faces of these people, looking out at her expectantly from their lost world, as though they wanted something from her. What if there were some reason they had been banished to the attic?

Her father and his stories were so large they cast a shadow all the way across the continent. But her mother was like driftwood, a branch that had broken off and washed up on another shore, with all the jagged places smoothed out and sanded down, so you couldn't tell where it had come from or what had caused it to break off.

Maybe she didn't know her mother, Zoe thought. Not really. Maybe she never had.

She could not bring herself to walk away from her relatives in the attic and forget about them. So she had begun bringing the photos downstairs to her room, lining them up against the mirror on her dresser, and studying them at night before she went to bed: how their hands rested, the expressions on their faces, how they leaned toward each other or turned away. Sometimes questions would drift up to the surface of her mind: Who are you? What made you happy? What did you hope for and never get? And what would you think if you knew we were what your life was leading to?

On one of her expeditions to the attic, Zoe found a fishing vest, tan with lots of pockets, that must have belonged to her mother's grandfather, the man who had left the house to them, his dead-end dynasty, the one responsible for their being here. Zoe unsnapped all the pockets and emptied the lures and lines out onto the attic floor so she could fill her vest with the fascinating and violent artifacts she was discovering under the hawk's roost tree.

The only thing she didn't find in the attic was a pair of binoculars. Those she had to borrow from Billy. Was "borrow" the word you used when you took something from someone without their knowing so you wouldn't have to ask for it, but you were going to give it back sometime when you didn't need it anymore? It was close enough. The other words she could think of weren't very flattering.

Billy had given Zoe a ride to town when her mother had sent her to pick up some groceries for supper. She would have been happy to walk, would have preferred it even, but he had passed her along the road on his way home and opened up the side door for her. She didn't know how to tell him what she was really thinking, which was "Get lost," so instead she got in.

Most of their conversation focused on a shotgun that was sitting behind the seat.

"It's not loaded," he said, when he saw her staring at it. "I go hunting in the fall: ducks, pheasants, a wild turkey, if I'm lucky. Mostly I just enjoy walking through the fields or sitting out in the blind, watching the sun come up."

"So why are you carrying it around with you now?"

"Skeet shooting," he said. "Skeet are always in season. Or I might want to use it to scare away a coyote. Lotta them been seen around here lately. They've been warning people to keep an eye on their dogs and cats. Can you beat that?"

"They're not really that dangerous," Zoe said, although it was more like a question than a fact.

"Not unless you're a poodle. Course, I wouldn't kill 'em, just the same. Too many poodles in the world anyway, if you ask me. But I'd fire a warning shot over its head."

He tried to make small talk, asking her questions about her life in Washington and the friends she left behind, but the conversation never really got off the ground.

"I'm not used to being around kids," Billy confessed.

"I can tell," Zoe said.

The binoculars were the expensive high-powered kind her father used on the boat. She saw them under the seat when she first got into the truck, but she didn't have a chance to "borrow" them until the next day, when Billy was in the basement supervising the men installing the jack to prop up their house. He never locked his truck. He probably wouldn't even notice his field glasses were missing for quite a while. You didn't need binoculars to shoot skeet. Still, she decided to keep them out of sight, shoving them into her backpack when she went out to the fields, along with the book and a water bottle.

She could get a much better view of the hawks now. There were actually two of them, a male the size of a crow and a much larger female. It made Zoe's blood run cold the first time she saw her magnified by the binoculars. She was beautiful and fierce, a sharp hooked beak made for cutting and tearing, glowing red eyes that looked right at you, sizing you up, dark slicked-back feathers on her head over a tan and brown barred chest, and talons like grappling hooks, that were used, said Virginia, for crushing prey, slashing it, or squeezing it to death. That's what the hawk did to a robin or squirrel before eating it. Another option was holding it underwater until it drowned.

Virginia and her descriptions of flora and fauna were good company on these outings. Her book was full of careful pencil drawings and firsthand descriptions of trees and flowers, birds and animals, fish and reptiles of the area. She seemed to have a special love for raptors. "It is easy to think of them as villains," she wrote, "until you remember how much they are like us."

Life at the top of the food chain wasn't all it was cracked up to be. The hawks had been driven close to extinction by hunters and poisons. Chicken hawks: That's what farmers called them. Killing them, even a nest full of newborns, had been considered a public service. Those that weren't shot for target practice, to protect chickens, or out of sheer meanness were nearly finished off by pesticides that thinned their eggshells.

Zoe's hawks were doing their best to make a comeback. They had been busy for days patching up an old nest, adding a few well-placed sticks. That was the female's job, according to Virginia: remodeling.

Now they had finished the nest and moved on to phase two: dinner dates. The male would go hunting and bring a juicy pigeon or starling back to the female, who would rip its feathers off and devour it, letting him have a few bites when she was done. After that there was a lot of lovemaking and wing-flapping, accompanied by their cackling call, *kek-kek-kek*ing, over and over, like madmen laughing.

She could have slept in on Sunday. The workmen weren't coming. For once the house would be quiet. The drills and buzz saws and hammers were locked away in battered metal boxes and stacked in a corner of the dining room, along with piles of scrap wood and wallboard, carpenter horses and coiled extension cords, like sleeping snakes. But she decided to get up anyway.

She glanced in each bedroom as she walked past, to make sure no one else was awake. It made her feel both smug and wounded to realize how easily she could leave and not be noticed. Just like that. She could slip away from them.

The temperature had dropped suddenly the night before. There was a coating of frost on the grass, and she noticed something else, something strange she'd never seen before. In the two weeks since they'd arrived, the bushes had started sprouting leaves. Now each leaf was encased in its own little prison of ice. They looked perfect, tender and green inside the ice, but they would be stunted and twisted by the cold. She felt a sudden pang of grief for this ugly place trying to grow, and dying young.

When she reached the woods, she found a frost-coated stump to sit on, and was grateful that she'd remembered at the last minute to bring along an old flannel blanket for a cushion. It made a nice platform where she could sit and watch her hawks. Her hawks: That was how she thought of them now, not Cooper's. Let him get his own.

The female had been sitting on her nest occasionally. Zoe could see her long black tail sticking out of the nest of twigs, and sometimes she spotted her hooked beak with those red eyes glaring at her when she approached. Occasionally the hawk would greet her with a single *kek*. Not a warm welcome exactly, but not unfriendly, either.

She greeted her mate with a series of excited *kek*s. When the big female spread her wings and sailed over to meet him, he would retreat to a high branch and let her feed on his kill awhile, before he came back for the scraps. Zoe hadn't seen him much lately, though, and that worried her, because it meant the female would have to go off hunting on her own. If she ever did lay eggs, they wouldn't be protected.

Zoe shivered, pulling her hands inside the sleeves of her fleece. What was it like, she wondered, to be inside an egg, waiting to be born, living each day in the darkness, wanting to break out into a world that was a mystery? When the babies' fragile world began to crack, would it feel like they were about to be born, or would it feel like they were dying?

There was a part of her that wondered, and a part of her that knew, a silent part of her that drifted to the surface when she was all alone. Sometimes when she was lying in bed, just before falling asleep, she could feel the darkness pressing down on her with so much weight that, even though she longed to escape, her body felt like it was made of stone, her arms and legs too heavy to move. It didn't feel like a dream. It felt like a memory; the oldest memory she had.

She was getting sore-bottomed, sitting there staring up at the sky all morning. Zoe wrapped the blanket around her shoulders to keep the cold wind from biting through her fleece and set off across open country to the road. She climbed up the hill and stopped to scan the gray sky with her binoculars before she left.

That was when she spotted the male. He was sailing high up, wings like a kite, riding an air current, waiting for unsuspecting mice to dart across the frosted field.

"About time you showed up," Zoe said out loud. Then she saw something else—a large animal, maybe—move out of the corner of her eye.

She put the binoculars down and scanned the field.

There was a boy—about her age—running flat out on the ground beneath the bird. From this distance he looked like a shadow, moving in perfect time with the hawk. His arms were spread wide, like he was flying, and his face was turned up to the sky.

Zoe's heart raced. What was he doing here? Who did he think he was? She could feel her face heating up, a jumble of feelings swirling in her. She almost called out to him, but stopped herself. He was so far from her. Would he even hear?

She hated him, felt invaded by his very presence. And she also wanted to know him. What was it that pulled at her, that feeling that pulsed deep beneath the anger and resentment?

She put the field glasses up to her face and studied him. He was tall and thin with electric brown curls ringing his head, and a face that was like a cliff, full of planes and angles. She watched him secretly, squatting low. It felt good to know him and not be known by him. She forgot about the hawk, and kept her binoculars trained on the boy as he turned and sidestepped, his face up to the sky, until he disappeared into the trees.

"One of the neighbors stopped by today." Her mother was bent over the oven, taking a roast chicken out, when Zoe came down for supper Sunday night. "Bridgeforth," her mother said. "Joanna. She has a daughter your age."

"She came all the way over just to tell you that?"

"That, and she wants to buy our house."

Zoe lifted her head. "She wants to live here. *Here?*"

"Actually, she wants to tear our house down. Her husband's a developer."

"What did you tell her?"

"No, of course."

"What do you mean, of course? It's already a wreck. We could sell it and buy a house in Washington, which is a better place for a bed-and-breakfast, anyway. Who would want to take a vacation here?"

"It's more than just a house to me, Zoe. We could go somewhere else, but it wouldn't be home."

"We don't belong here. It's *not* our home."

"But it might be. You haven't even given it a chance. When you go back to school tomorrow and start making new friends, then . . ."

"You think *then* I'll be happy? Do you know anything about me?"

Her mother sighed. "No, sometimes I feel like I don't."

"Maybe it's better that way. If you did, you'd only be disappointed."

"That's not fair, Zoe."

"What would you know about fair?"

Zoe stormed out the door into the yard. It was a brisk evening with a clear black sky, layered with stars. She was standing with her back to the house, hugging herself, when she heard her mother come up behind her. Her mother rested one hand lightly on her arm, but Zoe shrugged it off. They stood there silently for the longest time, both of them looking outward in the same direction, before her mother finally spoke.

"This is how it was the night you were born. Did you know that?"

Zoe didn't answer her. She flung her head back and looked up at the sky.

"Clear, like this. Cold. And stars. I'd never seen so many stars. Your dad insisted that we go out on the boat late that night. He said he had something to show me."

Her mother breathed a long sigh. "I thought he was just being crazy, you know? Your dad is so . . . well . . ." The unfinished sentence dangled in the air.

"But you know what it was he wanted to show me? A meteor shower: falling stars, hundreds of them sailing across the sky, one after the other. 'Wishes,' he said. 'There's no end to them tonight.'"

Zoe squeezed her eyes shut. She had heard the story many times. She could hear her father's voice in it.

"We fell asleep out there, looking up at them, making wishes. When I woke up, I was having contractions. Your dad started the motor and gunned it for shore, but I could feel you coming, and I was shouting at him to stop the boat. By the time he did, your head had already crowned. Your dad tried to pull you out, but then he saw that the cord was wrapped around your neck, and he had to unwrap it one, two, three times."

Her mother stopped talking, as though she didn't want to go any further. "And you didn't breathe, Zoe. He held you up and you weren't moving. You were small enough to fit in one of his hands. He tried to clear your mouth and breathe life into you. And all I could think was 'Please don't die.' That was all I wanted, 'Just don't die.'

"And then you cried, this beautiful gasping, wailing noise. You were so full of life."

Zoe kept her eyes on the fixed and familiar stars.

"But all of your life I've felt like you had one foot in this world, and one foot in another that I can't reach." Her mother turned to look at her. "I almost lost you when you were born. And, Zoe, sometimes I feel like I'm losing you again."

## CHAPTER 11

Like having your neck stretched out on a block, waiting for the ax to fall: That's what Monday felt like. Her life had been her own for nearly three weeks—first the move, then spring break. Now she had to go back to school.

They had moved eight times in the last seven years. The first few times, Zoe had made new friends, but it hurt too much leaving them. It was better, she found, not to get too attached. She'd taught herself to move in and out without leaving a ripple, like the otters that suddenly appeared next to the boat and then vanished beneath the water.

When she got to junior high, though, blending in became more of a challenge. The move to Anacortes last year had been especially hard, because everyone but Zoe had apparently spent their summer vacation growing breasts. She had shown up for eighth grade without the passport she needed to enter one of the tight little circles of girls talking about boys and bodies and makeup.

Fortunately, there was another outsider: a quiet girl who spoke almost no English when she arrived from Hong Kong.

She had become Zoe's best friend of the moment, and they had stayed that way when they went off to high school, even though they had very little in common except for oddness. The girl played music all the time, practicing three hours a day. Even her violin teacher told her to get out and have a little fun.

Now that the family was in Selena, Zoe was alone again. It was only Zoe who dreaded the start of school. Ollie was still too young to be bothered by what everyone thought of him. And Nelia wasn't interested in blending in. She took the opposite approach, arriving at each new school like royalty that had decided to mix with the commoners awhile. Here I am; lucky you. Something in her attracted people, and made them overlook her erratic moods and oversize ego.

It was only Zoe who preferred not to be noticed. Only Zoe wanted to be invisible.

It worked for a while. Her English teacher seemed to look right through her as she walked in the door, shoulders closed in around her blank notebooks. He just looked up hesitantly, as though he had seen something surprising, and then went back to what he'd been doing. Zoe wanted to hug him on the way out for ignoring her.

She got lost on the way to her next class, distracted by the unbearably painful sight of a locker decorated with ribbons, balloons, and a large poster board sign with blue letters that said, CONGRATULATIONS, MELISSA. YOU'RE A WOMAN NOW. By the time she found the room, the bell had already rung and everyone was seated.

"Yes?" the teacher said expectantly. She was young and

pretty, with large, even teeth. Zoe stood in the doorway a moment before starting to back out again.

"Oh, you're the new student," the teacher said, too warmly, too full of enthusiasm. This was going to be trouble.

"Your name is . . ."

"Zoe McKenna."

"Zoe. How beautiful."

She could smell an introduction coming, and winced.

"Why don't you take a seat next to Lorie over there. Lorie, will you hold your hand up?"

It wasn't necessary. She was sitting next to the only empty seat in the room—in front, of course.

"Let's welcome Zoe." The fresh-faced teacher started the applause and everyone halfheartedly joined in.

"Would you like to tell us something about yourself?"

There were so many things she could have told them: where she had come from, why they had moved here. All the standard things teachers asked her, like how many brothers and sisters she had.

But what came out of her mouth was this: "I almost died before I was born."

Thirty pairs of eyes locked on her. Two people in the back row had their heads bent together, whispering. A boy in front was trying to swallow a smile. She could see the tension in his cheeks. Next he would be laughing and it would spread like wildfire all over the room. Zoe looked directly at him. His gaze shifted to his feet. Silence filled the room like a bad smell.

Miss Brightness coughed. "That's very interesting, Zoe. I'm sure we'll be hearing more about this as time goes on." She went up to the chalkboard and started writing out some equations.

*Well, that's it,* Zoe thought. She was an untouchable.

❖

When she finally made it outside after school, there was a crowd gathered at the side of the building. She walked toward them, her gaze following a girl's hand as she pointed at something up near the roof. The sun was sinking down toward the horizon, shining directly into her eyes. Zoe put her hand up to shade them, and thought she made out something clinging to the rock wall of the building, about thirty feet in the air.

Zoe squinted at the dark shape and it came into focus: a lanky boy in jeans and a white T-shirt, which hung loose, exposing his tan back. His face was pressed against the stone wall and his arms were stretched out above his head, curled hands clinging to the limestone blocks. One leg was supporting him, a foot firmly wedged between two stones. The other leg was bent, struggling to find a foothold. At first she thought he might have fallen from a window or the tower, and was clinging there waiting to be rescued. But then he found his footing. His arm muscles rippled and strained, and she realized he wasn't going down at all. He was rising.

Zoe shouldered her way farther into the crowd for a better look.

"Hey, spider boy." Next to her a smarmy kid with a skateboard under his arm flicked his greasy hair out of his eyes and taunted him. "Hey, fly sucker." His friends, a skinny boy with blond hair, half his size, and a girl in a tight-fitting top, rocked back and forth snickering.

"Shut up," Zoe snapped. "I'd like to see one of you do that."

The mouthy boy scowled at her. "You think I'm that big an idiot?" he said.

Zoe leveled her eyes at him. "Yeah, I do."

The boy stepped in front of her, but the crowd closed in again. Zoe looked up to see the climber's hand slip. He was clawing at the rock, struggling for another handhold, his whole body tense, trying not to let go.

Suddenly his foot gave way, setting loose a landslide of little chunks of dirt and mortar that tripped down the side of the wall. For one terrible moment Zoe thought she saw his body fold inward.

"Don't do it," she said under her breath. She willed him to press flat, hold tight to the wall. Her teeth clenched. "Hold on," she muttered, as if his ear were next to her lips.

She saw his hand settle around a large block that jutted out to the right, almost beyond his reach, and she felt her body relax with his. The crowd moved back.

A big-bellied man with thinning gray hair burst out of the door, followed by two men in police uniforms. The man turned and raised his head toward the roof.

"Ivy! Get off that building. You're in enough trouble already."

The boy looked down, but said nothing. What was the matter with the man, Zoe thought, hating him. Did he want this boy to fall?

The policemen stood on the steps near a group of teachers, with their hands on their hips, heads tilted way back, like latecomers at a movie, forced to sit in the front row.

"Why don't they call the fire department and bring a ladder to get him down?" someone asked. "What if he falls?"

*Or jumps*, Zoe thought.

Zoe's eyes were riveted on the boy. Her heart was pounding. Her stomach tightened in knots. What was it she was feeling? It wasn't fear.

The boy came to life again and started to climb, slowly, but with more confidence than before. He scanned the wall for openings, crab-walking a little to the side, then moving up again. He was almost to the top now. He stretched out his left arm as far up as he could and his fingertips closed in on the floor of the bell tower. A few more moves and he had hauled himself up to his waist. Zoe could see his chest heaving as his breath went in and out. His legs dangled in midair.

She breathed relief as the boy boosted himself up the rest of the way, pushed up to his feet, and gazed back down at them, smiling. He stood with his hands on his hips, triumphant. Behind him, the sun glowed. His face was in the shadows, but there was something familiar about his lanky ease and grace, the pleasure he seemed to take in movement, the brown ring of curls that spilled over his forehead. And she thought . . . she was sure . . . he was looking at her.

Zoe had forgotten that school wasn't the only thing beginning that day. Weezy was coming to get the kitchen organized. She had talked Zoe's mother into letting her help out with the cooking. Weezy was standing on a chair in the kitchen, her head inside a cabinet and a bucket of Lysol next to her on the counter, when Zoe burst through the back door.

"Back already?" Weezy dropped her rag into the bucket and got down off the chair. "How was it?"

"Long."

"Meet anyone you like better than yourself?" Weezy's standard greeting.

"Not yet."

"Cat got your tongue?"

"Come up with any new lines lately?"

Weezy shot her a sly smile. "I'm going to crack you one day, Zoe. You know that, don't you?" Before Zoe could get out the door again, Weezy walked over to the table and pulled the lid off a tin of cookies she'd baked and brought over. "Oatmeal," she said. "No nuts, just raisins."

Zoe looked at them suspiciously. How did Weezy know she hated nuts in cookies?

Weezy climbed up onto the chair, fished the rag out of the bucket, and wrung it out again. "You can't hold out forever."

Zoe waited until Weezy had turned around and busied herself with the cabinet, before she wrapped two cookies in a napkin to take upstairs.

"Love always wins in the end," Weezy said.

# CHAPTER 12

How long were you dead?"

"What?"

Miranda Pikul stared at Zoe across the lunch table, her piercing brown eyes magnified into watery globes by her thick glasses.

"You said you almost died before you were born. Which, by the way, is the most interesting thing anyone's said at this school in the whole time I've been here. How long did you go without breathing?"

"I don't remember," Zoe said.

"I bet it wasn't longer than three minutes. The human brain can't go without oxygen longer than that without shutting down altogether. Although there was that girl in Alabama . . ."

Zoe's eyes wandered away from her, glancing at the churning bodies jammed into the lunchroom, but that didn't stop Miranda. She was perfectly capable of holding up both sides of a conversation. Zoe had learned that much about Miranda in the few days she'd known her.

There was the usual lunchtime mayhem going on: chairs

scraping; people laughing, shoving, teasing, and gossiping. And there were the usual divisions. It was always the same. Zoe could have been anywhere. But she was looking for one person in particular, someone who would have stood out like a silver dollar in a jar of pennies.

"One million, four thousand six."

"Huh?"

"The number of people who are born every year; it's one million, four thousand six."

Zoe looked at Miranda. She was definitely not one of the pennies, and she wasn't the silver dollar, either. But at least Zoe was not sitting alone.

"How do you remember that stuff?"

"I don't know. It's not that I try to. I can't help it. It's like my brain is made of flypaper. If a fact goes by, it sticks. I can't get rid of them."

Zoe had an image of Miranda's head, covered with index cards, each with some sort of fact written on it. She supposed it was her destiny to meet this girl. They were like hook and eye: the girl with the endless supply of answers, drawn irresistibly to the girl who has all the questions.

"What happened to that boy?" Zoe asked.

"What boy?

"The one who climbed the school the other day."

"You mean Ivy?"

"That's his name? Ivy?"

Miranda nodded. "Ivy Walker. His real name is Paul Walker, Jr. But everyone calls him Ivy because he's always climbing things. Last year he was arrested for climbing the courthouse."

"Do you think they arrested him again?"

"No. They suspended him. I heard Mr. Anzinger talking to

the principal, 'Looks like we're going to have to suspend Ivy again.'" Miranda's voice sank several octaves when she became Mr. Anzinger. "Those were his words, exactly."

So that explained why Zoe hadn't seen him around. The only kid in the school she might have been able to relate to had been thrown out.

"Don't you think it's kind of odd how they think they're going to fix Ivy by giving him a week or two off school," Miranda said, "when what he really needs is a good mountain?"

Zoe licked peanut butter off her lip and smiled. "You're a strange girl, Miranda Pikul."

"Thank you," Miranda said. "And by the way, it's not 'pickle,' it's 'pik-*cool*.'"

It felt like her first week of school would never end. When it did, Zoe fell into bed, exhausted after supper on Friday, and slept right through to mid-morning on Saturday. She took advantage of the fact that everyone else was already busy when she finally woke up, packed herself a lunch, and slipped out to the fields.

When Zoe reached the tree with the nest in it, she put down her backpack, dug out the binoculars, and lay down in the tall grass at a respectable distance, far enough so she wouldn't upset anything, but close enough to see what was happening. The hawk was there all right. She could see her head bobbing about. It looked like she was plumping up the pillows. She turned round a few times, then hunkered down again in her stick palace, returning to what seemed to be her only purpose, her only desire: just to wait.

You had to admire her patience, even though there was no

reason to believe that anything would come of it. Several times over the last few days when Zoe had trained her binoculars on the nest, there hadn't been a bird to be seen. If there were eggs in that nest, neither hawk had been there to keep them warm or protect them from marauding crows and blue jays. She was beginning to think they weren't the best parents in the world.

Still, the hawk always came back and took up her post again. Maybe she was just too birdbrained to give up when it was clear she should. Or, maybe you didn't have to be a perfect mother. Maybe if you were there even half the time, it was enough. There was really no way to tell if she had been a good enough mother, until something hatched. In the meantime, all the hawk had to go on was blind faith.

And for some reason she didn't understand, Zoe wanted to wait alongside her. They could be like that all spring, the two of them. She could see the long weeks stretching out before her, her coming home from school each day and lying in the field—until grass grew up around her, flowers bloomed, and roots sprouted from her body, reaching deep down into the earth.

As long as the hawk kept coming back to her nest, so would Zoe. Maybe the hawk knew something Zoe didn't. Maybe some bird intuition told her that even though it didn't look like it, in the end everything was going to be all right. Or maybe it was only a matter of time before the hawk decided enough was enough. Hope was a strange thing, Zoe thought. It could live without food or nourishment for a long time and then suddenly dry up and die for no reason at all.

When Zoe walked back into the yard, Billy was standing in front, talking to some dusty-faced workmen with leather knee pads and pointing up at the roof. "Zoe," he called out to her as she walked past him toward the house, "have you seen my binoculars?"

She felt her face get hot. "What makes you think I took them?"

The workmen bent over the blueprint that was stretched out on the tailgate of the pickup, as Billy walked toward her.

"I didn't say that you took them, Zoe. I was just asking if you'd seen them lying around somewhere. Things get misplaced, that's all."

She was no thief. She had intended to give them back eventually. But she had a need for them now. "I saw them under the seat of your pickup a while back," she said. It was the truth, if not the whole truth.

"That's where I usually keep them," he said. "I'm pretty careful about putting things back. But anyone can make a mistake." He hesitated a moment, as though it were her turn to say something now. But instead she just stared at the workmen.

"You don't like me very much, do you?" Billy asked.

"I don't see what that has to do with anything," Zoe said.

"I'm going to be around for quite a while," he said. "You don't have to like me, but it might be worth a little effort for us to try to understand each other."

Zoe slung her backpack over her shoulder. "I understand you just fine."

"Letter, Zoe," Nelia said as she walked into the kitchen just before supper with a handful of mail. Her mother was at the stove, stirring a big pot of soup. Zoe and Ollie were sitting at the table breaking the ends off string beans. The kitchen was where everyone lived now, the only room in the house that hadn't been torn up.

Nelia set the pile of mail down in front of them. Zoe picked an envelope off the top and read the return address: Bridgeforth. She set it back down.

"You're not even going to open it?" her mother asked.

Reluctantly Zoe ripped off the top of the envelope and pulled out an invitation. "It's from that girl, Jordyn Bridgeforth. She's having a pool party April 28."

"It's a little chilly for swimming, isn't it?" Nelia remarked.

"They have an indoor pool," Zoe said sullenly. "And a horse barn. And a tennis court. Miranda told me."

Her mother tapped the spoon on the side of the pot to clean it off and laid it down on the stove, then came over to look at the invitation. "Nice of them to think of you," she said.

Zoe stared at her. "I'm not going."

"It wouldn't hurt you to be friendly."

"Yes it would," Zoe said. She threw the invitation back down onto the table, knocking another letter off the pile. The first thing she noticed about it was the handwriting: her father's. She picked it up gingerly and looked at the postmark: Dutch Harbor. He must have sent the letter in with one of the freezer boats that shuttled crab back to the factories. Zoe started to tear at the envelope, but Oliver slapped at it.

"That's my letter."

"What are you talking about, Oliver?"

"It's got my name on it."

She flipped the envelope over and read it.

Oliver leaned across the table and pointed at the letters. "That's an *O.*"

"I know how to spell your name."

"Let me open it."

He tried to take it from her, but she pulled it back.

"Mommmmm." Oliver was starting to cry. She felt like a bully, taking a toy from a baby. But she wanted that letter bad.

"Stop fighting. You're going to rip it," Nelia said.

Zoe pried Ollie's fingers off.

"I'll read it for you, okay? Here," she handed it to him, looking him straight in the eye. "You can open it."

Oliver tore into the envelope, and the contents spilled out onto the floor. Photographs. Zoe knelt down and started sweeping them back into the envelope, while Oliver raced to pick them up off the floor one by one and flip them over to look at them. He let out a squeal.

"It's Booda!" he said.

"Lemme see."

The photograph showed a close-up of Oliver's bear, hanging on to the rigging of a boat, with a rough shanty town and snow-covered peaks in the background. On the back there was a caption written in her father's large print. Zoe read it out loud. "Chilly, homesick, and missing his boy, Liver, Booda arrives in Dutch Harbor, Alaska. He had not planned on taking this trip, but being a brave and adventurous bear, he makes the best of things."

"Read me this one." Oliver handed Zoe a picture of their father, bearded, sunburned, and tired, standing near the ship's rail with Booda on his shoulder. Something dark floated in the water behind them. "Booda and a harbor seal. Look close at the right. He is eating a crab. Fine dining in the Bering Sea. One less crab for us."

There was a third picture of two men in orange slickers, hoods up, facing out toward an endless stormy, churning gray sea. "A typical day," Zoe read the caption. "The work is hard and the same thing over and over. Often we work two days before we sleep, and then it's only three or four hours, then back on deck. After ten days of this, we're ready to deliver our crab to the processors. Maybe sooner if the catch is good."

Oliver stared at the picture. "He's coming back."

Zoe said nothing.

Oliver picked up the other photo. "Booda looks happy," he said. He pressed the photo to his chest and ran upstairs, while Zoe flipped through the pictures, as though she were looking for some secret in them.

In the last photograph her father stood facing the camera. His face, under his orange hood, was too dark to see. He had one gloved hand raised, waving halfheartedly, and the other hand clung to a metal crab pot. The deck was iced over, and so were the railings. Except for his slicker and the orange buoys, the boat, the sky, and the ocean were all the same color—gunmetal gray.

This is what she knew about water: It was cold, dangerous, and unforgiving. It could break a boat like a matchstick and swallow a man whole and never spit him back.

# CHAPTER 13

There was a knock on the half-open door. Her mother stood in the hall with a two-piece swimsuit folded neatly in her hands.

"What's that for?" Zoe asked.

"The pool party."

"That's not my suit," Zoe said. "I had to throw mine away last year, remember?"

"Uh-huh. That's why I picked this one up back in Anacortes. End of season sale; I couldn't pass up the bargain. I bought it a size larger, thinking you might grow into it."

She said this in an offhand way, but Zoe knew exactly what she meant. She had been slow to develop. That was her mother's way of putting it.

Breast budding was what the doctor called it. When she went in for her back-to-school checkup each year, the doctor would glance casually under the white paper sheet and announce, "No sign of breast budding yet," like a farmer waiting for a field to bear fruit, who was, every year, disappointed.

"Why don't you try it on?" Her mother laid the suit down

on the bed. "I never thought I'd be able to locate it in all those boxes, but there it was right on top. Lucky, huh?"

"Lucky," Zoe said. There were so many things she had left behind, so many things discarded or forgotten. Why did this have to be the one thing that had made the cut?

Zoe dangled the suit from her finger. It was turquoise with green flowers.

"I'm sure it won't fit," she grumbled.

"We'll see," her mother said.

Zoe trudged down the hall to the bathroom. Loud music throbbed from behind the door. She knocked sharply. "Can you please hurry up? I have to get in there."

Inside she could hear Nelia howling along with the music. "Ooohoooh. You can try to resist, but you know it's true, don't you know, don't you knooooowww, can't stop the—"

"Nelia!"

"I can't hear you!" Nelia shouted, her voice barely audible above the thumping bass.

"Turn the radio down!" Zoe shouted back.

"What?"

"I need to get in there!"

Zoe banged on the door with both hands. The door opened so suddenly that she nearly hit Nelia's face, which popped out like a jack-in-the-box. She was wearing a towel on her head, and there was green cream, the color of seaweed, smeared all over her face. Nelia peered at Zoe with two owl eyes, through the cloud of steam in the bathroom.

"As you can see, I'm very busy," she said. "This had better be an emergency."

"I have to try on this suit," she said.

"You have a bedroom." Nelia began to push the door closed,

but Zoe stuck out her foot. "There are workmen outside my window. I don't even have curtains."

Nelia sighed. "Okay, but hurry up. If this stuff dries on my face, I'll need a jackhammer to get it off."

Nelia stepped into the hall and leaned against the wall, her arms folded over her terry cloth robe. "Three minutes. I'm counting, Zoe."

Zoe went into the bathroom and closed the door. She slipped off her T-shirt and jeans and stepped into the suit. Normally she didn't pay much attention to how she looked. She never wore makeup and was usually content with a few quick brushstrokes to tame her hair.

She stood on tiptoes and gazed through the thick fog in the bathroom to see how the swimsuit looked. There was something wrong. One side of the swimsuit top was rounded, but the other was flat as a pancake.

She wiped away the steam to make sure she hadn't made a mistake, and looked again. Was she growing breasts? No, she was growing a breast. There was a soft swelling on one side of her suit, and on the other side there was just an empty poof where her breast should have been.

What was going on here? Didn't they come in pairs . . . like eyes and ears, arms and legs? She pulled the top of her suit away from her skin. One of her breasts had finally begun to grow. It was an unmistakable bud. The other was apparently a dud.

Zoe sat down on the edge of the tub. What if they stayed like this? What if one kept growing and growing, trying to make up for the lazy breast, until it turned into one of those giant water balloon breasts?

Worse yet, she might be dying. She had never heard of anyone dying of lopsided breasts. But on the other hand, it was probably one of those things you wouldn't tell the truth about.

Zoe stared through the mist at her shadowy reflection in the mirror. Even if she survived this, she might as well be dead. She was going to be a freak. A unibreast.

There was a loud pounding on the door. "Are you coming out, or do I have to force my way in?"

Sadly, Zoe unlocked the door and Nelia pushed past her. She wetted down a washcloth under the faucet and swiped at the green cream on her cheeks.

Zoe hesitated. "Can I talk to you about something?" she murmured.

"This stuff is like pond slime." Nelia said, staring at her face in the mirror. She wrung out the washcloth and wiped her top lip. "Smells like it too. What did you want to talk about?"

"Breasts," Zoe said.

Nelia bared her teeth at herself in the mirror. "Did I get any in my mouth?" She dabbed at her big front tooth with the cloth. "I bet they dig this out of swamps."

"You're not listening to me."

"Yes, I am."

"What did I say?"

"I don't know. Something about bad breath." She turned around and looked at Zoe for the first time. "Nice suit," she said, raising her green crusty eyebrows at the splashy display of flowers. "You look like a window box."

Zoe went back to her room, threw some sweat clothes on over her bathing suit, and went outside. Her mother was talking to Billy and one of the workmen about some problem with sending in a deposit so they could get more materials ordered. "I need to ask you something," Zoe said.

Her mother put her hand up and turned toward her. "I'm

a little busy right now, Zoe." She glanced down at her sweat clothes. "Weren't you going up to try on that bathing suit?"

"Yes, but . . ."

"I know what your question is, and the answer is no, you can't buy another one. We can't afford it. And I still want you to go to the party, okay?"

She turned around again, picking up where she'd left off. Zoe went back to the house, shoulders collapsed over her hollow chest with its uneven breasts. There was no one to talk to; no one at all.

# CHAPTER 14

"What's wrong?"

Miranda Pikul was sitting next to Zoe on the bus, studying the side of her face.

"What are you talking about?" Zoe pulled open the window and let in some fresh air.

"There's something wrong. I can tell by the way your mouth droops at the corners." Miranda made a face to show her what she meant. She looked like a sick monkey.

"You're the one with all the answers. You tell me."

"Trouble at school," Miranda said.

Zoe shook her head.

"You're in love with an older man."

Zoe rolled her eyes.

"Someone died."

"Worse."

"What could be worse than death?"

Zoe dropped her head back on the seat and closed her eyes. She could think of lots of things. "What do you know about breasts?"

Miranda looked over her shoulder to see if the boys sitting behind them were listening, but they were busy throwing wads of paper at someone across the aisle. "I know they're overrated," she said. "But then, my opinion may be warped a little because I don't have any. Why?"

Zoe considered whether or not she could count on Miranda. "You won't tell anyone, right?"

Miranda's eyes widened. "You can trust me completely."

"I only have one breast."

Miranda stared at her. "Are you sure? I mean, have you counted them?"

Zoe turned her face away and looked at the cars whizzing by outside the window.

"Okay. That was an idiotic question. Maybe you should see a doctor. There must be something they can do. I saw this girl on television who was born with a penis—not a big one, just a little sprout or something—and she went to a plastic surgeon who turned it into a vagina. I mean, they can do miracles. . . ."

"Could you keep your voice down, please?" Zoe said.

Miranda bit her lip. "I'm sorry. Really. Have you talked to anyone? Like your mom?"

Zoe shook her head. "No one listens to me."

"That's the trouble with parents," Miranda said. "All they want to do is talk. No one wants to listen. Don't worry, Zoe. I'm there for you." She put a hand, reassuringly, on Zoe's arm and fixed her with a steady gaze. "You are not alone."

When Zoe was ten, they moved to Forks, a little town near the Hoh River rain forest on the Olympic Peninsula. It was little more than a crossroads. But her mother had found a job waiting tables at the Log Cabin Café on Highway 101, which specialized in homemade blackberry pies and venison steaks. And a friend of her father's had offered them the use of a trailer he'd hauled down from Alaska, and a job at the sawmill when he wasn't out fishing. It was a long way from anywhere, surrounded on every side by national forest and rugged coastline. But there was a good, if somewhat small, school; the Calawah River was nearby, where you could fish for steelhead and salmon; and the town had a public library, housed in a mansion that had been donated to the town by a man who'd gotten rich during the lumber boom.

That was the summer Zoe had decided to read all of the books in the world. Oliver was still a toddler. They had found space for him at the Darling Dumpling, a day care that advertised on the bulletin board at the Safeway. It was the perfect place for a two-year-old: a little white ranch house at the edge of town with crayon-colored rooms, a fenced-in yard with a climbing gym and big toys, and a large, laughing, endlessly patient woman named Wendy who kept a noisy mob of sticky preschoolers happy with ample amounts of apple juice, graham crackers, and homemade playdough.

Zoe was too old to be a darling dumpling, but too young to be on her own. So her mother came up with the inspired idea of paying Nelia to watch Zoe. What actually happened was that Nelia, who was going into high school that fall, gave half the money to Zoe as payment for staying out of her hair, and kept the rest to buy lip gloss, magazines, and tickets to the movies for her and an ever-growing stable of boyfriends.

It was a good bargain, for both of them. Nelia had privacy, Zoe had freedom, and they both had plenty of spending money. Zoe used her earnings to buy fifty-cent sodas from the machine outside the Safeway and useless trinkets at the Dollar Store, where she would generally head right after breakfast. After that she would ride her bike down the winding streets, looking for excitement, or at the very least a little fun. It was a small town, without too many loose children in it, so when she tired of exploring its limits, she would usually wind up at the public library.

It was so unlike all the other buildings in town that when you stepped into it, you felt like you had crossed into another world. A gray stone building with turrets and beveled glass windows, in the middle of a park surrounded by an iron fence, the library was originally built by the lumber baron as a castle for his wife, who had died before it was finished. It was as out of place in that town of small wooden bungalows as Zoe felt herself to be. And she loved it, as much for the fact that it didn't belong as for its air of melancholy and longing.

She also loved the librarian, Ms. Belleville, who had an air of being out of place too. She had a neck like a swan, long white hair she wore pinned up on top, and a mysterious past as a dancer at a nightclub in Ketchikan, which contrasted nicely with her long gray skirts, cashmere sweaters, and sensible shoes. She pronounced her name with a French accent, so it rhymed with "eel."

Ms. Belleville had befriended Zoe, and made her feel welcome there. She recommended books and liked nothing better than to help Zoe find answers to her questions.

That was the best part. She was half librarian and half bloodhound. Sometimes it took days to find the answer, but once she was on the scent of something, she never gave up. Zoe would climb the long staircase on a hazy summer afternoon, swing open the large carved wooden doors, and find Ms. Belleville waiting at her desk, smiling with deep satisfaction as she slid a white slip of paper across her desk with the name of a reference book or magazine article penciled on it.

How many galaxies are there besides the Milky Way? What is the capital of Haiti? How do you remove spaghetti sauce stains from tablecloths? Why do elephants have trunks? No concern was too silly, no topic too wide-ranging, and no question too obscure for her.

"Now, there's a conundrum for you," Ms. Belleville would say. It was the first time Zoe had heard that word, and she liked the sound of it so much, as it echoed through the wood-paneled walls of the library, that she adopted it as her own. "I have a conundrum," she would say. Although she stopped saying it at home, because Nelia would always say something like, "Maybe you can have it removed."

If she was occupied with something else, Ms. Belleville might suggest a section where Zoe could look for answers. More often, her face would light up, as though she had waited her whole life for someone to ask her that question. "I have always wondered that myself," she would say, and they would be off on another search. It did not occur to Zoe, until long after they had left, that perhaps Ms. Belleville had been as lonely as she had been. Except for the tropical fish in the children's room, Zoe was generally the only other living soul in the library.

All that summer she had gone to the library for the same reason other people went to church: for comfort, for understanding, for answers. Sometimes Zoe would bring questions that even Ms. Belleville couldn't answer. Like "Why do people kill each other?" or "Where do you go when you die?"

"There are some questions," Ms. Belleville would say, "that do not lend themselves to easy answers, Zoe."

That was what gave Zoe the idea of reading all the books in the world. If she did, then she would *know*.

Had they stayed in Forks, she might have still believed it was possible to accomplish her goal. The library there had a small and eccentric collection, top heavy with books on celestial navigation, forestry, and the history of the Northwest.

But they had moved the next spring, this time to Seattle. The closest library was the big one downtown, where Zoe discovered that there were more books in the world than barnacles in the ocean, more than she could read in ten lifetimes.

As a going-away present, Ms. Belleville had given Zoe the name of a good reference librarian in Seattle and a brand-new copy of *The World Almanac*, with library binding. Inside the fly leaf there was this inscription: "To Zoe, a fellow searcher. May you always have questions to keep you company on your journey, and may the roads you travel lead you home."

At first she thought that was all she had written, but later, when she was looking up information about Kiribati (Question: What do you call the people of Kiribati? Answer: Kiribatians), she discovered that the whole book was embroidered with messages from Ms. Belleville.

Sometimes they were the kind of things that Ms. Belleville herself would have said, had she been there. On the page listing endangered species of the world, for example, she had written, "Imagine, Zoe, only 6,000 tigers left in the wild. I hope someday you get to see one."

Some of it was shameless propaganda. Above the heading for Health and Medicine, she had inscribed this quote: "I have never known any trouble that an hour's reading would not dissipate.—Charles Louis de Montesquieu."

And sometimes they were simple words of encouragement

and advice, like the one Ms. Belleville had inexplicably chosen for the Science and Technology section: "That Love is all There is, is all we know of Love.—Emily Dickinson."

The next spring, when they moved again, Zoe called the library in Forks to let Ms. Belleville know they were now in Bellingham and that the library there was quite nice, but not as good as hers. She was upset when a new librarian answered the phone. So upset that she hung up without leaving a message or asking what had happened to Ms. Belleville. Zoe didn't want to know.

"She probably retired," Nelia said to Zoe, as she sat slumped on the chair next to the phone. "Or died," she added thoughtfully.

It was only her anger that kept Zoe from overflowing with tears.

"I'm just being realistic," Nelia muttered in her defense. "She *was* old, you know."

"You don't know the first thing about her."

Nelia, nudged by guilt, had offered to call the library herself and find out how Zoe could reach Ms. Belleville. But Zoe wouldn't let her.

She never did call the library back. She preferred to write her own ending. On the long bike rides she took that spring, she made up lives for Ms. Belleville. Perhaps the grandson of the lumber baron and true heir to the family fortune showed up and asked Ms. Belleville to marry him. Or perhaps her mysterious past in Ketchikan finally caught up with her and she was in the witness protection program, living on some remote island with new fingerprints, a new identity, and a new name, possibly Smith.

Zoe regretted her childishness, now that she was faced with such a hard question and there was nowhere to turn. Why hadn't she asked for Ms. Belleville's address so she'd be able to write to her and ask for help?

Not that it really mattered. She'd never get an answer in time to fix her problem. It was too late. *The World Almanac* would have to be enough. Zoe took it down from the shelf, flopped down on her unmade bed with the book propped open on her chest, and flipped through it, comforted by the familiar handwriting in the margins.

She looked under Female Population in the index and found a dozen topics, which said a lot about what the almanac thought was important about women: death rate, childbearing, marital status of, income of, number in the armed forces, ACT scores. No help there.

But on the last page of the index, after ZIP Codes, Zodiac, and Zoroastrianism, she found what she needed to know. Written in Ms. Belleville's round, clear letters at the bottom of the page were these words: "Remember, Zoe, that wherever you go, you will always have a home at the public library."

The library in Northfield, the next town over, was a simple redbrick building with white shuttered windows and large white pillars. A short, dark-haired woman was bent over the reference desk filling out papers when Zoe walked in. She wandered over to take a book off the shelf and pretended to look at it while she studied the woman. She was wearing a white blouse with a little black velvet tie at the neck, under a pin-striped vest. A silver charm bracelet jangled at her wrist.

Zoe flipped through the pages, wishing she'd asked Miranda to come with her so she wouldn't feel so alone. What was she going to say to this woman? "I'm looking for information on how to grow breasts"? The librarian seemed rushed, businesslike.

Not the kind of person you could easily ask questions of a personal nature. Not Ms. Belleville.

Zoe shoved the book into its place on the shelf and walked toward the back wall where a row of computers hummed quietly, waiting for someone to wake them from their dumb machine sleep. She sat down at the far end, pressed a key, and the screen blinked to life. Friendly, impersonal, and eager to please: This was better.

She clicked on the screen and typed in the words "female troubles."

"Sorry, no match found."

Then she tried "female mutants."

"Sorry, no match found."

She poked the backspace key and typed in the word "freak."

Power freak, control freaks, but no freaks quite like her.

Nervously she glanced around, then typed in the word "breasts." She scrolled down the list of books that came up, stopping at *The Man Who Grew Two Breasts and Other True Tales of Medical Detection*. At least she was getting warmer. Then she read the next title: *The Puberty Book: A Guide for Children & Teenagers*.

Bingo.

Zoe scribbled down the call numbers on a scrap of paper and slunk over to the juvenile shelves. There was an empty space between *The Period Book* and *Growing Up Isn't for Sissies*, right where *The Puberty Book* was supposed to be. Great. She would need to reserve it. More humiliation, more time, and they'd probably call the house and leave a message to let her know her puberty book had come in. She'd just have to make do. Zoe reached for the period book and the sissy book. Then she retraced her steps back to nonfiction adult and grabbed *The*

*Man Who Grew Two Breasts* for good measure, adding *Statistics for the Terrified* and *Letters of E. B. White* for camouflage.

The woman with the charm bracelet and tinted glasses looked down at Zoe's stack of books when she dropped them on the desk. "E. B. White," she said. "He's one of my very favorites."

Zoe's throat tightened. Was she going to read all the titles out loud?

A young man about Nelia's age walked over and got in line behind her. Zoe rested her hand on top of the books, as though they needed to be held down. She cleared her throat. "I'd like to take these out."

"Certainly. May I have your library card?"

Zoe pulled out her wallet, and handed her a card from the Bellingham library.

"You don't have a Northfield card?" The woman fiddled with her button earring.

Zoe shook her head.

The librarian reached under the desk. "If you fill out this form and have a parent bring it in with a tax bill—"

"I'm just passing through," Zoe said.

"Oh?" The woman looked puzzled.

The boy behind her scuffed his feet impatiently.

"I'm visiting . . . a friend," Zoe said. "She's outside waiting. I'll just go see if she can come in."

She started backing toward the door, hoping she'd be outside before the librarian lifted E. B. White off the stack and exposed Zoe's real taste in books.

There was no way she was ever going back inside that library. She was just going to have to think of something else.

# CHAPTER 15

How do they find their way back?"

"What's that, Zoe?"

"The salmon. How do they know the way back to the place they were born?"

It was the time they'd gone upriver to see the salmon spawning: big silver fish, glittering in the sunshine, flinging their bodies into the air, over and over, trying to get back upstream. She couldn't have been more than eight years old, but she remembered it now as she sat outside the library, as though it were still happening: the roar of the falls, the smell of wet rocks and cedar, the streams of light reaching down through the trees like silver fingers. They were sitting on the banks, the two of them, Zoe and her father, watching the fish leap into the air at the base of Little Bear Falls.

"Ahhh, it's a hard thing isn't it, this swimming upstream business. Makes you wonder why they do it."

"I know why they're doing it. They want to go home," Zoe said. "But I don't know how they find their way."

Her father picked up a stick and flung it into the churning

water. "The thing is, Zoe, there are some questions I don't have answers for. That's a hard business too."

"There's an answer," Zoe said. "I just haven't found it yet."

Her father ruffled her hair. "Not a quitter like your old dad, eh?"

He threw an arm around her shoulder and pulled her close to him. "Let me see something, here." He rubbed his fingertips behind her ears. "Gills!" he said. "Just as I thought. You're half-salmon yourself, aren't you, then? Always pushing against the current."

Zoe had to wait nearly a half hour for the red station wagon to swing into the entrance of the library parking lot. Garrett was in the passenger seat. He'd been teaching Nelia to drive, ever since her mother had decided the job required someone with more of a risk taker's personality. He reached a well-muscled arm over the seat and held the door open for Zoe against the cold wind that seemed determined to close it.

"You could have waited inside," he said.

She didn't bother to explain why she preferred the outside of the library to the inside, and probably would for a long time. She let the door slam shut behind her and smoothed out her windblown hair. "Where were you?" she grumbled.

"Shopping," Nelia said. "I went to three stores looking for a new hairbrush for you and still couldn't find the right kind."

"I don't need a new brush."

"Yes, you do. I lost yours."

Zoe stared out the window, watching a crumpled white bag tumble down the sidewalk in the wind.

"Look, I'm sorry, okay?" Nelia said. "Just who do you think

you are, making a big deal out of a little brush, when you're the one who's always—"

Garrett's smile flickered across the seat. "Settle down, Nelia." He put his hand lightly on her shoulder. "Zoe wasn't even complaining."

Nelia's room was like a riptide. Some mysterious force sucked things into it: Spare keys, lip gloss, bike locks, went down there and disappeared. Zoe wouldn't have gone in, if she hadn't caught sight of her hair in the mirror when she'd walked into the house and decided she'd better find that brush. She looked like she'd been electrocuted.

While Nelia and Garrett sat in the kitchen talking, Zoe went upstairs and pushed open the door. Nelia always kept it closed to keep her mother from complaining about the carpet of wet towels and dirty clothes. The room was decorated with an assortment of old papers, gum wrappers, and empty glasses with milk rings dried around the edges. Zoe stood in the center of the chaos, nudging blue jeans and underwear aside with the toe of her shoe, but didn't see the hairbrush.

The mattress pad had slipped off the bed, taking the sheets, blankets, and pillows with it. Zoe got down and thrust her arm underneath, reaching in all the way up to her shoulder. She groped about, trying to identify the objects her hand fell upon: papers, panty hose, books, mismatched shoes. She stuck her head under, tilting it sideways, peering into the darkness, and thought she saw something blue at the back.

She tried to get a clear shot at it by pulling out the papers and magazines blocking her view. A wrinkled copy of *Cosmopolitan* fell open to the classified ad section at the back. She was about to shove it aside, but something caught her eye. In between the columns of ads for $10 love horoscopes, free cosmetics, miracle weight loss, and painless facial hair removal, there was a picture of a big-bosomed statue, naked from the waist up. Floating above her head, like a flag, was the word "Maxibreast" in big red letters. There were three exclamation points after it, just in case the "maxi" part didn't get the message across.

Zoe sat back on her knees and smoothed out the page. "Why not have the bust you've dreamed of? Gain three cup sizes in just thirty days. No harsh chemicals. No surgery. 100% herbal, 100% natural. Results are permanent. Why wait to be the woman you want to be?"

The door swung open. Zoe slapped the magazine shut. Nelia gawked at her. "What do you think you're doing?"

"Looking for the hairbrush you stole." It was always best to take the offensive in dealing with Nelia.

"In *Cosmopolitan*?" She handed Zoe her hairbrush. "I found it in the bathroom right where I left it," Nelia said. Then she dug into the white plastic bag she was carrying and pulled out a Dove chocolate bar, Zoe's favorite. "For the pain and suffering I caused you," Nelia said. She gave it to Zoe, then stepped past her and tossed the bag onto the bed.

Zoe stood up and brushed off the crumbs she had been kneeling on that were now embedded in her clothes. She looked down at the bag on Nelia's bed. MEDIKWIK, it said in bold, black letters. FOR ALL YOUR HEALTH AND BEAUTY SUPPLIES.

"And I'd better not find you rifling through my room again," said Nelia.

"Thank you," Zoe said.

Nelia turned to face her, hands on her hips. *"What?"*

"I said, 'Thanks.'"

Nelia looked at her suspiciously. "You're welcome."

❖

"Did you know the condom is five hundred years old?"

Miranda had stopped several feet behind Zoe, eyeing a display of contraceptives with the curious detachment of an anthropologist.

"Sshhh." Zoe hushed her. She pulled Miranda by the wrist.

"Not this particular one. Just the idea of them. They were invented in the sixteenth century by Gabriel Fallopius, as in fallopian tube."

Zoe clamped a hand over Miranda's mouth. "Not so loud," she whispered. She dragged Miranda into the next aisle.

"May I help you?" The young woman in the green lab coat had her name, Jennie, sewn in flowing white letters on her pocket. She had perfect long red hair, perfect white teeth, and the casual confidence of someone who had always lived in a perfect body and took it for granted that she always would. Not someone like Zoe: the kind of girl you'd find skulking around the aisles of the MediKwik looking for Maxibreast with a friend who couldn't shut up.

Zoe could have worked up a good case of envy. But the young woman seemed so kind. Zoe wanted to pour out her heart to Jennie. Tell her the whole story, one girlfriend to another. How her mother had dragged them across the country, away from everyone and everything she cared about, and if that weren't bad enough, now she was growing one breast.

"We're just looking," Miranda chirped, unaware that they were now in the incontinence aisle.

Zoe was beginning to think that Maxibreast wasn't the kind of thing this store carried. She walked toward the back wall and spotted a shelf full of herbal supplements with a sign that read WOMEN'S SUPPLEMENTS. She motioned for Miranda to come on over.

Mysteriously, Jennie appeared, carrying a stack of boxes, walking behind Miranda. Were there two of her?

Zoe picked up a bottle of Joint Juice and studied it as though she were going to be tested on it, glancing up every now and then to scan the labels on the top shelf. Miranda pulled a bottle off the shelf. "Horny Goat Weed. That doesn't sound right," she said. She put it back and picked up another. "Nu Hair: Wrong 'nu' thing. Healthy Woman Estromax. Hey, this sounds like it has possibilities."

Jennie was kneeling down beside an open box, loading bright yellow bottles of Foot Fungus Treatment onto the lowest shelf. Zoe nudged Miranda hard with her elbow, but she went on reading as though nothing had happened.

"Stay in control. That's appealing. Supports healthy estrogen balance. I think we've got something here." She ran her finger under the fine print. "Stabilizes mood: Nice side benefit. Reduces hot flashes. I guess not."

A voice over the loudspeaker interrupted her. "Sales assistant to cosmetics." Zoe's heart pounded. She waited until Jennie stood up and walked toward the front of the store, and then she turned on Miranda. "Go outside and wait for me, would you?"

"What?"

"Everyone's looking at us."

"Don't be so sensitive."

"*Please . . .*"

Miranda shrugged. She walked toward the front of the store. It was now or never. Zoe's eyes searched the rest of the women's supplement shelf and stopped abruptly when she reached the end. Tucked into the farthest corner of the shelf were not one but three "breast enhancers."

A gallery of beautiful women smiled down at her from the boxes, over the tops of their large, perfectly matched breasts. She passed over Maxibreast pills and New Bosom oral supplement because she saw something even better: MiracleBust, a topical breast enhancement cream.

"Revitalize and awaken your breast cells. Rapid results. As seen on TV," the box said. She passed over the part that said "recommended for women 18 or over." It was probably like R-rated movies. They didn't want your breasts to send you into shock before you were ready. Then she discovered a bigger drawback: the price. It was $29.99. She had only ten dollars.

A harried-looking woman about her mother's age came around the corner pushing a cart with what looked like a two-headed octopus hanging out of it. Two very noisy children about three or four years old waved their arms and grabbed things off the shelf that their mother had to pry out of their little fingers. Zoe noticed them too late to put the MiracleBust back on the shelf. Panicked, she dropped it into her pocket.

"I want vitamins," the girl said, hanging over the edge so far she almost fell out.

Their mother ignored them while they jostled each other. Zoe stepped aside and let the woman take a bottle off the shelf, then watched them round the corner, her thoughts jittery.

*Now what?* Maybe she should pretend to be eighteen and ask if they had any free samples. Fat chance. She looked like she was twelve, and she didn't even have the nerve to take the box up to the checkout.

Then she had another thought, a thought she didn't even want to admit to herself. She put her hand down and felt the box of MiracleBust inside her coat pocket.

No one had seen her drop it there. She could just leave.

❖

"What do you mean you took it?"

"I put it in my pocket because I was embarrassed, and I left, that's all."

"You walked out without paying for it?" Miranda let go of her bike and had to grab it to keep it from falling over. "You stole it?"

"No!" Zoe looked at her feet. "I just took it."

"You'd better go in there and tell them what happened."

Zoe's mouth fell open. "I'm not going back in there, Miranda. I can't."

"Then, I'll do it."

"You're going to turn me in?"

"No, no. I'll just tell them something. I'll tell them I found it outside. It must have fallen out of someone's bag, or off the back of a delivery truck."

"No one's going to believe that."

"It doesn't matter. The thing is you have to give it back."

She thrust her hand toward Zoe's pocket and its load of contraband drugs, but Zoe's fingers tightened around the box.

Miranda bit her lip and glared at her. "You're not the kind of person I thought you were," she said. She swung a leg over her bike and looked over her shoulder at Zoe one last time. Then she turned her back and pedaled off into the parking lot.

Thief. Zoe didn't say the word or even think it at first. She tried to think of nothing at all, as she walked over to her bike, then bent over and twirled the combination on the lock. It took her three tries to remember the combination—her birthday. When she finally heard the click and felt the lock release in her hand, she glanced around to see if anyone was watching before she swung her leg over the seat, as though taking her own bike were a felony.

She didn't even remember the ride home, except for feeling empty all the way, and starting to cry so hard that she missed seeing a stop sign and a car that was starting through the intersection.

"Don't be so careless," she railed at herself. "You could have died." She was surprised that the thought didn't upset her as much as it should have.

Not until that night, sitting on the edge of her bed with the MiracleBust directions spread out on the quilt, did she allow herself to say it. "I am a thief. I stole drugs."

Now that she heard herself say it, it sounded even worse than she had thought it would. *I am a drug thief.* The kind of person you see on *Real Cops* with their legs spread, leaning up against a car.

She looked at the jar of MiracleBust on the bed and felt sick. Was she really that bad? Drug thieves go to jail. She tried rephrasing it. "I stole an herbal supplement." It sounded less sinister somehow. And more intelligent.

She hated people who stole things. She had stopped speaking to a girl in Bellingham when she'd bragged about shoplifting from the Wal-Mart. But this was different. She hadn't stolen jewelry or designer clothes or expensive shoes. She had taken something she really needed, something to treat her "condition."

She had once read a story Ms. Belleville had given her about a father who was too poor to buy medicine to save his little boy from dying. So he stole it and went to jail for the crime. Wasn't this the same sort of thing? Now that she thought about it, it was really the MiracleBust company's fault. They were the ones demanding outrageous sums of money for something that could do so much good for suffering humanity. Greed was as bad as lying, wasn't it?

No matter how she twisted it, her mind felt better but her heart didn't.

Zoe picked up the jar of MiracleBust and twisted the cap off. Inside there was a glistening green gel that smelled like sour apples. *Like the Garden of Eden*, she thought. For an instant she considered sneaking the bottle back into the MediKwik. But her crime had become like a rock pushed over a cliff, much harder to stop than it had been to set in motion.

She hesitated a moment, then dipped two fingers in, swirled them around, and rubbed the gel on her pancake breast. If she was going to be a criminal, she might as well be one with boobs.

"Grow three cup sizes," the directions said. Better do this gradually. If she woke up in the morning with great big breasts, her mother would suspect something. Zero to AAA would be plenty. At least, at first. Maybe later she'd consider going up another cup or two. Or more, depending on how she liked it.

It was too bad you couldn't try them on first, like a new bathing suit. Once you grew three cup sizes, they were probably there to stay.

Zoe pulled her T-shirt over her head and cast it off onto the bed, then walked over to look in the mirror. She tried to picture herself with enormous breasts, doing the things she always did. She swung her arms from side to side and up and down. Despite what all the boys her age thought, when it came to breasts, it was entirely possible to have too much of a good thing. Big hooters would only get in her way.

Still, an A cup, or even a B, might be nice. She decided to

use a double dose on the good side and a triple dose on the flat side to even them out. The gel felt cool, but not unpleasant. She slathered it on thick, so it didn't all sink in.

*This is the last time I will see myself this way*, she thought. Her breasts were wet, like something newly born. They sparkled with a faint iridescent light.

She put her T-shirt back on, then added a sweatshirt in case she got up to go to the bathroom in the middle of the night and ran into her mother with her new breasts. She wasn't even going to tell her. It served her right for humiliating her at the doctor's office every time they went, asking "Are you sure something's going on there?"

Zoe crawled into bed and curled up with her arms crossed over her chest. She felt like she was on the edge of some great change in her life, as though she were going to wake up the next morning and be someone else. No, that wasn't right. She was already someone else, and sometimes she was not so sure she liked who she was.

*This is what it is like*, she thought, *to lose the life you understand, and walk off into the unknown.*

# CHAPTER 16

She dreamed of fire, raging out of control, flames eating up forests, smoke blotting out the sun. Zoe woke up in a sweat, facedown, her hair lying damp and stringy across her cheek. She rolled over. Her skin felt hot. Did she have a fever? Was she sick? Then she remembered the MiracleBust.

Foggy and half-asleep, she flung the blanket onto the floor and stumbled down the hallway. Closing the bathroom door behind her, she flicked on the light and pulled up her sweatshirt. Nothing had changed. Her chest looked just as it had yesterday: a long, flat plain interrupted by one gentle slope. The only thing different was the color. She looked like she had a good case of sunburn, all the way up her neck. Her face was flushed too. Even her wide-open, frightened eyes looked red.

Zoe tiptoed back to her room and fell back into bed. There was no reason to panic. Maybe this was how it happened. Like a volcano. You had to build up a big load of heat and steam and then suddenly, without warning, there was an explosion that pushed everything out. A picture of Mount Saint Helens flashed through her mind, two of them, twin peaks.

She lay perfectly still and listened. She didn't *hear* any rumbling in there. Her heart was beating wildly, blood thundering in her ears. What would it be like when she finally erupted? How could it not hurt?

*I am not only a thief,* she thought. *I am a natural disaster.*

She closed her eyes, trying to sense what was going on inside her. She felt somehow as though she were hovering above herself, looking down at her pathetic limp body on the bed. Wasn't that what happened when you died? Last week she had known everything there was to know about her body. But now, it seemed, her body was a secret to her. All those mysterious processes that went on in the darkness inside her were somehow taking place without her will, without her permission, and without her knowledge.

She had always enjoyed her body for what it could do: her lean and muscled legs, her sun-browned arms and tapered fingers. She trusted it, relied on it. She took it for granted that it would always be there for her, heart beating, breath going in and out, without the slightest effort on her part.

But now she was a passenger on a journey she hadn't chosen. Her body, it seemed, had its own idea of where it was headed. She could either go along quietly, or get dragged behind.

There was a knock on the door. "Time to wake up, Zoe." Her mother's morning voice: cheerful, senselessly optimistic. "I'll make you breakfast before I drop you off at the Bridgeforths."

April 28, the pool party. She could not have felt worse if her mother had invited her to come downstairs to be flogged.

Zoe slouched at the breakfast table in a gray hooded Columbia sweatshirt, stirring her soggy cornflakes in milk, which by now was as warm as soup, pretending that she was actually going to eat it.

Nelia sat across from her, digging pink, juicy flesh from a grapefruit.

"I thought you were going to Jordyn's party today."

"I am."

"So where's, 'the Suit'?" Nelia emphasized the last word like it was a looming danger. "I thought Mom rescued it from your wastebasket before it got taken out to the trash."

Zoe dropped the spoon into her bowl with a clatter, splashing some milk over the side. She pulled a flowered strap out from under the neck of her sweatshirt. "She did."

"I could have told you that wouldn't work, by the way," Nelia droned on. "She already knows that trick. I tried it when I was thirteen. Mom bought me a polka-dot chiffon dress with puff sleeves for a Valentine's dance. Picture that one."

Zoe did. It made her feel better, but not for long.

Nelia rolled a piece of grapefruit around in her mouth. "Red with white dots . . . as in Minnie Mouse."

She winced as she dug her spoon into the grapefruit and it spit back at her. "You could have at least put it in a different box before you threw it away, Zoe. Besides, it's not that bad. It's actually kind of cute . . . in a window-boxy sort of way."

"Just leave me alone, okay?"

"No, I mean it. With your body, it will be great."

"You don't have to try to make me feel better. And it's not working. You're only making me feel worse. I just want to get this over with."

"It's a party, Zoe, not your execution."

Her mother walked into the kitchen, opened the refrigerator, and took out a carton of eggs and a tub of butter and set them on the counter, next to the stove.

"Aren't you too warm in that, Zoe? You look a little flushed."

Nelia and her mother both stared at Zoe. She felt like there was something crawling up her back. She squirmed in her chair, craning her neck as she rubbed it against the back of the chair, trying to stop the itch. The more she thought about it, the worse it got.

"Is it some kind of crime to wear a sweatshirt around here? Can't I even dress myself without everyone picking at me?"

"Of course you can. I was only saying that it's a beautiful day and . . ." Her mother's voice drifted off. She turned on the stove, sliced off a piece of butter, and dropped it into the pan.

The sizzle of the butter made Zoe think of heat, and the thought of heat made her itch again. She shimmied a little too hard in her chair and the table began to shake.

Nelia reached for her glass of milk and steadied it to keep the liquid from sloshing over the sides. "Stop fidgeting, will you?"

Zoe could feel Nelia's eyes on her as she ate. She tried to look nonchalant.

"Why are you staring at me?"

"It's just . . ." Nelia scowled and peered at her like she was an exotic bug. "I just thought . . ."

"Stop looking at me." She hung her hair like a curtain between them.

"Your lips; they seem so . . . I don't know. Big."

"I have big lips. Okay? Is that a problem?"

"I think full lips are very attractive," her mother said.

"But they seem somehow bigger than I remembered them. Really big. You didn't hurt them, did you? Look at this, Mom. Her nose seems bigger too."

"Nelia, for heaven's sake."

Their mother set down the spatula she was using to scramble some eggs and looked intently at Zoe. So did Nelia.

"Here . . ." Zoe held her arm straight out toward Nelia and pulled back her sleeve. "Why don't you just take a slice off and slide it under a microscope?" She slammed her fist down hard on the table, sending some silverware clattering to the floor. "I'm not a freak, you know."

"Well, excuse me for being concerned about you," Nelia said.

"No one said you were a freak," her mother said. "We just want to be sure you're all right."

Zoe licked her lips and chewed on them. If she could, she would have eaten them. But the more she chewed, the more they hurt.

Her mother walked over and peered closer at her, cocking her head like Zoe was a problem that refused to be solved. "Turn your face this way." She put a hand lightly on Zoe's chin.

Zoe jerked her head away.

"Is there something wrong?" her mother asked, so gently that Zoe had to lash out at her to keep from crying.

"Everything's wrong, okay?"

She shoved her chair back and it fell down with a crack like gunfire. Zoe wheeled and stormed into the hallway, fighting back her tears until she made it to the landing.

Quarreling voices drifted up the stairs after her. Her mother muttered something she couldn't make out, drowned out by Nelia's counterattack, edgy and self-righteous. "It's not *my* fault," she proclaimed. "Why do you always blame me?

Safe behind the locked door of her room, Zoe leaned on the dresser and studied her damp, red face in the mirror. She touched her lips and nose with her fingertips. Puffy; just like Nelia had said. Her eyes looked swollen too, and crying wasn't helping matters. How could she go to the party like this? Maybe she should tell them she was sick. But then her mother would take her to the doctor and they'd find out what she'd done.

Zoe opened the door a crack until the sound of clattering plates told her that Nelia and her mother had gone back to eating breakfast. She went down the hall to get her yellow and blue striped beach towel from the linen closet and aloe vera cream from the medicine chest.

Back in her room she smoothed the cool cream on her already red face and neck. If anyone at the party was rude enough to say something to her, she'd just tell them she'd been out in the sun too long the day before.

She screwed the cap back on and dropped the cream into a bag, then pulled open the middle dresser drawer and fumbled around under the stacks of T-shirts and jeans until she found a pair of silver-rimmed sunglasses: her father's, the ones he wore on the boat. He had left them behind when he'd gone to Alaska, and Zoe had rescued them from a box. She slipped them onto her balloon face for camouflage. They made her reflection in the mirror look almost normal. The metal pinched her swollen nose, but the pain gave her something to be aggravated about, and anger felt better to her than self-pity.

Zoe slung the bag over her shoulder and trudged back down the stairs. Her mother was waiting for her, car keys in hand.

"Zoe, are you sure you're feeling well enough to go?"

Her eyes misted up behind the dark glasses. Here was a way out and she couldn't take it, because then her mother would find out everything she had done. She wiggled her nose like a demented rabbit. It was stinging with salty tears.

"Fine, I'm fine," she muttered as she shuffled out to the car.

❖

To begin with, she was late. If that didn't make her stand out, the hooded gray sweatshirt, baggy sweatpants, too large sunglasses, and blue Seattle Mariners baseball cap did.

Jordyn's mother walked her back through the great room, to the sliding glass doors that led to the indoor pool. There were ten or twelve girls clustered around a wrought iron table. One of them glanced over her shoulder as Zoe walked in, then turned back and whispered something to the clump of girls, who dissolved into laughter. Zoe found a lounge chair nearby and slumped into it, hoping they would go back to their gossip and let her disappear into the scenery.

"He did *not* say that," an indignant high-pitched voice complained from the center of the clump. "You're not joking about this, are you? Because I swear I'll kill you if . . ." More murmuring and nervous giggles.

"One of your guests is here, Jord," her mother interrupted them. The girl group swung open like a set of jaws. Zoe recognized Jordyn from the group that had been standing outside the school when Ivy had climbed the wall. She was seated at the table with a thin frizzy-haired redhead behind her. In the back Miranda was standing off to one side, looking deeply uncomfortable. Miranda, who was only invited because her mother worked in Jordyn's mother's office.

Jordyn smiled at Zoe, a smile you might see on the face of a cat that has just discovered that a bird has somehow gotten into the house. She looked like someone who could cause trouble, someone who enjoyed it and was good at it. She had a swimmer's body—strong, broad shoulders; slim hips; and long legs, wound around each other and tucked neatly under the chair. Her hair was long and dark and her skin faintly tan.

Jordyn came around the table toward her. Zoe stood up. It made her uncomfortable to have someone looking down at her. Jordyn's face was changeable, hard to pin down. She smiled and looked Zoe straight in the eye, but when she turned away, her mask slipped a bit, revealing another face, one Zoe neither understood nor recognized underneath.

"Everyone, this is Zoe. She just moved here . . ."

Everyone smiled on cue. Behind her dark glasses Zoe grimaced. It felt like something was crawling down her neck. She swatted at it and then tried to pretend it was nothing by running her hand through her hair.

No one said anything for a long time. Zoe figured she was supposed to say something now, but she didn't know what and she was distracted by the flesh-crawling feeling, which was now spreading down her shoulders and back. She tried to squirm it away but it only made her look like she was having some kind of seizure. Beads of sweat drizzled down her forehead and cheeks. Smiles disappeared like lights going out.

Jordyn glanced at Zoe's baggy clothes.

"Aren't you hot in that?" she asked.

"Not really," Zoe muttered.

"I'm hot looking at you, and your face is *so* red. Why don't you skim off a little and we'll go for a swim?"

"I don't like to swim."

Jordyn looked at her as though she had just announced that she didn't enjoy breathing and was considering giving it up. "You mean you don't know how?"

"No, I mean I don't like to."

Jordyn's mask slipped again. A challenge; she liked that. You could tell. She studied Zoe with cool detachment. "You're not afraid of the water, are you? I mean, you *can* swim. Remember that what's-her-name girl who practically drowned when Hector threw her in?"

Nervous laughter. Apparently everyone remembered.

"I don't *like* to swim," Zoe repeated. She decided to stop short of adding, "Are you deaf or something?" and felt like a coward for being kind to someone who so clearly did not deserve it.

Jordyn nodded. "My party." She shrugged. "Swimming is a required activity. Lizzie, get the ball. We're playing water polo. And you," she said, pulling Zoe's sunglasses down a bit to look directly into her eyes, "can be the other captain."

Lizzie, a tall blond girl with wary green eyes stooped to pick up the ball and tossed it to Jordyn.

"Who wants to be on Zoe's team?"

There was a long silence. No one stepped forward from the safety of the pack. Zoe shifted from one foot to the other. She scratched frantically at the back of her leg with the other foot, so hard that she scratched her skin with the metal of her sandal. Why had she come? Why didn't she just leave?

"Anyone?" Jordyn rolled the ball affectionately between her palms. Behind her a girl in a bright yellow suit smoothed her streaked hair back into a ponytail. She smiled without pleasure or warmth, a bored spectator at a game that had been lost before it had started.

Zoe pulled at the neck of her sweatshirt. She wanted to claw it off. It felt like there were insects running all over her chest. A gangly girl at the edge of the clump whispered something to a pale blond in a black Speedo, and giggled.

"How about this," Jordyn said. "I'll throw the ball in the air and whoever catches it goes with Zoe."

"I'm not playing." Zoe pursed her lips.

Jordyn ignored her. She tossed the ball high into the air above the pool. It seemed to hover there above the glistening blue water, caught up for one breathless moment, before it plummeted downward, hitting the water with a smack.

Ripples grew from the center of the pool and licked at the deck. The ball bobbed along on waves of its own making, sailing alone, drifting toward deep water.

Jordyn watched it, a self-satisfied smile spreading across her face. No one made a move or a sound. Maybe they would just stand like this forever, waiting. Zoe went into another spasm of itching. She felt everyone's eyes burning her skin.

Finally the silence was broken by a loud splash. A slick head popped up out of the waves and reached a thin arm out for the ball. It was Miranda. She bobbed in the center of the pool, clutching the ball to her chest like a priceless treasure, smiling.

Jordyn turned to Zoe. "Well? Are you going in or are you going to let your *friend* sit there and soak?"

Anger boiled inside her, hot steam rising with nowhere to escape. Why would they do this to her? She hated Jordyn for being cruel and being so good at it. She hated all of them.

Her body blistered with rage. She was no coward; and she was not going down without fighting back. Nothing, not even that awful flowered suit, was worse than that. She started tearing at her clothes, shrugging her sweatshirt off and hurling it onto the deck. Then she kicked off her sweatpants. With what little dignity she had left, she strode over to the side of the pool and hesitated, toes curled over the edge, gripping, ready to dive. She looked back over her shoulder, expecting to see the girls laughing, but instead she read something else on their faces. Horror.

"Oh my God," Jordyn whispered. Her mouth hung open; her eyes riveted on Zoe.

"Oh my God," she repeated.

"Disgusting," someone said. The word floated in the air and settled at Zoe's feet, as though she had dropped it.

She jerked and slapped at her leg, screaming through clenched teeth at that maddening itch that wouldn't leave her alone. Then she looked down and realized what everyone was staring at. She was a monster. An angry red swath of swollen lumps cut across her thighs and leaked up onto her back and chest.

The sight of it sickened her: hundreds of glowing scarlet bumps, a whole galaxy of them, pulsing with fiery itching and pain. She looked like she had been on the losing end of a boxing match, with wounded and puffy skin the color of raw meat. And whatever it was seemed to be spreading. Her stomach churned violently. She felt like she was going to vomit.

It must have been the MiracleBust.

# CHAPTER 17

Zoe sat on the edge of the cold metal examining table, as pink and naked as a baby pig, with only a flimsy paper sheet between her and complete humiliation.

The nurse was brisk, but sympathetic in a homey, purposeful sort of way. "Did they keep you waiting out there very long?"

Zoe's thick tongue got caught in her throat and she didn't answer. Instead she scratched frantically at a nasty spot behind her elbow that by now was rubbed raw, while the nurse wrapped a blood pressure cuff around her arm.

"I've never seen it this busy." The nurse squeezed air into the cuff until it gripped Zoe's arm like a vise.

"Does that hurt a bit?"

She had to grit her teeth to keep from crying out in pain.

"You just sit tight. The doctor will be in any minute."

The nurse patted her on the knee and left, leaving her alone in her little white womb.

Zoe slumped like a forgotten doll, legs dangling over the side of the table, hugging herself to keep the paper sheet from slipping down and to give her hands something to do besides scratching her skin off. The sucking sound of some machine drifted in from another room. At least her mother had agreed to wait outside when she'd asked her to. So why did she now suddenly wish that she had let her mother stay?

The door opened and a huge man with a stethoscope slung around his neck appeared. Dr. Herbstrett held out his hand to shake hers, a man willing to touch even a leper. He was a big, solid hulk, standing with his legs splayed out. Dark, hairy arms the size of Zoe's thighs stuck out of his short sleeves. A brown bushy mustache bobbed along on his lips when he spoke, giving him the appearance of a great and friendly walrus. He looked like someone you could trust, like somebody's daddy.

"What seems to be the trouble?"

*I'm dying,* she thought.

"I have a bad rash," she said.

There was a gentle kindness oozing from this big man that made her want to burst into tears. "Mmmmm." He flipped through the notes the nurse had entered on a clipboard, then held her arm straight out and ran his finger over the bumps. "How long have you had them?"

"What?"

"The hives."

"Hives," she repeated. She felt better already, knowing that the bumps all over her body had a name and it was not smallpox, not leprosy, not an outbreak of hundreds of tiny breasts.

"Urticaria," he said.

He moved the stethoscope around on her chest.

"That's the medical term. We like to scare people with big words."

Dr. Herbstrett smiled under his mustache at the small joke he had told on himself and pressed the stethoscope to her back. The cold metal felt good on her hot skin.

"When did it start?"

"This morning. My sister told me I looked like a blimp when I woke up."

He nodded his head. "I have four daughters," he said, as though that explained something, "and three older sisters. Any pain?"

"My skin burns."

He wrote something down on the chart.

*Patient feels like she's being tortured by demons with flamethrowers.*

"Itching?"

She twitched and slapped at the back of her head like a sorry dog with fleas.

"Let me guess. Yes." His whole body jiggled. He had the kind of laugh that made you believe life was not a tragedy after all. Someday they'd let you in on the joke and you'd see what good fun it had all been and everything would be set right.

Dr. Herbstrett held Zoe's foot and pressed a thumb into her ankle. It left a dent. "Edema, one point five." He wrote that down. Then he stuck a tongue depressor into her mouth and peered down her throat.

"Nice and roomy in there. Not much swelling. And you're still breathing. That's a good sign."

Zoe raked her ankles and Dr. Herbstrett put a hand on hers.

"You'll probably be more comfortable if you try not to scratch too much."

She gripped the sides of the table as though it were a lifeboat in a stormy sea.

"Allergic reactions before this? Seasonal allergies . . . pets . . . antibiotics . . . ?"

"No . . . no . . . no . . . no."

"Eaten any strange foods? Mom tried any new laundry detergents? Any new cosmetics?"

From where she sat on the table, Zoe could see her backpack sitting on a chair with a corner of the MiracleBust box sticking out of it. She had brought it with her, just in case, but she was hoping, somehow, miraculously, she wouldn't have to show it to anyone. Inside the pack the MiracleBust lady was sneering at her, mocking her with her big breasts and self-satisfied smile.

". . . ointments, creams . . . ?"

"No. Yes."

Zoe pulled the white paper sheet up to her chin, exposing her thighs. The sheet seemed to be about the size of a large dinner napkin.

"That box over there."

He handed her the backpack. She fished out the MiracleBust box, took the jar out of it, and gave it to him. Then he skimmed through the ingredients.

Dr. Herbstrett looked at her with his merciful blue eyes and waited. She was grateful to see no trace of shame or judgment in them. Here was a man she could tell anything and he would just nod and smile as though he heard stories like this every day, as though he had once been that foolish himself.

"I only have one breast." She gagged on the words. "One of them started growing and the other didn't . . . and . . . I was trying to fix it with that stuff." She did not tell him she had stolen it. She did not tell him about overdosing, or her dreams of a B cup.

A sympathetic smile appeared under his mustache. "Let's have a look."

Zoe lay back on the table and stared at the ceiling, wishing she could have an out-of-body experience. Dr. Herbstrett folded the paper sheet back and examined her. He looked at his chart again. "You're fourteen?"

"Yes."

He offered her a hand and pulled her back up.

"Looks to me like you're perfectly normal," he said.

Normal. The word rained down on her head like a pardon. You are not a freak. You are normal.

"Everything's happening right on schedule. This sort of thing isn't unusual. Your body knows what it's doing. The other breast will catch up.

"We'll give you some antihistamines to make you more comfortable." He scribbled out a prescription and handed it to her, then gave her the MiracleBust. "The hives should go away by tomorrow, as long you stop using the cream. From now on leave the drugs to people like me who've been to medical school and have the loans to prove it."

Dr. Herbstrett put the clipboard down on the counter.

"You can put your clothes on. I'll go out and have a talk with your mother."

"Wait," Zoe said. "You're not going to tell her I used that stuff, are you? I thought you could tell doctors things and they wouldn't repeat them."

He sat down on the stool as though he had nowhere to go and nothing to do, no line of patients waiting for him outside. "Is there some reason you don't want me to tell your mother?"

"I just . . . I mean, I want to tell her myself."

He clipped his pen closed and shoved it back into his pocket.

"All right, then. I'll let her know about the contact allergy and the treatment. The rest is up to you. You haven't talked to her about your breasts yet?"

Zoe looked down at her naked feet and shook her head.

Dr. Herbstrett stood up and put his hand on the door. "Things like this run in families. You may find she went through the same thing herself."

He turned back to look at her, and she wished suddenly that she were one of his four blue-eyed daughters with their charmed and effortless lives. Why hadn't she been born in a family where parents handed down good things?

"There's nothing to be ashamed of," he said.

But there was.

If her mother had been angry, Zoe would have known what to do. Arguing was easy. It gave you something to push off against. But instead, when she opened the door to the crowded waiting room, her mother's face was like her own heart, full of fear and confusion, worry and pain. Zoe couldn't look at her mother without feeling as though she were falling into a pit too deep to climb out of. That was when it came to her: She would have to find a way to fix this herself.

"May I help you?"

The woman behind the cosmetic counter at the Medikwik was a study in too much: too much makeup, too much hair spray, too much cheap perfume, and too much attitude. Her orange hair was swept up into a knot, held together by hairpins with green enameled butterflies on the ends; another butterfly dangled from a gold chain around her neck.

"I'd like to see the manager," Zoe said.

Madame Butterfly was not pleased. She seemed to take Zoe's request as a personal affront. She looked down at Zoe from the stepladder, where she stood whisking bottles with a feather duster. "Do you have something to return?"

Zoe fingered the paper bag with the MiracleBust in it, which she held gingerly at her side. "No," she said.

"Is there something I can help you with?" The saleswoman stepped down off the ladder for a closer look. Her green eyes glistened behind her wing-framed glasses. She stared at the bag, and Zoe moved it farther behind her hip.

"I don't think so." She rummaged through her mind for a convincing excuse. "It's a personal matter," she said.

Madame Butterfly raised her penciled-on eyebrows and sashayed out from behind the counter. Zoe followed her down an aisle of cold remedies to the back of the store, where she left Zoe in a waiting room outside the manager's office. "You'd better sit down, honey." She pointed at a row of molded gray plastic chairs. "You might have to wait awhile."

Except for a boy a few years older than she was in a white shirt and tie, who sat at a long folding table filling out an employment application, she was the only one there. Zoe hunched in the chair closest to the door, stood up and paced awhile, then sat down again in another chair. She crossed and uncrossed her legs and tried to think of what to do with her hands.

It was so quiet, she could hear the whirring of the brass clock next to her head. Why was it taking so long? The hands of the clock clunked to life, startling her. She hadn't expected to have time like this: time to think, time to change her mind.

A queasy feeling gripped her. She jerked to her feet and hurried back down the hall toward the sign for the women's restroom, shoving the door open and leaning with both hands on the sink, waiting for the feeling to subside. Her face in the mirror made her woozy again. She barely recognized herself. She looked old, hard, like someone who was past help, someone with dirty little secrets.

Out of the corner of her eye she noticed a sign on the wall and looked over her shoulder to read it. "Shoplifting is not a game," it sneered. "It's not a thrill, a dare, or a challenge. It's a crime, punishable by imprisonment or fine. You WILL be prosecuted." She felt sick again. *Get out,* she told herself. There's still time.

Zoe bolted for the bathroom door and yanked it open. She was hurrying back down the aisle when she remembered that she had left the bag with the MiracleBust sitting on the waiting room chair. They'd find it and realize what she'd done. There would be blurred black-and-white videos of her on the news with a voice-over: "Suspect is shown leaving the store, in possession of stolen breast enhancement cream. . . ."

Zoe wheeled around again. She could feel Madame Butterfly's eyes on her back as she walked toward the chair and reached to pick up the bag. There was a woman in a black pants suit talking to the young man at the table, and as Zoe swept past her, she turned around and stepped into Zoe's path.

"Sorry you had to wait," she said. "You can come in now."

"No!" Zoe didn't realize at first that she was shouting. "It was all a mistake."

The woman looked at her curiously, then down at the bag she clutched in her hand.

It was no use. They would know. If not now, then later, when she walked out the door and they asked to see what was in the bag and wanted to know what had happened to the receipt. Maybe they'd even arrest her for stealing it twice.

The woman held her hand out. "Perhaps we should talk about it inside."

Zoe sunk into the upholstered chair across from the store manager's desk. The bag containing the MiracleBust was sitting on her lap, pinning her down like a lead weight. Her hand trembled as she reached into the bag, brought out the box, and set it on the desk.

"I'd like to pay for this," she said.

The manager spun the box around to read the label, which Zoe had placed facing away from her.

"This is our merchandise," she said, picking it up to read the sticker.

"Yes."

"Do you have a receipt?"

Zoe tried to swallow away the lump in her throat, but it stuck there, gagging her. "I took it without paying for it. A few days ago . . . last week."

"I see." The woman rolled her tongue over her teeth.

"But I'm going to pay for it. I just don't have the full amount yet."

The store manager folded her hands and leaned back in her chair. "It must have taken a great deal of courage for you to come here. I respect that. But I still have to call the police."

"You don't understand. I am going to pay. I just have to get some more money and then—"

"It's not that I don't trust you," the manager interrupted her. "It's store policy."

Zoe's eyes burned. "I could pay more. I could work it off."

The manager's red lips curved upward into a trained smile. "Even if you paid me twice what it cost, I'd still have to report the theft to the police. I'm sorry. I can't change the rules."

"Yes, y-you can," Zoe stuttered. "If they're stupid rules, you can change them."

"I beg your pardon." The woman stood up. "The police will be taking you to the station." She picked up the phone and handed it to her. "Is there someone you'd like to call?"

# CHAPTER 18

They didn't speak. All the way home from the police station, Zoe and her mother were like strangers on a bus; passengers with different destinations, sitting side by side not because they wanted to but because those were the only seats left. Zoe stared out the window, glancing every now and then in the rearview mirror, as though she expected to see an undercover car tailing them. Her mother held the steering wheel in both hands, kneading it like a coil of dough.

It would have been fine, just fine, Zoe thought, if her mother never spoke to her again. Except that her silence cut deeper than her words could have. Zoe reached for the knob on the radio, punched a button, and scanned through several stations before finding one with enough driving rhythm to drown out her thoughts.

"Zoe, please," her mother said. "Turn that off."

"Is it all right if I breathe," Zoe said sullenly, "or would that be too loud?"

"I am in no mood for that kind of attitude from you," her

mother snapped. "In case you've forgotten, you're the one who's in trouble here."

"Right, I'm in trouble. You're perfect." She reached for the knob and flicked the radio off, glaring at the side of her mother's face. "Except for the fact that you have me."

The car jerked to a halt at a stoplight, and her mother looked directly at her. "I'm not *pretending* to be perfect. But if you'd only asked me. I had the same problem when I was growing up. If you'd only talked to me . . ."

A horn blared behind them. "All right, I'm going," she shouted into the rearview mirror. Silence echoed through the car again. "Maybe this is my fault," her mother said. "I'm too busy, too tired. I snap at everyone and I don't have time to listen. I know you want more from me."

"I don't want anything," Zoe seethed at her. But she did. She wanted to stop hurting. She wanted to take a break from living in her own skin. She wanted to be left alone and she wanted not to be. She wanted to cry until her eyes dissolved and poured down her face like rain.

Her mother sighed, as though she were the one carrying the unbearable burden. "We'll talk about this later."

That was another thing Zoe wanted. Not to think about later and all it might bring.

They pulled into the driveway, and her mother slammed the car door and walked upstairs to the porch. Billy had begun ripping it apart. He had torn off the railings and spindles, so the porch floated in front of the house like a raft, waiting for the order to abandon ship.

It was going to be replaced with something more solid. But it occurred to Zoe watching her mother step through the missing door of their battered house, that she liked wrecks. They asked so little of you and your broken and defeated life. They set no standard for you to live up to, and the people living in them generally didn't expect you to amount to much either. She felt at home in the atmosphere of melancholy that this house breathed out. It was like the pleasure of listening to a sad song over and over when your heart was breaking.

Nelia came out finally and walked over to where Zoe was sitting, leaning against a tree.

"What happened?"

"I stole something and then returned it."

Nelia looked at her quizzically. "Isn't that a good thing?"

"The store manager called the police."

Nelia raised her eyebrows and let out a long low whistle. "Even I never got in that much trouble. Was it ugly?"

"What do you think?"

"I think Mom's lost it. She's in there chopping tomatoes as if she had to kill them before she cooked them."

"Why do you always have to make me feel bad about everything?"

"Well, you asked me," Nelia huffed.

She couldn't sleep that night because she kept hearing voices in the kitchen: first her mother's and Nelia's, then just her mother's. Zoe went down the stairs in the dim light. Her mother was standing in the kitchen with her back to Zoe, holding the telephone. Her voice was muffled, so Zoe could hear only the last few questions: "He did? When? . . . Do you have any idea where?" Zoe waited until her mother hung up the receiver and then walked out of the shadows. Her mother turned, startled, her face drawn.

"What's the matter?"

"I tried to call your dad to tell him what happened."

"Was he mad?"

"I couldn't reach him."

"The boat's out of range?"

"No." Her mother rested her forehead on her hand. "He was causing some kind of trouble on the boat. Albain put him ashore and took on someone else."

"So, where is he now?"

Her mother shrugged. "He got angry and threw a punch. Albain told him to get off the dock or he'd get the coast guard to haul him off. That was the last time he saw your dad."

Zoe's hands tightened into fists. "You've got to find him," she said.

"He's not lost, Zoe. Just because Albain hasn't seen him doesn't mean there's anything wrong. He probably gave up and went home. I'd bet good money he's on the ferry right now, heading back down the inside passage."

"Then why didn't he tell us?"

"I don't know. Maybe he decided to tell us when he got back to Anacortes. Maybe he was ashamed."

"We could call the ferry."

"Zoe, he's a grown man, and he's made his own bed."

"Why do you always want to punish him for everything?"

Her mother straightened. "I don't want to punish anyone."

"Then why are you always hurting us?" Zoe shouted at her.

"Keep your voice down."

"If you hadn't made us come here, we wouldn't have lost Dad and I wouldn't have turned into a criminal."

Ollie came down the stairs in his pajamas. "Is Daddy lost?" he whimpered.

"No, Ollie. No. It's all right," her mother said. She put her arms around him and he pressed his face to her chest. "You're just like your father, Zoe."

"Is that why you hate me?"

"Zoe!" her mother shouted. But Zoe wheeled around and stormed back up the stairs. Not until the door was shut behind her and her face was buried in the pillow did she let herself wail.

The house seemed darker than it ought to have been when she woke up at five thirty the next morning. Outside, the wind was lashing at the trees. It whistled through the chinks in the house and tore loose the blue plastic sheets Billy had used to cover piles of wood in the yard. Zoe could see them flapping wildly outside her window, like sails straining in a hard wind.

A dream still hovered at the edge of her mind. She had seen a girl in a long dress standing at the shoreline, clutching an armload of red roses to her chest. Water washed up around her legs, tugging at them. Her knees buckled when the waves receded.

"The tide is coming in," Zoe called out to her. It was knee deep and rising. But the girl stood stock-still, facing out to sea, white foam swirling around her drenched skirt. Zoe ran down to the water's edge and waded in, fighting to keep her balance in the strong, swirling current. She reached out to touch the girl. Then she pulled back, afraid the girl would turn around and look her in the face.

Every time she closed her eyes, she saw the girl again, standing in the rising water. She couldn't erase the picture in her mind, because it was more than a dream. It was a memory from her uncle's funeral.

She had learned the language of sorrow early. In the fishing towns she'd grown up in along the coast, everyone knew someone who had gone out and not come back. You had to accept that. It was just the way it was.

But it was always not you; always the other child's father, always the other woman's husband, always the other family's brother, grandpa, or cousin. At least that's what you told yourself in the middle of the night.

They were the men her father worked with. The children they left behind were the ones she went to school with, standing wide-eyed and frightened beside their mothers with not even a coffin to prove their fathers weren't coming back. One of the boys who lived near them when they were in Bellingham refused to let anyone say his father was dead all through seventh grade, after his boat went down. If his father was really dead, why had the boy seen no body? Why hadn't his father said good-bye?

Sometimes there was an explanation: bad weather, equipment failure, a crab pot came loose or a sailor was washed overboard in a storm. There were a hundred ways to die. Sometimes it was, her father said, "their own damn fault." They were drinking too much, or exhausted. Sometimes people just disappeared, set out for an island and never came back. And sometimes there was no reason at all.

When her uncle died, it was the first time that lightning struck so close she could feel the hair on her arms stand on end. Their boat was headed back to the processor with a load of crabs when a storm battered it with thirty-foot waves. They were twenty miles offshore when they capsized. Wes Albain and Zoe's father were picked up by another crabber trolling nearby. Her uncle and three deckhands were never found.

They had a service on the waterfront at Seafarer's Memorial, a stone statue of a woman holding a lantern—with a little child clinging to her skirts—that stood near the harbor, looking out to sea. Underneath it was a plaque that listed all the men from her uncle's town who had been lost at sea, along with the date and the name of their vessel; three columns of them. Zoe counted them as she waited for the service to begin. Her uncle's name was inscribed at the end of the list.

Her father gave the eulogy, and had to stop several times to gather the wits to go on. It was the first time Zoe had seen him cry. There had been fishermen in his family ever since his great-grandfather had come over from Ireland in 1877. Her father had been crabbing in Alaska since he was nineteen years old.

At the end of the service they took the flowers that were piled around the base of Seafarer's Memorial and threw them out onto the waves. But when it was Zoe's turn, she clutched the bouquet of roses to her chest beneath her crossed arms.

"It's time," her father whispered to her.

She did not move or speak.

She clutched the thorny roses so fiercely that when she finally let go of them, there were pinpricks of blood on her skin.

Her father waded out into the ocean and flung the roses, not in grief but in anger, a fist shaken in the face of death. She could see his back, bent over in sorrow, waves licking at the legs of his trousers, his only suit, the one he had bought to say good-bye. And she could see the roses roll under the waves.

She was that girl in the dream. It was her face.

Zoe got out of bed, pulled her backpack out of her closet, and started throwing things in. She didn't think about what she might need. If she thought about it, she might not go. And she had to go. She always knew the time would come. Nelia and her mother could get by without her. Ollie might miss her at first. But her father needed her.

There was nothing holding her here, except a date with the Rock County Juvenile Authority. She was already in trouble. What difference did it make if she was in trouble here or there?

Outside, she shouldered her pack and started toward the road amidst wind-whipped trees, dead leaves, and debris swirling around her feet. The wind was gusting in powerful bursts that pushed her back as she leaned into them, pushed her almost as hard as she pushed forward. Muscled clouds raced through the dark sky, hauling bad weather in. She rifled through her mind, trying to remember everything she had learned about wind, ticking off the Beaufort scale. Force five, fresh breeze: White horses form on moderate waves; be prepared for stronger gusts. Force seven, moderate gale: Sea heaps up; white foam blows in streaks. Force nine, strong gale: Crests topple and roll; spray makes it hard to see. Force ten— What was force ten? She had never been out in a storm that bad, so she hadn't listened.

Her father was always teaching and testing her. "Spindrift, see it?" "A ring around the sun: far halo, near rain." "And what's happening ashore?"

"Why does it matter what's happening on land?" she had asked him.

"You have to know whether to stay at anchor or take your chances at sea. And what your craft can handle. Hard weather will turn up every weakness in your boat." Her father's voice was calm and steady, guiding her over the landscape of swells, troughs, and confused seas, reading the chance of rain in the clouds, cirrocumulus, altostratus; his body a finely tuned instrument that sensed the properties of water, the run of the waves, and the fetch of the wind. Why had she been wrenched away from him, when there was so much she still had to learn, so much she had learned and already forgotten?

In the distance she could see a storm line, a black wall of water moving toward her across the fields, squirming and changing like a living thing. Squall. It wasn't the wind you had to fear, it was the quiet that came just before the storm changed direction and struck.

She stumbled across a long stretch of open field. The sky had taken on an eerie look, an unearthly green light. The wind suddenly went still. Zoe turned, as though she could outrun it, her feet stumbling on the rutted dirt, heading for shelter under the nearest tree. Better the danger there, than to be a lightning rod with a metal-framed pack on her back.

She wriggled out of her pack and hunched down, leaning against the trunk and hugging her knees as the wind surged again, howling and churning, ripping off dead leaves and twigs. The tree thrashed wildly back and forth.

A wild animal noise filtered down through the leaves above her. Zoe tilted her head back. In the topmost branches she could see a nest. She must have wandered in a circle and hadn't known it. The hawk was there, riding uneasily back and forth as the wind battered her, threatening to spill her out. She stood up, as though she were going to take off. The nest tilted at a precarious angle to the ground, but she beat her wings and held on. Was she brave or crazy?

"I'll stay with you," Zoe whispered, as though it mattered. "Don't leave."

# CHAPTER 19

Brenda Davidson closed the door to her office and motioned for Zoe and her mother to sit down as she rifled through a stack of papers on her desk, making them wait like two children who'd been instructed to just sit there awhile and think about what they'd done.

"So, Zoe," she said. Her voice was raspy, startling in such a small space. "It looks like you've been assigned to court supervision."

"Which means what?" her mother asked.

"It means that Zoe is mine. At least for the next six months. Your grades will come to me. Your teachers will tell me if you show up for class. Your mom . . ." She stopped and flipped through the papers again. "Dad's not around right now, is he?"

"He's fishing," Zoe said. "That's his job."

"Well, then it looks like I'll be calling your mom to make sure you're in every day after school, hitting the books. And I don't even need to tell you that you'd better not find yourself outside the house after curfew, do I?"

Zoe leaned back in her chair and folded her arms across her chest.

"Then there are the classes twice a month."

"Classes?"

"Girls night out, every other Friday: Everything you ever wanted to know about sex, gangs, drugs, and how to keep yourself out of trouble. No drinking, no smoking, no drugs. No illegal substances of any kind. No walking out of stores without paying for things ever again. And did I mention community service?"

"No."

"You're on the work detail at a nature preserve just west of here, every Saturday from now until mid-July. They'll be sending me time sheets, so you'd better show up. And no, you will not be paid. And yes, you still have to pay restitution to the drug store." She stopped and flipped through her papers again. "$32.95 for the breast enhancement cream, which, by the way, you do not get to keep."

"It was only $29.99," Zoe muttered.

Ms. Davidson looked up from her papers and gave Zoe a wry glance. "You forgot the tax," she said. "*And* you owe them an apology. You play by the rules and we'll wipe this whole thing off your record, assuming you don't reoffend. You break any of the rules—curfew, grades, skipped classes, slacking off at community service, back-talking, and generally being obnoxious—and you'll find yourself in front of the judge instead of me."

"That's it?" Zoe asked.

"Pretty much."

"What if I don't want to do it? Can I go to court?"

Ms. Davidson sat back in her chair and smiled tolerantly. She had clearly heard this question before. "You can, but you'd be making a bad trade: two years, maybe, instead of six months. The judge will most likely assign you a probation officer, put you on home confinement, and fit you with an ankle bracelet and monitor so they know if you go anywhere else, outside of school. And you'll have a record."

Ms. Davidson leaned forward and folded her hands on her desk. "I know it doesn't seem like it, Zoe, but landing in my office is a good thing."

Zoe stared at the wall of the windowless room. It was not a good thing, though she didn't say it. Even her thoughts were prisoners. A good thing would be if they had never moved here in the first place.

"Zoe, get the door, would you?" Nelia called from upstairs.

"I can't hear you!" Zoe shouted over the grating noise of the vacuum. She was shoving it angrily back and forth, as though it were personally responsible for all the trouble she'd had.

"The *door*, Zoe."

She gave the machine one violent push that pulled the cord right out of the socket. There was another knock at the door, probably Garrett, and this time she couldn't pretend not to hear it. Was it too much trouble for Nelia to come down and let him in herself?

Zoe stalked over to the door and swung it open. "The door's unlocked. You could have just—"

It wasn't Garrett. It was Miranda. She was facing away, as though she were about to give up and go home.

Zoe folded her arms across her chest. "If you're here to say I told you so, get it over with and get out."

"That's not it. Really, I just wanted to see if you were all right."

"I'm not sick," Zoe said.

"I know that. It's just that, I heard what happened."

Zoe moved back from the doorway. "Everything?"

Miranda shrugged. "Anyway, I came over because I wanted to say . . . Well, the truth is, I didn't know what I was going to say. I was hoping it would come to me on the way over, but it didn't."

Answer Girl's well runs dry.

"I understand," Miranda blurted out. "That's what I wanted to say. Not that it was right, but I understand why you'd do it." She walked toward the porch stairs, and then turned back. "And by the way, it's 'pickle,' not 'pik-cool.' I got tired of everyone making dimwit jokes, but I guess at some point you just have to accept that a Pikul is who you are."

Zoe watched her step gingerly off the porch. Billy still hadn't replaced all the steps, so just walking in and out of their house took a certain amount of courage. "Hey, wait," she said.

Miranda stopped and looked back.

"C'mon in," Zoe said. "Maybe we can read the encyclopedia or something."

Zoe met Brenda Davidson at her office on Saturday morning. A few other girls straggled in after Zoe, and Ms. Davidson loaded them all into a white van with Rock County Juvenile Authority written in large black letters on the side. Three girls sat down in the backseat, girls who seemed like they'd been through this before, laughing loudly at each other's stories, as if they were on their way to soccer camp instead of a work release program. A wisp of a girl with limp brown hair and skin the color of skimmed milk chose the seat in front, huddled in the corner, staring out the window, her body closed in on itself, like she was trying to make herself disappear.

A large-bosomed girl, the ringleader of the backseat, greeted Zoe as she climbed in the side door and sat down in the middle by herself. "Hey, new girl," she said, her voice pleasant and lilting. "What'd you do to deserve all this?"

Brenda slid into the driver's seat. "Angela," she said sharply, her dark eyes watching them in the rearview mirror, "no cussing, no gang talk, and no talking about other people's offenses. Got it?"

"Yes, Ms. Davidson. I got it."

"I got so much of it my socks are brown," she murmured into Zoe's ear.

They turned onto the highway, Brenda in her blue tinted sunglasses with the window open, letting in a hot stream of air that ruffled through her tightly braided dyed red hair, setting a few springy hairs loose. They drove past endless stands of subdivisions that sprouted in open country like persistent weeds. Mill Pond, Quail Hollow, Indian Boundary, Deer River. Why, Zoe wondered, were these places always named after things they had driven out?

All the houses were gray, white, or beige fake wood, with grass that had been rolled out like carpets. They had pathetic little scrub bushes in front of them and short, scrawny trees tied to the ground with wire, as though they might sprout legs and try to get away.

Strip malls grew up alongside the housing developments, first gas stations and convenience stores, then fast-food joints, and finally gigantic swollen stores, like ValueMart, with "ugly" written all over them. They were surrounded by huge parking lots where people drove in endless circles, honking at each other like geese. Nothing wild, nothing that wasn't tame. Everything wild had been buried under asphalt and coated with concrete.

Eventually they turned off the highway onto a much smaller side route that wound back, toward Selena. If Zoe hadn't known better, she would have thought Ms. Davidson was driving her home. Empty fields began to appear in between the scattered ranch homes, with split rail fences in front and an occasional horse barn. At the top of a hill the van made a right turn onto a gravel drive. In the tall grass by the roadside, Zoe saw a log sign that read MESQUAKIE PRAIRIE, NATURE CONSERVANCY at the top.

They drove up to a small equipment building with an office in front and stopped beside a pickup truck. Two women wearing jeans and rubber work boots got out of the front seat. There was a lot of scuffling as the girls in the van gathered up water bottles and lunch bags, and then lined up, Angela first and the mouse in the back. Zoe started to get up too, but Brenda stopped her.

"You just can't wait to get away from me," she said, sidling by her. "Your time will come, honey."

As they climbed out of the van, Brenda handed each girl a fluorescent orange vest with D.O.C. stamped in huge black letters on the back. Department of Corrections; that was subtle. At least, Zoe thought, she would be spared that humiliation. Zoe waited in the van as the women passed out shovels and rakes and took off with the girls across open country.

Then Brenda climbed back into her seat and turned the key in the ignition. "Are you nervous?" she asked into the rearview mirror.

"No," Zoe said. She was, but she was trying not to think about it, even though a vague feeling that something awful was about to happen prowled at the edge of her mind.

"Sometimes people are on their first day," Brenda said, "especially first-timers. People like you: good kids who just slipped up. The ones I don't expect I'll be seeing in my office again, once they're finished doing their time."

"Mmmm." Zoe nodded, to show she was listening.

"Everybody's allowed one mistake," Brenda said.

"Only one?" The words slipped out of Zoe's mind and into her mouth.

Brenda grinned into the rearview mirror, a good-hearted smile full of teeth.

They drove a little farther up the road until it reached a dead end at a thicket of trees, next to an old farmhouse. "This is it," Brenda said. She dangled an orange vest over the seat, the one Zoe thought she wouldn't have to wear.

"Do I have to put it on?"

"Until you earn the right not to."

Zoe stood by the van and put the vest on like it had razor blades sewn inside. Brenda came around the side and slammed the door.

"I have some business up at the DNR office we passed on the way in," she said. "After ten years of doing this, I'm smart enough to know which kids I can trust and which I can't. You go on up to that house over there and ask for Hub. He's in charge of things. He'll get you oriented, show you what to do."

She had only gone a few yards when Brenda called to her.

"Zoe."

She turned. Brenda's head was sticking out the window on the driver's side of the van.

"Don't you go spoiling my good opinion of myself," she said.

❖

Zoe heard the sound of the engine starting up and the crunch of tires on gravel as she walked up to the old farmhouse. She was surprised at how forgotten and neglected it looked. On one side of the driveway there was a collapsed toolshed and on the other side there was a falling-down barn, with daylight showing through, and a corral that might have once had cows or horses in it, but now had only tall brown grass and sapling trees.

The sign on the front door told her to go around to the back. She knocked, and when no one answered, she pushed the door open and stepped into a dark passageway, so small even Zoe had to stoop to get in.

"Hello," she called out. She squinted into the darkness, but didn't see anyone. There was a dank, musty smell, the scent of things living underground.

"Hey, Hub," a voice called out. "The county kid's here."

A big man in a flannel shirt stepped out of the shadows, from behind a rack piled with shovels and rakes, a hairy man with bushy eyebrows and salt-and-pepper stubble all over his face. There was an energy about him, even though he was old enough to be her grandfather. She could feel him in the room even before her eyes came into focus. Even then, she might have mistaken him for some animal living in this den.

Hub squinted at her. "I thought they were going to send us more DUIs" he said.

Another man stepped from the shadows, a scrawny man with a red beard that camouflaged the long scar across his cheek. The man made quick darting movements like a fox. Without meaning to, Zoe moved back a few steps.

"Maybe if you didn't run 'em all off," the scrawny one said. "The last two said they'd rather go to jail than work for you."

Hub muttered something under his breath.

"For now, this is what we've got."

What was she supposed to say? Sorry I'm not a drunk? Was there no one she didn't disappoint?

"You're a little small, aren't you?" Hub said.

Zoe folded her arms across her chest. "No one told me there was a height requirement for getting arrested."

The little man snorted.

Hub got his back up a bit. He looked over the top of her head, probably searching for someone else to choose from.

"I'm almost fifteen," Zoe said, as though that somehow made up for all the things she lacked.

He shook his head slowly, studying her, eyes narrowed. She felt like he was testing her somehow, taking her measure, figuring out what she was worth. "I guess she'll have to do. But you tell those people over at Department of Corrections to send us the DUIs next time. These kids aren't big enough to bend a reed with a good wind to help them."

"Don't mind Hub," the fox-man said, loud enough for him to hear. "He only talks that way to people he likes."

Hub took some tools off the shelf and walked out into the sunlight, expecting her to follow like a puppy. He handed her lopping shears, a pair of leather gloves, and a rake, and then he loped over to poke his head in the front door of the house, barking an order at someone inside. Then he walked toward the prairie, eating up the ground with long strides, with Zoe lagging behind him, memorizing his back.

They crossed a dirt road, then waded waist-high into a field full of dead dry grass with green shoots sprouting up at the bottom. Hub stroked his arms like a swimmer as he made his way to the center. The lopping shears and rake started getting heavy, but Zoe couldn't set them down to rest without falling behind.

They reached the place where Angela and the other members of the orange-vest club were dragging branches into a pile, while one of the women in jeans mowed a long thin strip around the perimeter of the area. The girls straightened up and waved to them as they passed. Zoe set down the tools, thinking she'd be joining them, but Hub kept walking toward a gently sloping area that backed up to the woods, shouting "Well, c'mon" over his shoulder.

"We just passed them!" she shouted after him.

Hub stopped. "That crew's big enough to handle things. I've got another job in mind for you."

Apparently she was being sentenced to solitary confinement. Did he think she was going to breed discontent, start a revolution? They were too far out now to see the house they had come from. It made Zoe uncomfortable, and she began leaving landmarks, a rock here, a branch broken there, something to make her feel less lost.

When they reached the crest of the slope, Hub stopped and stood with his hands on his hips, his hat shading his face from her, looking out at the surrounding prairie. Zoe stood beside him, shifting from one foot to the other, not knowing what was supposed to come next. There was a long silence, interrupted only by the dry rustle of tall grasses in the wind. He reached into his pocket and unfolded the sheet of paper the D.O.C. had sent him, the record of Zoe's crime and punishment.

"Where did you come from?" he asked.

"Selena." He knew this, didn't he? It must have said so on that sheet of paper, along with everything else they thought was worth mentioning about her.

"And before that?" Hub asked. "I saw you marking the path. You weren't born here, were you?"

She scowled at him. "The islands, north of Seattle," she said.

Hub nodded his head. He turned and stared into the distance.

Zoe looked around her at the faded grasses and leftover seed heads from last year's flowers. A chorus of frogs began.

"What do you see?" he asked her suddenly.

She shrugged, but it wasn't enough to satisfy him. Hub waited. Her heart raced. She didn't want to get it wrong. Even though he infuriated her, she didn't want him to think she was ignorant. A cloud passed over the sun. The wind roared in her ears.

"Weeds," she said finally.

He hung his head, the way someone does when they've just heard terrible news. Was she missing something? What had he expected her to say?

Hub looked at her carefully. "You're not afraid of hard work, are you?" he asked.

Was he goading her? She didn't answer quickly enough. He set off down the hill again, heading straight for a patch of dense brush. Zoe struggled to keep up, weighed down by the loppers and rake, tripping on downed wood and tangled vines. He finally stopped in the middle of an area overgrown with scrubby bushes, hemmed in on the back side by dense woods.

Hub pointed to a prickly bush. "Buckthorn," he said. "Clip it back as low as you can. Drag the branches way off into that corner over there, and pile 'em up butt end out. Rake the litter up when you're done."

A man of few words; you'd think he was being charged for them.

Zoe stared at the bush. It was taller than she was and covered with mean-looking spikes. She yanked the gloves on and picked up the clippers. If he thought she was going to whine and beg to go back to the house and stuff envelopes, he had another thing coming.

"If you need help, yell. That crew we just passed is close enough to hear."

"Hey," she called out to his retreating back. "What should I do when I'm done?"

"Find another one," he said. "I'll be back later with herbicide and hit the stumps. I don't like to use the stuff, but you've got to kill the root, or it will just sucker back."

He walked away, leaving Zoe alone with her festering thoughts, baking in the sun, whacking away at the thorny branches, which seemed to want to hurt her as much as she wanted to hurt them.

Did he purposely give her this job because it was endlessly boring and painful, or was that just a happy accident as far as he was concerned? Why did he stick her out here all by herself instead of with the rest of the work crew? She was no worse than anyone else. Why should she be the one who got punished?

Zoe was sitting down, nursing her raw skin, aching back, and cramped fingers by the time Hub came back for her at the end of the day. Her anger had burned its way down to embers and ashes, and her spirit had gone with it.

Hub circled the piles of severed and mutilated buckthorn branches before he walked over to her. "Looks like you got the best of it," he said.

He offered a hand to pull her up. Her arm shook when she held it out.

"Tired?" he asked her.

"A little." She had never in her life been so exhausted, but she wasn't going to tell him that.

"It'll get easier as time goes on."

Zoe winced. "I have to do this again?"

A sympathetic smile crept across his face. "Yup. And when we get the buckthorn out of here, we'll start on the Canadian thistle and garlic mustard."

Maybe an ankle bracelet wouldn't have been so bad. "Why can't you just poison everything or plow it up?"

Hub tipped his hat back and swiped at his forehead with a wrinkled handkerchief. "Because you'd kill everything. And the things you don't want are all wound up with the things you do."

"But it's all just a bunch of weeds."

Hub glanced out at the motley plants and the space where the buckthorn used to be. There was nothing beautiful about this place. Surely he knew that.

"There's something worth saving here," he said. "Most people can't see it, but it's here. All we have to do is give it space to grow, and it'll come back."

They walked up to the top of the hill. Hub carried the tools and Zoe trudged behind him. The sun was beginning to go down in the west, and it gave an orange glow to the edge of the world.

When they reached the crest, they could see the whole surrounding area: the prairie they had walked through, the houses that huddled on the east end of the preserve, the little patch by the woods where Zoe had spent herself that day, and something else. When she looked farther south, she was surprised to see Selena and, at the edge of it, her own house. She had been so close the whole time.

"Tell me what you see," Hub said.

"Home," she said.

❖

Nelia was alone when she drove up to the Rock County Juvenile Authority building late in the afternoon. Zoe took a long time sliding gingerly into the station wagon, one sore leg at a time.

"How was the chain gang?" Nelia asked.

Zoe winced as she eased her aching back against the seat. "Not as much fun as you'd expect. Where's Garrett?"

"He couldn't come. Billy sent him off to get some studs before the lumber yard closed."

Zoe cut her a sharp glance. "You drove all the way here without him? What are you going to say when the cops pull you over and find out that you're driving on a permit without—"

Nelia held up a laminated square of plastic, pinched between two fingers.

Zoe snatched it from her. It certainly *looked* like a real driver's license. "You passed?" she said.

"Third time's a charm."

Zoe flipped it over and studied Nelia's photo. She was smiling into the camera, a look of surprise and disbelief on her face. It *had* to be real.

Nelia leaned over her shoulder. "I'm not sure that picture does me justice. Do you think they do retakes? " She took her license back, tucked it into her bag, and zipped the bag shut.

Zoe put her head back on the seat and closed her eyes. "I wouldn't go around looking for justice if I were you."

# CHAPTER 20

How do the waves know when to turn back?"

"What's that you're asking now, girl?"

How old was she? Eight, maybe nine. They were sitting in the boat, down at the dock, mending nets before her father went fishing. Zoe was watching the fingers of the waves tossing shells up onto the beach as the tide went out.

"What is it that tells the tide to stop going out and start coming in again?"

"Ahh," her father said, "the waves. Let me think on that awhile." He laid the web of ropes down on his lap and poured himself another mug of coffee. A thinking cup, he called it. He gazed at the waves, as though they would answer.

"I think it's like this," he said. He placed the mug in her hand and rocked it from side to side, watching the deep brown liquid slosh back and forth. "Things can only go so far one way before they have to come back again. The sun goes up and comes back down. The flowers come and go. It's the way of things, Zoe."

"Are you sure that's the answer?"

His blue eyes—oh, she remembered them so vividly, as if she

were staring into them now—his blue eyes danced like light on water. "There's very little I'm sure of, girl," he said. "And when you're as old as I am, you'll be smart enough to know that too."

She did not know exactly when it happened, but when she looked at the house now, Zoe felt less like things were coming apart and more like they were coming together. For a long time the future had been something only her mother could see, a vision of what their house could be, as she pored over stacks of catalogues and magazines, picked out fixtures and thumbed through paint chips. It was only her mother's fantasies, spun at night, as they sat around the dinner table, the fate she imagined for the house and its inhabitants, the force of her dreams applied to the dead weight of their doubt and resistance that kept them from sinking altogether.

But there was a point when things had changed. Lately Zoe had begun to think her mother's blind faith hotel was more than just an empty hope. Maybe the place of shelter their mother imagined for them was something they would actually one day inhabit.

Billy and his crew were done jacking up the front of the house, tearing down walls, and replacing the siding. Now the driveway was crowded with the trucks of carpenters, plumbers, and electricians, with wood and pipes sticking out of the top. All week long the house was full of men nailing, pounding, and fixing, and the air was full of the promising scent of new lumber.

Something was missing, of course. There was no trace of their father in this place. Their lives were coming together again, but they were built on a new foundation. Sometimes days would go by and Zoe didn't even think of him.

❖

Several postcards had arrived in the last few weeks from her father, each with a different postmark, and all of them short on words and information. "Took some time off," the first one said, on the back of a picture of a mountain and a blue lake. Nelia had received one a week later with a picture of a bear cub and two words, "Working harborside," scribbled on the back.

The last one was addressed to Zoe. "Shipped out aboard *Kenai Lady*," it said. "Done with Albain for good. Tell your mother. She'll be glad to know."

"Do you think he means it?" Zoe asked.

Her mother searched her face. "It's hard to read the truth in someone's eyes when they're three thousand miles away from you."

He would be gone a long time. That was what "shipping out" really meant, the truth that was written between the lines. And maybe it was just as well. At least it was a loneliness they could understand.

They would not hear from him now, and that was just as well too. Each new round of postcards lifted their hopes and dropped them again. "When Dad gets back . . ." Ollie would say for a while after they got each one. But a week later he'd stopped talking about him at all.

Zoe alternated between feeling a terrible sadness for Ollie, the boy with no father, and seeing him as a big pain in the neck. Ever since she had taken him out to see the hawks' nest, he had been pestering her to take him back. He and Miranda and Zoe had become a threesome after school each day, wandering out to the fields to check on the progress of the eggs.

Sometimes Zoe would share some tidbit she had learned

from Virginia. "The Cooper's hawk is sometimes called the black widow of the bird world," she would say casually, waiting for them to take the bait.

Of course, Miranda resented it when Zoe knew more about something than she did. Sometimes she'd try to fake it, with an "everyone knows that" sort of shrug. But sooner or later her curiosity would get the best of her.

"I give up," she would say. "Why the black widow?"

"Because," Zoe said, savoring the moment, "she sometimes eats her mate."

Miranda pondered. "It makes a certain amount of sense," she said. "You know, in times of famine. It's better than eating your young. For one thing, there's more meat."

It would not have surprised Zoe to discover the bones of the male hawk underneath the nest. If she hadn't eaten him, she had most certainly driven him off with her *kek-kek-kekk*ing demands. She often had to hunt for her own supper now, wandering away for hours at a time, then suddenly reappearing and settling back down on the nest, tail sticking out over the side, as though she'd never been gone.

There were plenty of birds around waiting for her to pluck. Their town was a rest stop on the Mississippi flyway. Virginia's flora and fauna book had told Zoe so. Zoe had watched the hawk hunt, and it seemed to be mostly a matter of sitting perfectly still, keeping her eyes peeled, and waiting until some bird wandered close enough for her to launch a midair attack. Zoe found the whole business of tearing the beating hearts out of your victims more than a little disturbing, but she and Miranda still watched in awful fascination whenever the hawk treated them to this spectacle. Miranda, the ever logical and ever practical seeker of facts, and Zoe, whose main interests were why and why not.

She had more sympathy for some of the bird victims than others. It surprised her to learn this about herself. She didn't mind losing a few gray sparrows and dowdy pigeons. It was only the bluebirds, cardinals, and songbirds she mourned, the pretty and the talented. Not that it mattered to the hawk. Judging from the assortment of feathers they found beneath her nest, she ate everything she could get her talons on.

Still she was beautiful, gliding soundlessly through the air, wings spread as wide as a kite, appearing from out of nowhere and rising up at the last minute to settle into her nest. She would sit there alone for hours, full of foolish hope.

There was a note on Hub's door when Zoe went back to Mesquakie at seven o'clock the next Saturday morning. It was scribbled on a scrap of lined paper. "Back at eight" was all it said. Zoe tried the doorknob and found it unlocked. She thought of going inside the little dugout rabbit warren that passed for his office, but she was afraid he might find her nosing around and have her sentenced to a life of hard labor.

So instead she squatted down on the three-legged milking stool she found outside near the barn, and sat with her legs splayed out, watching the clouds glide over the prairie. It had been cool the night before, and the ground was still coated with prisms of dew that shimmered on the delicate grass and the lacy spiderwebs. It was almost beautiful in the morning light.

She tried to stay still and blend in, something her father had taught her how to do. A garter snake slithered through the grass. Birds sang all around her. She got up and stretched her legs, walking around to the back of the house, breathing in the damp earthy scent of things coming back to life again.

When Hub didn't show up by eight, she began to get restless, and by eight thirty she was just plain mad. Maybe the things he had given her to do weren't important. Maybe it was all busywork, something he'd come up with just to punish her. And today he was going to let her sit there and stew.

"Prickly old man," she muttered to herself, kicking up a dust ghost. "We'll just see who wins this one." She was pacing in front of the office door, thinking of leaving, even though she knew it would mean trouble, when someone came up behind her.

"You lookin' for Hub?" the fox-man asked.

"Where *is* he?"

"He'll be here. Just got tied up with training some new volunteers is all."

She picked a stick up, snapped it in half, and threw it down.

The fox-man put down the load of rakes he was carrying. "You don't like him much, do you?"

"They told me I had to come here. I don't have to like him."

"Yeah, well. He grows on you. I thought he was the biggest horse's ass I'd ever met when I first came here. And I've seen plenty."

"Why didn't you quit, then?"

"He was the lesser of two evils. The other evil being an all-expense-paid trip to Rock County Jail. Same deal they offered you, only a little worse."

He pushed his sleeve up and showed her a trail of dark spots on his forearm. "I've been clean seven years. I owe most of that to Hub. That's why I'm still here, horse's ass or no."

"You don't seem like a junkie."

"You don't seem like you'd be wearing an orange offender vest. Everybody's got scars of some kind. Just that most of them you can't see. Even old Hubert. That's his real name, you know. Hub suits him better. Funny how people live out their names, isn't it? Like Kellermann," he said.

"Huh?"

"I thought you might like to know what my name is. Hub never told you, did he? He's not much on ceremony."

"Is that your last name or your first?"

Kellermann threw his head back and laughed. Gold teeth glittered in the back of his mouth. "That's the one I inherited," he said. "It means 'cellar man.' But you can call me by my given name, Pete."

"What's that mean?"

"Rock. I'm trying to grow into it." He held the door open for her. "You ever wonder what Zoe means?"

"It means life," she said.

"Well, there you go." The fox-man smiled at her.

Hub finally showed up at nine, with the lopper and rake and no apology.

"Which do you want me to carry?" Zoe asked.

"Both. It will balance you off better."

"I don't mind being unbalanced," Zoe said.

The smile that appeared for a moment under the brim of his hat was like a prize, something you didn't get often. "Everybody's got to carry their own weight around here."

She picked up the scent of smoke just before they reached the area with the mowed swath around the perimeter. There had been a fire. A whole field had been destroyed by it, leaving the earth black, barren, and ashy, with nothing standing except a few charred stalks. Even the lone oak that stood in the center of the field was singed knee-high on its trunk and exposed roots.

"What happened?" Zoe asked.

"We burned it off yesterday, this section and part of the woods."

"*You* did this?"

"Yup. Had some trouble, too. An updraft; the fire jumped the creek and spread so fast the fire department had to put it out. We had volunteers out there with flappers and water packs. But that's the thing about fire. You can worry about the weather, watch the wind, check the fuel load, and it can still take you by surprise."

"Then why did you burn it?

"Prairies need fire. Indians called it red buffalo. They set fires to drive game and to make better pasture. But even if they didn't, sooner or later a lightning strike would. If the winds were high and the grass bone-dry, there'd be a wall of flame thirty feet high, and a hundred acres long, moving faster than a horse could run. Now we keep it small, mowing firebreaks, setting backfires if we need to."

"What good does it do to kill everything?"

"It's not dead. Prairie roots go deep, sometimes fifteen feet. They tap into groundwater so the plants can survive fire or drought. Fire only kills the invasives that aren't adapted to it. What's worth saving will come back from the roots; what's not will be burned away."

The day was turning out to be unseasonably warm. Zoe battled the buckthorn alone for three hours, the sun getting hotter as it rose in the sky until the air above the field shimmered. She had run out of songs she knew the words to, jokes she could remember the punch line for, and grudges she held against various family members. Now she was keeping her mind occupied with a question: Which was worse—the dead stalks of last year's grasses, which scratched at her arms and legs, or the dirt caked under her fingernails and glued to her skin with sweat?

Zoe straightened up like an old woman, pressing her palms into the small of her achy back. Too bad she hadn't worn the straw hat her mother had offered her on the way out the door. Then she could have looked *and* felt like somebody's grandmother.

She found a tree at the edge of the woods to sit under, and she spread her orange offender vest on the ground to sit on. At least it was good for something. Then she ate lunch by herself. In the bag was a hard-boiled egg, an apple, and half a peanut butter and jam sandwich made from the last jar of blackberry jam her mother and Ollie had put up last spring in Washington. Zoe ate like it was the first food she had touched in a week, grateful not only for the way it soothed her empty stomach, but also for the way it connected her to home.

When she was done, she got up and wandered back to see the section of forest floor they had burned. There was something about it that drew her, the horror or the power of it. It stirred up feelings in her, something ancient and unreasoning, like the terror that gripped you in the middle of the night.

A flock of crows were picking through the ashes, scavengers looking for fried bugs. The flames must have swept through quickly. The trees were scorched, but only at the base, and there was an eerie carpet of leaves as black and shiny as tar. She found one fallen limb still smoldering, wafts of smoke rising from its burning core. It made her uneasy so she stooped to scrape up some dirt to smother the embers.

On the way back she crossed through another field and stopped short. She thought she had been alone the whole day.

The other county girls had been transferred to a work crew at another preserve. But as she turned to go up the hill she saw a boy facing away from her. Zoe crouched in the high grass so he wouldn't see her and her orange fluorescent vest and know her for what she was, someone doing time.

He looked like he was her age, a little older maybe—tall, lanky, and tan-skinned, with a shock of brown curls cascading down the nape of his neck. He was wearing khaki shorts and was bare-chested. With his back to her, she had time to study him. It excited her to watch him this way, without his knowing.

He was yanking up plants with both hands, and he had a kind of grace when he moved, as if it were a dance. He seemed to be making a game of his work, tossing the plants, root and all, over his shoulder into a white plastic bucket behind him, spraying clods of dirt in his wake like sparks. She could see the muscles in his arm ripple when he did this and had a sudden impulse to put her hand on them and see how it felt when they moved, or to touch those curls that came to life around his face, that hair with so much energy, hair with a mind of its own.

Every so often he would crouch down and stare at something, his back arched like a question mark, bony knees all the way up to his chin. He looked like something curled and ready to spring, a wildcat on a cliff, something that might at any moment leap into furious motion.

She wanted to speak to him. But if she did, he might ask her what she had done that landed her here, and then what? She would have to lie, of course. And what if he found out? She was a fool and a liar. He would know that then.

Zoe pushed herself up higher, peering over the top of the grass, heart thumping like a rabbit's, trying to get a better look. There was something about him. She felt like she knew this boy, as though she had waited for him her whole life. Like someone you look for in a bus station, a face you pick out of a crowd because it belongs to you.

He turned toward her, and Zoe dropped to the ground, lying close to the dirt, breathing hard. Had he seen her? She didn't think he knew she was there. But as he walked back toward the house, he looked over his shoulder one last time and she could see his eyes, nearly black, glistening. There was so much darkness in them that you barely saw white at the edges. His mouth turned up only slightly at the corner, a smile that had something of weariness in it.

She knew now what was so familiar about him, why her heart pounded at the sight of his naked back. It was the boy who had climbed the school.

Hub came back late in the day. She had managed to clear out all the buckthorn, and was standing there, rubbing her sore neck and admiring her work, when he showed up.

"Not bad," he said.

She looked at him sideways. She supposed that was a compliment, but it was a pretty thin one. "You could have just burned all this, too, couldn't you?"

"Come over here," he said.

He walked to a corner of the field and parted some brown stalks, exposing tender green shoots underneath.

"What's that?"

"Lakeside daisy," he said. "Take a good look at it. It's what tells you this place is more than a weed patch. I was walking through here last summer and spotted some blooming. Might be the last ones in this state. You want to see a grown man cry? That'll do it. A few years back we were harvesting seeds by the railroad—they were tearing it up to lay new track—and we stumbled on some of it. By the time we came back to save it, they'd already bulldozed the place. I'll be damned if I'm going to let that happen again."

"What's so special about it?"

"It's an indicator species, a sign that tells you there's something rare, something worth saving here. Lady's slipper orchid, golden alexanders, hoary puccoon, blue gentian—you find those growing and you know that what you've got is a piece of original tallgrass prairie that somehow didn't get destroyed like the rest of it. Underneath this damned mess there's a remnant of it, hanging on by its teeth. Thousands of acres of prairie grew here for thousands of years before we came and plowed it all under. Now prairie is rarer than the rain forest. One twentieth of one percent, that's what's left. And that will die too, if we don't stop it. Just like the passenger pigeon. Lost. Extinct."

Hub walked up the rise, and Zoe trailed after him. "What do you see?" he asked.

Zoe looked hard. She closed her eyes and opened them again. From the hill, at this distance, the sloping fields that surrounded them looked like the ocean. The wind made waves in the grass, rippling patterns of light and dark. Clouds sailed overhead in a dome of blue sky.

"Water," she said.

Hub stared at her as though she'd just sprung full-bodied out of the dust.

"What do *you* see?" she asked.

"I see an orphan," he said.

Zoe hugged her chest. Something ached in her, and she was trying to keep it from leaking out.

"That little patch of prairie you're working on is dying. That's what happens when things are cut off. They can't regenerate. Next thing you know, the buckthorn and thistle move in. And for some reason even I don't understand, I believe you're the one who's supposed to save it."

He looked straight at her, neither right nor left, a glance like flint. Why did she always feel like he was looking all the way through to her beating heart? "What would that take?" she asked. "To save it, I mean."

Hub picked up an armload of tools and started back down the hill. "To begin with," he said, "you have to love it."

## CHAPTER 21

All week she thought of Ivy. At school she'd hear a voice and turn, or glimpse dark curls bobbing among the sea of heads and follow them like a fish chasing a lure. But it was always someone else.

In the middle of algebra class the smooth brown curve of his back, the one her hand wanted so much to touch, would appear floating in front of the board, and the sight of it lifted her out of her chair, transporting her back to that field, her fingers stinging and the hot sun licking her neck, as she watched him through the tall, waving grass. All day long, while the voices of her teachers droned on about subjects and predicates, polynomials and mitosis, she lived another life with him, so real that she could hear the buzzing of insects, smell the pungent bite of the grass, and feel the rub of windblown seed heads on her face.

Who was he that her thoughts orbited around him so tightly? What gravity did this boy have?

When she didn't see him at school, she began looking forward to Saturday. He would notice her this time, get up and walk over. She could feel the heat of him close to her, and see his lips moving. What would he say to her? She could not imagine. The only thing she knew was this: that he would look at her and see, with those black animal eyes, that she was not what she appeared to be. That she was more than this, more than the thin, small girl who was only half a woman, branded in black and orange by the D.O.C. His eyes would look past all her imperfections, all that was not enough in her, and lift up what was good, like gold from a muddy stream.

But she did not see him when she went to work at the prairie the following weekend. She began to think she had conjured him up out of her own fierce longing. Maybe he was no more real than water in the desert when you're dying of thirst.

She thought of asking Hub about him as they walked back to the field Saturday morning, but she was ashamed, afraid he would tell Ivy. "You know that new girl, that little runt not strong enough to bend a reed? She asked about you; got her eye on you, Ivy." And then he and Pete would laugh and throw their heads back, and Ivy's face would darken.

"What do you know about Ivy Walker?" Zoe asked Miranda.

They were walking back to the nest after school on Friday the following week, while Ollie ran ahead of them, carpenter apron cape flapping in the breeze and goggles pushed up on his forehead. He had changed his name from Hammer Man to Hawk Man, but the outfit was still the same.

Miranda stopped walking and looked carefully at her. Zoe tried to put on a blank face, but she knew it wasn't working.

"Only that it's hard being him. It's hard being anybody different in this town. You know those invisible fences they put up over in the subdivisions so the dogs can only run so far before they come yelping back?"

"Yeah."

"They've installed them for the humans, too."

"Don't be dramatic."

"I'm telling you. It's true. You're not the only prisoner."

Zoe looked up to see Ollie galloping toward them, full out, yelling, "C'mon! Hurry up!" She was sure there was something wrong. He had wandered far ahead of them because she hadn't been paying attention, and now she felt a wave of guilt wash over her as she started running to meet him.

"What's wrong, Ollie?"

"Run!" He grabbed her by the pant leg and pulled her forward, then let go and charged ahead. He was standing under the tree, swinging his arms in big arcs and jumping up and down, as though he actually believed that with a little more effort he'd be airborne.

"Pick me up," Ollie said. "I wanna see the babies."

Zoe was standing directly under the nest and could see nothing. She tilted her head and stumbled back a few steps, trying to get a better look at whatever was up there. Ollie grabbed on to her shoulders and started shinnying up her back. She bent down and reached for his leg, shifting him up to piggyback position. "What is it, Ollie?" He had one hand over her eye, the other in a choke hold around her neck, and he was kicking her in the flanks like she was a stubborn horse.

Miranda arrived, panting. "I see it," she yelled.

Zoe was miffed that they'd seen something she hadn't. She fell backward and shook Ollie loose. He ran over to climb Miranda. Zoe stumbled over to the other side of the tree. She could see the mother hawk bent over the nest, her head poking about, and then something else moving back and forth. A leaf? No, it was a tiny head.

She let out a whoop of triumph, as though it were all her doing. It should have scared the birds right out of their stick nest, but it didn't. The mother peered down at them over the edge, annoyed, but not enough to do anything about it. Wings shot up on both sides of her like the opening of a fan. Four wings, maybe six.

Ollie took off, running a victory lap around the tree, then ran back and threw both arms around Zoe's legs and squeezed.

"Why are you crying," Ollie asked her. "Isn't it a good thing?"

Zoe swiped at her eyes with the back of her hand. She hadn't even known she was crying, and even if she had, she surely wouldn't know why.

Why did she care so much? Because they were wild. Maybe that's what it was. She needed that in her life the way other people needed oxygen. There was one hope that hadn't died in her, like all her other stillborn dreams, and it was this: She wanted what was wild to survive. No, not wanted it—ached for it.

"It's a good thing, Ollie," she said, sweeping him up in a ferocious hug. "It's a very good thing."

Nelia, her mother, and Weezy were sitting in the kitchen, sorting through recipe cards when Zoe came in and pulled out a chair next to them. Weezy had been teaching Nelia how to cook, which was a little like teaching her to drive, only the consequences of the inevitable disasters weren't as great.

"I think I'll make banana bread for dessert," Nelia said. She picked a card out of the box and ran her finger down the list of ingredients. "Flour, sugar, salt, bananas. . . . You need bananas to make banana bread?"

"What did you think you made it out of?" Weezy asked.

"I don't know, essence of bananas maybe?"

"Nelia." Her mother said her name like it had one-hundred-pound weights attached to each end.

"Oh, all right. I'll make peanut butter cookies. Do we have any essence of peanuts?"

Nelia was humming as she rifled through drawers and cabinets, stacking bowls, measuring cups, canisters, and jars noisily on the counter. She was always happy now, even when she had to help around the house. There was Garrett, of course. There was the freedom, new territory, and power over Zoe that having a driver's license had given her. And she had managed to find a class at the high school that could hold her interest: psychology.

"I like it," she had told them the first afternoon she'd come home and dropped her books on the sofa, "because it's all about me."

Whenever there was a lull in the conversation, Nelia filled it by telling everyone what was wrong with them. These were actually things she had believed her whole life, but now she had the weight of science to back her up.

"We started a unit on parenting techniques today," Nelia said. She was scraping essence of peanut out of the Skippy jar and slapping it into the mixing bowl.

"Oh?" her mother said. She appeared to be flinching. "How am I doing?"

"Not very well, I'm sorry to say." Nelia dumped a cup of sugar into the bowl and worked away at it with a wooden spoon. "You get high marks for basic needs, but your discipline techniques need a little work."

"Well, you've managed to turn out pretty well despite her, Nelia," Weezy said.

"It's been an uphill climb. Zoe, get your finger out of that bowl." Nelia slapped at her with the wooden spoon, but missed.

"I wouldn't take advice on how to control your children from someone who can't even control her own temper," Zoe said. She stuck her finger in her mouth and sucked the sweet brown batter off of it, then licked at the spatters the wooden spoon had made on her forearm.

"It's my stage in life," Nelia said. "I'm *supposed* to be impulsive and ruled by emotions. You see this prefrontal cortex?" She tapped herself on the forehead. "It's not fully developed in adolescents. I take orders from my animal brain. In short, nothing I do is my fault."

Zoe looked around warily. Nelia had the spoon raised in the air ready to swat away any other fingers that tried to work their way into the bowl. "What happened to Ollie?" she asked.

"He asked me if he could take Billy back to see the hawks' nest you two found," her mother said.

"Billy! What's he doing here so late?"

"Billy and Weezy are staying for dinner," her mother said. "I figured we'd better start practicing on some friendly guests before—Zoe, where are you going?"

"Out," she called back over her shoulder.

She was too late. By the time Zoe reached the edge of the field, she could see two figures walking back toward the house, a tall man in jeans and a plaid shirt with his arm around a small boy with a cape. Even at this distance she could see the binoculars hanging around Ollie's neck. She stood and watched them as they approached.

"I need the binoculars now, Ollie," Zoe said when he ran up to her. She held her hand out, but he balked.

"You said I could use them," he pouted.

"I know," she said. "But they're Billy's."

Reluctantly, Ollie handed them over to him.

"He didn't take them," Zoe said quietly. "I did."

Billy looked at her hard. "I know," he said. Then he waited, as though he expected her to say something else.

Zoe's throat went dry. She tried to swallow, but couldn't.

"People make mistakes," he said, finally.

"It wasn't a mistake. I did it on purpose."

He nodded, his eyes narrowing. "I'm glad you told the truth. Either road is a hard one to go down. But the thing about lying is that you find you're even lying to yourself. Here," he said. "Why don't you keep them until those hawks of yours fledge."

"So I hear you like to garden," Weezy said.

"Garden?" They were sitting around the table that night at dinner.

"Your momma told me that you had a job at Mesquakie."

"Job?"

"I guess volunteer work would be a better way to describe it."

Zoe felt Nelia's heel under the table, pressing down on her foot, rousing her. "I didn't exactly volunteer," Zoe said. "It was more like something that was suggested to me, strongly suggested."

"Well, the point is, you like to work outside, to grow things. Am I right about that at least?"

"Yes," Zoe said. She smiled in order to prove that she wasn't extremely dumb, rude, or both. And also because she realized, as she heard herself say it, that it was actually true. She looked around the dining room table, set with a blue and white embroidered tablecloth and wild-rose-patterned china, which contrasted nicely with the bare wood lath and studs. She looked at Billy, Weezy, Nelia, her mother, and Ollie in turn. Everyone was nodding and smiling, like sunflowers in a gentle breeze. "Yes," Zoe said. "I like to grow things."

Weezy said, "She takes after your mother, Annie. Don't you think?"

"Mmmm," her mother said. She took a bite of chicken, put her fork down, and laid her hands on the napkin in her lap.

"You should have seen that garden when she was alive."

"Garden?" Zoe said.

"Here we go again," Nelia muttered.

Zoe took a wing shot at Nelia with her eyes, but Weezy went right on talking. "It used to be at the back of your property, off by itself, beyond the barn. I think she must have put it there, far away from the house, as a kind of refuge, if you know what I mean. Oh, it was a beautiful thing, the peonies as big as Ollie's head each spring; pink and white and burgundy . . . The lilac bushes, the climbing roses. It was different in every season. And the scent of it! You'd think you'd made a wrong turn and found yourself on the road to heaven."

Weezy stopped abruptly, remembering. "She had a thumb greener than God's own. My father used to say she could grow a field of wheat from a sack of flour."

She turned to Zoe's mother. "Annie, well, you know it broke my heart when your grandpa let that garden go. I don't think he was the same man after your mother died, losing a daughter like that."

Her mother's eyes shifted.

"You know the strangest thing of all? Remember how she

had your dad build that fence around the garden the summer before she died? That fence came to life."

"Now, Weezy," Billy said.

"I mean it. I bet you can still see pieces of it. They made it out of willow branches, and you know as well as me, Billy, all you have to do is put green willow in water or earth and it will send down roots and sprout leaves."

Zoe's mother pushed her chair back abruptly, and the scrape of her chair on the wood floor startled them all. "Nelia, why don't you come in the kitchen and help me serve those essence-of-peanut cookies you made," she said, reaching over the table to clear the plates.

Billy turned to Zoe. "You'll have to forgive Weezy. She tells a lot of stories. A few of them are actually true."

Weezy gave Billy an affronted look. "Well, this is one of the true ones. If you don't believe me, go look for yourself."

After Weezy and Billy had gone home, Zoe wandered outside, walking back toward the field in the moonlight. She had never paid much attention to the part of their property that was overgrown. It was just something she walked past on the way to the fields. Now she could see the shape of what it used to be. There was an arbor with a gate, so completely covered with weeds and vines that it was barely recognizable as a way in. And it was walled in on every side by a mass of shrunken and distorted trees. Zoe pushed through the brush and picked a leaf off a yellow branch. Willow.

"Zoe?" Her mother walked up behind her.

"Why don't you ever talk about them?" Zoe asked.

Her mother looked away. "I was so young when they died. It was so long ago."

"How did they die?"

"An accident. My father was driving. He was drunk. His car veered into the other lane. My mother died instantly, and so did two of the people in the car he ran into: a woman and her child. My father lived several days. If he hadn't died, I honestly believe my grandfather would have killed him. My grandfather never wanted my mother to marry my father in the first place. The crash was just one more reason to hate him."

"Is that when you left? When they died?"

"No, not then. Zoe, some things are better forgotten. What good does it do to drag all this up again?"

"If you wanted to forget, then why did you bring us back here?"

Her mother squinted, straining to see something in the distance. "There were good things here too. But they're mixed in with the pain. I thought I could come back and start over, make a fresh beginning for us. But it's not like that. All you get to do is go back and pick up where you left off."

Zoe's mother looked out at the forgotten garden. "We were made for Eden. My mother used to tell me that all the time. She said it was the reason why, when you walk into a garden, you always feel like you're coming home.

"Weezy was right, Zo. Your grandma would have loved you. I just wish she had lived long enough to tell you that herself."

# CHAPTER 22

The otherness of him is what pulled her in. The friends she'd had before had often looked and acted different from her, but inside there was a way in which they had been deeply alike. But she found herself drawn to Ivy because he wasn't like her at all, wasn't like anyone, really. Most people were different because they wanted to be noticed. Ivy was different because he couldn't be anyone else.

He was a mystery to her, endlessly fascinating and frightening in a way that wasn't unpleasant, like standing toe to toe with a canyon and looking over the edge. She had gotten into the habit of bringing the binoculars to work on Saturdays, and on her breaks she would go and lie down on the hillside in the tall grass where she couldn't be seen, and she'd watch him, propped up on her elbows with the field glasses glued to her eyes. It made her mildly uncomfortable, spying on him this way.

But there was such pleasure in studying him, without having to take a chance on the rejection that might come from being up close. It wasn't, she told herself, that different from the hawks. She wasn't peering in his window. He was there in full view.

She merely wanted to get a better look at him, to know him, everything about him.

The thought of seeing him each Saturday was the one thing that kept her going through the next few weeks of classes and the chaos of the construction at home. On these late May days Ivy worked with his shirt off. She thought he should have been a statue, so beautiful were the bony lines of his broad shoulders and the working of his muscled arms.

He was too alive to be a statue, of course. Ivy was always in motion, swinging his arms as he worked, bent over at the waist so Zoe could see the parallel lines of his ribs rise and fall with his breath. And oh, the curve of his hip—what a thing it was! He moved with the fierce energy and grace of an animal. When her field glasses wandered up to his face, it was like looking in the eye of something half-wild. What could go on in a mind like that?

Sometimes she would see him lie down and look up at the sky. She imagined herself lying beside him, sharing secrets as they traced the path of the clouds. The life she invented for them together was so vivid that she almost didn't want to talk to the real boy.

And besides, she was ashamed to talk to him. Zoe had been sentenced to Mesquakie, but Ivy got paid to work there. She'd seen Hub hand him an envelope, that was how she knew. Maybe later, when all this was over and she'd burned that orange vest, she'd find a way to talk to him, but not now. When it finally happened, she knew how she would feel. *I still don't know you,* she would think. *You could talk all day and I still wouldn't really know who you are.*

School would be over in a couple of weeks, and the thought of all those long summer days of freedom ahead filled her with a powerful mix of restlessness and yearning, as she made her way alone out to the back corner of the field, *her* field, each Saturday morning, or walked through the woods where a carpet of wildflowers had sprung up in the wake of the fire, green shoots pushing through the black ash. Trout lily, Solomon's seal, May apples, shooting stars, jack-in-the-pulpit.

Ephemerals: That's what Hub called them; flowers that bloomed and died in a matter of weeks, before the trees leafed out and shaded them. She liked the way the word sounded in her head. *I am an ephemeral.* It made her feel like something passing and precious.

There were days so clear and skies so brilliant blue, with white clouds scudding across them like ships under full sail, that she felt she could lift right off the ground. One moment she was ambling down a path, and the next thing she knew, the wind would take hold of her, like a hand pushing against her back. Her feet would start running without her even willing it, even knowing it. And she would run faster and faster across the prairie, until her heart jumped like a rabbit and her breath came in deep gasps and her feet barely skimmed the ground.

It felt good to spend herself this way. The air tasted fresh and delicious; it smelled like damp earth, grass, and flowers. And her body felt strong, supple, and hungry for more of everything life could serve up.

She ran and felt like one of the animals, as though her feet were growing up out of the earth. And she knew what they knew, that sometimes you ran just because you could, because of the way the rush of air felt on your face and how your legs reached out, eating up longer and longer patches of ground.

She ran until the blood pounded in her ears, so loud she couldn't hear the voices that said, *You're not good enough*, *You're not old enough, You're not beautiful or smart or lovable, and you will always be alone.*

She ran because there were ghosts chasing her, shadows that pursued her, heartaches she was leaving behind. She was running for her life, and those phantoms couldn't catch her; not here, not anywhere. She would outrun fear and sadness and worry and shame and all those losses that had lined up against her like a column of soldiers with their guns shouldered and ready to fire. If she had to, she would outrun death itself.

She would keep on running until she dropped, exhausted. Then she would roll over onto her back and breathe in the endless sky above her, sun glinting off her face.

To be an animal, to have a body like this that could taste, see, hear, and fly through space, to lie down and smell the earth and feel the heat of the sun on your face was enough for her. She did not need anything else but this: just to be alive, cool air caressing her skin, dreaming of Ivy and what might be ahead.

There was no school on Memorial Day, no workmen to keep Zoe from the luxury of having a morning to sleep in, and a whole day with nothing pressing to do. After breakfast Zoe walked back into the wilderness that used to be her grandmother's garden, armed with a rusty shovel and a pair of clippers.

In the box of photos she'd brought down from the attic, she'd found a faded picture of her grandmother, standing under the arbor in a frame of climbing roses, with a spotted dog lying at her feet. She was wearing a man's shirt, loose white shorts, and a broad-brimmed hat with wisps of dark hair sticking out underneath. It must have been midsummer, judging from the dense leaves and exuberant flowers. She was holding a pair of cloth gloves in the hand that rested on her hip, and the other hand held up a spade, as if she'd been interrupted at her work. She was looking past the camera, at someone or something in the distance, a squinty smile on her face from staring into the sun, and her mouth was half-open, as though she had just begun to speak.

It made Zoe ache, thinking of how happy her grandmother had been in the midst of all that beauty, and how fragile a thing her life had turned out to be. She almost put the photo back into the box, but as she studied it in the dim light of her room, it occurred to Zoe that perhaps she could bring at least part of that world back to life. Maybe the garden was like the prairie. Like Hub said, it was mostly a matter of giving it some space to grow.

Zoe stood beneath the arbor, exactly where her grandmother had stood, but facing inward at what used to be the garden. She held the faded photo up, moving and turning it, trying to find some landmarks that would help her locate any remnant of the flowers that had once filled the space.

The photo showed a stone path that led from the arbor into the garden. Zoe bent over and began ripping out plants, handful after handful, and didn't see anything but dirt. Then she dug until the spade clanked on something hard, about three inches below the surface. Zoe squatted down and scraped away the dirt with her bare hands until she exposed a flat white rock. One by one she dug the stones out of the ground, cleaned them off, and set them back in place again. By late afternoon she'd made a path six stone steps long. A day's work, and all she'd managed to create was a clearing, a path in. She wouldn't have time to tend to the whole garden with all the other things she had to do. Well, she thought, leaning on the shovel, her body sticky with sweat, it was a start.

❖

Zoe went back to the house to hose off the dirt that coated her arms and fingers. Nelia was out in the yard getting a leg up on her tan. She was lying facedown on a lawn chair, wearing a pink straw hat, sunglasses, and a two-piece suit a little larger than a tissue. Every now and then she would lean over to pick up a can of bug spray and fog the entire area.

"You can't kill everything," Zoe said.

Nelia looked back to where Zoe was standing with the hose, running water down her bare legs. "I can try." She made a pillow with her hands and put her head on it, peering over her sunglasses at Zoe. "You missed a spot."

"Where?"

"Here," she said, pointing at her forehead.

Zoe dropped her head down and splashed water up to her face. When she looked up, her hair was hanging in wet threads.

"Make yourself useful and put some suntan lotion on my back," Nelia said.

Zoe was sorely tempted to soak her down, but instead she wiped her wet hands on her shorts, then came over and squirted white cream out of the tube.

"Remember the time I drew a pattern on you with sunblock, so you woke up with a red bull's-eye in the middle of your back?"

Nelia pitched a surly glance over her shoulder. "Another great moment in the history of passive aggression," she said.

Zoe wiped a big smear of cool cream across Nelia's hot skin. Her back was broad and strong, compared to Zoe's thin frame. "Looks like the mosquitoes got in a few shots before you exterminated them," she said. "You know why they want our blood?"

"They sell it to buy beer?" Nelia said under her hat.

"No, they feed their babies with it. Good thing you came out today. Now they'll live to see their children's children bite you."

"Just goes to show you," Nelia said.

"That nature always wins in the end?"

"No, that you're reading too many field guides."

Nelia sat up and reached for the sunblock to grease the other side. "Why are you looking at my chest?"

"I was just wondering."

"What?"

"Were they always that way? The same size, I mean?"

Nelia put down the sunblock and rubbed her hand down her arm. "Oh, that again. You're not thinking of robbing a drugstore, are you?"

"Funny."

"They'll grow, Zoe. Boobs are like boyfriends. You go around wishing for them and trying to figure out what you have to do to get them, and worrying about all the things you're probably doing wrong, and then one day, who knows why, you wake up and find you've got more than you wanted."

"That's very comforting."

"I do my best." Nelia leaned back on the lounge chair and folded her arms. "Besides, you shouldn't compare yourself to me. I'm in the prime of my boob life." She took her sunglasses off and looked intently at Zoe.

"What is it?" Zoe asked. "What's wrong?"

"Turn sideways," Nelia said. She wagged a finger at Zoe. "Now stick your chest out." She nodded her head. "Mmm, hmmm. I thought so. You're going through a developmental leap."

"That's a bad thing, isn't it? I can tell by the way you say it."

"No. It's good. Your boobs are growing, that's all."

"Both of them?"

Nelia considered the question, but didn't answer it directly. Zoe's face melted.

"You're too sensitive about it, Zoe. It will all even out in the end."

"I'm not worried about the end. I'm worried about now."

"You know what would be good for you? A day of shopping with me."

"Thanks, but you don't have any money, and neither do I."

"I will soon. I got a job up at the Rack—Saturdays and Sundays starting next week. Weekdays, too, once school gets out. Plus I get a discount. As soon as I get my first paycheck, I'm going to blow it on my little sister. And you can bring that factoid friend of yours. What's her name . . . Miranda. I sort of like having her around."

Nelia eyed her curiously. "There's something else different about you, Zoe," she said. She pulled the pink hat down over her face. "If I didn't know better," the hat said, "I'd think you were in love."

They decided to celebrate the last day of school, June 8, with a shopping trip that began with a compulsory makeover. When Miranda arrived, Nelia was already assaulting Zoe with a mascara wand in the bathroom.

"Stop squirming," Nelia said. She leaned into Zoe, who was sitting stiffly on the toilet seat, and jabbed at her eyelashes, missing them by at least an inch. "How can I make anything out of you if you're fighting back?"

"What difference does it make what I look like if you blind me?"

"Everyone else can see you."

Miranda peered at Zoe over Nelia's shoulder, tilting her head. "Is that blue streak on her cheek a bruise or did the eye shadow slip?"

Zoe shoved forward, trying to get up, but Nelia blocked her escape. "It's all right. I'll get it off." She dabbed at her with a washcloth.

"Why are you trying to make me into another version of you?"

"I'm not. Well, I guess I am—sort of an abridged version. But it wouldn't be a bad thing if I did." She put down the mascara and came after Zoe with a tube of red lipstick. "Sit still, would you?"

Zoe jerked her head away and pursed her lips. "Not red. It makes me look like a clown's mistress."

"You're right. That color's not good on you. Not with your hair. Your hair is really beautiful, Zoe, if you'd just fix it up a little."

"I *like* it this way. It's easy."

"Easy is not what we're after here."

Nelia switched to a pale gloss and stood back to admire her work. "Well, what do you think, Miranda?"

Miranda tilted her head, studying Zoe from several angles. "Nice look," she said, "for a Kabuki dancer."

Zoe stamped her foot. "I knew it," she said.

Miranda threw her hands up. "I'm kidding, okay?"

Zoe stood up and looked at herself in the mirror. She barely recognized her own reflection. But the truth was, she did look good.

Nelia held the mascara wand aloft and turned to face Miranda. "Next?" she said.

"Let's get you some nice big ones," Miranda said. She stopped rifling through the lingerie rack and held up a black lace bra with cups the size of soup tureens.

"Believable, Miranda," Nelia said.

Miranda moved down past the little white tab on the rack that said 32D. She flipped through several hangers and pulled out a bra that appeared to be made from metal funnels wrapped in pink satin. Miranda held it up to her chest and grinned. "What do you think?"

"Too pointy," Nelia said. "Imagine hugging someone who was wearing that thing. Think soft and round." She sketched curves in the air with open hands. "The idea is to create the illusion of reality."

Zoe was in the corner, halfheartedly flipping through the 28AAs, her real size, trying to pretend she didn't know them.

"Just what we need," Nelia said triumphantly. She held up a package of Natural Wonder Bust Pads. "The new Kleenex."

Zoe, moritifed, picked a bra at random and skulked toward the dressing room.

Nelia walked over to the salesclerk. "Can you buy one of these," she asked, louder than she needed to, "or do you have to take them both?"

"Nelia!" Zoe wheeled around, so enraged that she barely stopped herself from raising the 28AA into the air like a bullwhip and whacking Nelia with it.

"They're on *sale*, Zoe." Nelia turned the tag around. "Buy one *package*, get the next one free."

Zoe could feel her face turning red like a stoplight.

"Oh, forget it," Nelia said to the salesclerk. "We'll take them both." She took her wallet out of her purse. "Maybe Miranda would like a set."

Zoe looked for Ivy the next Saturday but didn't see him. He wasn't out on the prairie working where he usually was when she went to look for him on her morning break. He might have been working in the office or he might have taken the day off. Then again, he might have gone away now that school was out, and disappeared from her life altogether. She'd never forgive herself for being such a coward if he had. She hadn't even given him a chance to reject her. And there was nothing she could do but go back to work.

Until now it had never occurred to her to be lonely when she was outside by herself. She liked having a place that was only hers, a place she could be not someone's sister or friend or daughter, but just herself. In the quiet, hauling branches or clipping brush, things that took all her strength and concentration, she was no longer even Zoe. She was someone without a face and without a name. Sometimes on the way back she had to stare into the river at her murky, quivering reflection, just to remember what she looked like. It felt good for a time. Forgetting her face helped her remember who she was.

But today there was a dull pain gnawing away at the back of her mind as she worked alone under the hot sun. "Lonely" wasn't really the word for that pain. "Longing" was the word. She longed for something; ached for it. The future maybe, or something the future held, something she couldn't even imagine or dream of yet. And somehow Ivy was at the center of it. He had wound his way into all her thoughts, so much so that she could barely remember what it was like to have an idea that didn't include him.

It had been warm and dry the last two weeks. The ground was cracked and the plants looked thirsty, all except the Canadian thistles, which could have grown just as well in a concrete parking lot. Hub had brought her out in the morning and given her the job of yanking the thistles out of the edge of the prairie near the woods, where they were starting to muscle their way in among the grasses.

"There's your victim," he had said. He'd pointed at a plant that was covered with tiny needles.

"Grab it low like this so you won't get pricked. And make sure you get the roots, or they'll come right back like a bad meal."

She'd brushed one arm against a pricker, bending over to try it, and then she'd kicked at it with her boot.

"They're just trying to survive like the rest of us," Hub had said.

"Well, they don't have to stick me to do it." She'd looked around her. There must have been hundreds. "I suppose you want me to pull them all."

"Now or later. They're not going anywhere."

Neither, apparently, was she.

It was hard to pull them out of the dry ground. And she hadn't counted on them fighting back, jabbing her right through her cotton gloves. Sweat dripped down her neck, and horseflies buzzed around her face. She was tempted to dig them out with her shovel, but Hub had told her not to; it would just damage the root systems of neighboring plants and stir up the thistle seeds underneath, giving them an opening so they could come back with a vengeance.

She tried pouring water from the jug she'd brought, to loosen the packed earth. That helped for a while, until she ran out. Then she got angry and began hacking at the thistles with her shovel, chopping them into pieces, madder than a dog at a cat show.

One blow was too hard. Zoe lost her balance, fell back, and

landed with her arms and legs spread wide, a snow angel in a patch of thistles, prickers stinging every inch of bare flesh from her neck to her ankles. They stung her palms as she pushed the heels of her hands back and boosted herself up again.

In a blind rage she stomped back and forth, trampling every thistle she could find, smashing them with the heel of her boot, scraping their guts through the dirt. She threw her head back and howled, waving her arms in a violent dance, until there was nothing but green and purple pulp beneath her feet.

Zoe stood on the wreckage, her chest hot and heaving, and looked around her. She had smashed them all right. But now, how was she going to get the roots out? She flung her gloves down onto the ground. "I hate you!" she shouted. "I hate you. I hate you. I hate you."

There was no answer, except for the dry wind. She had poured her whole jug of water onto the ground, and those demon plants had just drank it all up. She wiped her sweaty face against her shoulder and considered whether or not to walk all the way back to the house and refill the jug.

There was another way: a pond in a little hollow in the woods. It was a scummy thing, coated with bright green duckweed the color of fresh limes. But it was a good enough place to swish her jug down and get water. She wasn't going to drink it, after all, just moisten the earth and make it easier to dig. Zoe picked up her jug and started off toward the woods, looking back one last time at the thistles. "I'll kill you when I come back," she spat at them.

She found a path and followed it as it wound back into the trees. She had been to the pond before, and thought she recognized this as the way. But as it went deeper in, the path got smaller, the bushes so close together that she had to squeeze through sideways at times and still caught her clothes on low-hanging branches. Birds squawked alert calls over her head. "Watch out. Here comes a two-legged." She looked back to where she had come from. It seemed as though the path was closing up behind her.

She eased her way through a thicket of crab apples. The path came to a dead end in a thick stand of sumac. There was a small opening, but she could get through it only by crawling. Beyond it there was a circle where the grass had been pressed down, a sheltered bed enclosed by branches. She'd been following a deer path. A crow cawed in the distance. How could she have been so careless? Something skittered above her head and she shrunk down. She scanned the dark web of leaves above her, but saw nothing. She crawled backward to where she could stand up again. There was nothing to be afraid of. She knew that. But she couldn't shake the feeling that someone had been following her.

Here was the price to be paid for all the hours she'd spent spying on Ivy. For the first time it occurred to her that someone else could be watching her, another pair of eyes, following her movements, her arms reaching out to push back thorny branches, the swing of her hips and the flexing of her legs. This was what it was like to feel the crosshairs on your back.

She stopped and listened, but heard nothing except her own breathing. Her hand worked the handle of the jug. The sound of something crashing through the brush shoved her into motion. Her feet started running. Then she caught sight of a rack of antlers. *A buck*, she thought. What a baby she could be. She couldn't see the deer path anymore. Her heart banged like a fist on the wall of her chest. The woods looked the same in every direction. She didn't even know which way to go.

"Stand still." That was what her father always told her. "If you get lost, stand still." She took a deep breath and waited, even though she wanted to bolt. Water; she could smell it. For a moment she thought she was lost not in the here and now but in some fantasy of the past. But when she turned her head, she caught sight of the pond. It was right behind her.

The pond had a prehistoric look. There were trees rising up in the middle of it, with moss dripping from them, and dead stumps coated with algae near the banks. She looked for a place to dip her jug in, but it was too muddy and rank in the shallow end. Finally she found a fallen giant of a tree that stretched out from the bank to the center of the pond. Its roots had been pulled right out of the ground when it had fallen. There was a huge tangle of them at one end, still embedded with dirt. She had to hold the handle of the jug against the tree while she clawed her way up on top of it, feet digging into the soggy bark. Then she pushed herself to her feet, spread her arms like a tightrope walker, and began weaving unsteadily along the part of the tree that jutted out into the water.

Halfway down the length of the trunk, she dropped to her knees, gripping the damp, rotting tree with her fingertips, and inched her way forward. Every so often her sneaker would slip on a piece of loose bark and she would lose her balance, holding on to the tree as though it were a lifeline. The trunk got narrower as she went, until she reached a place that was ten feet or so from shore. She leaned over the side and swished the jug through the water until it was half-full, bringing it up with great effort and resting it on the log. The water seemed much deeper than she had expected. Then she stopped again.

It hadn't occurred to her to wonder how she would get back. She was too afraid to stand up and too unsteady to back up on her knees, carrying the jug. Out of the corner of her eye, she saw a dark shape moving in the water behind her. Slowly she turned her head around. A long black snake slithered along on the surface of the water, a few inches from where her foot dangled over the edge. Terrified, she jerked her leg up. Her body rolled sideways. She dropped the jug and reached out for the tree, but the rotting bark crumbled in her hands and she fell, arms stroking and legs kicking even before she went down into the muck.

The water was only up to her neck, but Zoe's feet sunk into the soft silt at the bottom and it sucked her down. She tried to free herself by pressing her heel in, but that only made her sink down farther. She dunked her head under, grabbed her leg, and pulled it, and came back up gasping for breath, crying out, even though she knew no one would hear her. She dunked down again, but this time her arm got tangled in the weeds. She clawed at it with her other hand, kicking furiously, lungs bursting, breath running out, but she couldn't get her head above water.

Then she felt something move in the silty darkness underwater, untangling her. A body, strong and solid beneath her own, pushed her toward light and air. She came up struggling and choking, and behind her another head appeared at the surface. It was Ivy.

His arms locked around her, pulling her back to the shore. He leaned over her, where she lay gulping air. She could see his eyes, through the blur in her own, and his lips parted and moving. He must have been saying something, but her waterlogged head couldn't decipher it. Had he been watching her the whole time?

She looked at him staring down at her, his face gradually coming into focus. And she understood, at last, what it was he was saying. It was the very thing she wondered herself.

"Why are you here?"

# CHAPTER 23

"Why are you here?" She'd had no answer when Ivy had asked her that question after he had dragged her out of the pond, and so she had answered him with another question: "What do you want?"

"To save you from drowning." He sat back on his heels, water dripping from his hair and a wry smile breaking at the corners of his mouth. "If it's all right with you."

The next week she'd seen him coming toward her as she'd worked in the field, and she'd held her breath.

"Hub told me to come over and give you a hand," he'd said.

"I don't need any help." It was the first thing she thought of, and the words spilled out of her mouth before she had time to stop them.

He planted his rake on the ground and rested on it. "If I promise not to save you," he'd said, "will you let me stay?"

They'd worked side by side, mostly in silence that day, both of them testing the waters, sneaking shy looks at each other, a careful move closer, then apart. And when he'd turned to go, wiping his hands off on his khaki shorts, without thinking she had called after him, "Are you coming back?"

"I could if you want."

She looked away from him.

"Hub didn't send me out here to help you. I asked him if I could," Ivy said finally. And that was the truth. She could see that in the clear, unflinching way he looked at her with those bottomless eyes.

*Why are you here and what do you want?* She didn't know the answer to either question then, but now she did. She wanted to know him. She had never wanted anything as much as she wanted this.

Once summer vacation started, Zoe volunteered to work some extra weekdays at the prairie, along with her regular Saturday community service. She told herself she had nothing better to do. Nelia was working at the Rack, Miranda had a summer job babysitting for her neighbors' kids, and her mom could handle Ollie most of the time. But there was more to it than that.

There was Ivy.

They worked together out on the prairie. They drank ice-cold water from the same jug, their heads flung back and rivers running down their chins. Then they rested under the tree that stood alone in the middle of the section Hub had burned in the spring. By late June the black scars from that fire had disappeared under a thick cover of grasses spotted with butterfly weed, coreopsis, and the first purple coneflowers. Zoe had thought the burned area would be slow to bounce back, but it had grown up even taller and stronger once the matted weight of the old had been burned away.

The tree was a massive bur oak with limbs like inviting arms that reached all the way to the ground, and above that was a dome of gnarled branches and leaves, as wide as it was tall. Hub said the oak was at least two hundred years old. It had been there before the elk, the bears, and the bison in those parts had all been killed off or driven out. The great dying, Hub called it. The tree had been a silent witness when the clouds of curlew and swallow-tailed kites had vanished. Now it stood alone, waiting to see what the future would bring.

They usually ate their lunch together under the bur oak, lying down afterward in its shade, looking up through the web of branches and the leaves that were always moving in the restless wind, and still not seeing the top of it. It was more like a small world than a tree. Sometimes they climbed up into the branches, Ivy grabbing hold of her hand and pulling her up higher than she would have gone alone, until they reached a place where they could see far off in all directions.

When they weren't working, they were exploring. Going out into the prairie with Ivy was like wading into water, the grass so tall it came up to your waist. And it was swimming with life: birds singing, bees buzzing, and butterflies sailing on the wind that made waves in the grass.

One day there was a good soaking rain and Hub put them to work indoors, the smeared world disappearing outside the window. At noon they stopped to eat lunch, sitting in the cool dark of the cellar, leaning on musty bales of straw, legs hunched up, eating peanut butter and honey sandwiches and carrot sticks spread out on an old red blanket at their feet. Something about being alone together in that place of shelter, the grayness of the day, the drumming of the rain outside, and the comforting smell of damp earth made Zoe crack open.

She told him things she otherwise wouldn't have: about her

father being away fishing in Alaska, how it had seemed he was always in another place or wishing he was. She told Ivy about her mother and her pipe dreams, Nelia and her oversize ego, and how Oliver was always getting in her hair.

She did not tell him how she cried sometimes in the middle of the night. She would rather have stripped naked in front of him than let him see that side of her. And she did not tell him she longed to go back home again. Because it seemed to her suddenly that what she longed for was to be out on the prairie, under the bur oak, her body stretched out next to his and the wind cooling her sunburned skin.

Ivy didn't tell her much about his life, but what he did made her feel like there was a wound in him, and it ran deep. His mother was dead. The one thing Ivy told her about his father was that he tried to stay out of his way. Ivy was silent sometimes, and distant, but it was the price, she decided, of being different the way Ivy was.

He seemed to be connected to life in a way that other people weren't. Hub knew names and facts and reasons, but Ivy understood things. He felt the swells and changes in life around him as though they were all a part of his own body, as close as his hands and feet. The wild part of him spoke to the wildness in the world.

He noticed things that escaped her: crayfish hidden in the marsh grass and turkey vultures circling in the air. She didn't need to take Virginia's flora and fauna book along when he was there, because Ivy kept everything in his head. He knew the tactics of ambush bugs, the favorite food of dogbane beetles, the song of field crickets, and the winter retreats of monarchs.

"Monarchs: They're the ones that migrate each year," Zoe said when they were resting one day. She was watching a butterfly folding and unfolding its wings as it hung suspended from the fiery orange seed head of a purple coneflower. "Do you know where they go?" she asked.

"Mexico. They spend the winter in the Sierra Madre."

"Why do they go so far?"

"Wouldn't you if you had wings?"

"But they come back."

"That's the strange part. The butterflies that come back aren't the ones that left. They're the next generation. What I don't get is how they find their way back to a place they've never even seen."

Zoe shrugged. "Something in you knows when you're finally home."

Ivy stopped abruptly. "Don't move."

Zoe froze. "What's the matter?" She kept her head still and shifted her gaze. There was a butterfly high-stepping across her yellow shirt. "They like bright colors," she said.

He smiled at her, those dark tameless eyes, half-bold and half-shy.

"They like beautiful things," he said.

Ivy was like the prairie. He belonged to a forgotten time when the world still spoke and people still had ears to hear it. The lives most people lived seemed like a kind of poverty compared to his. He wasn't a lost boy, as Miranda called him. No, not that. He was one of the found.

One afternoon when Zoe was taking some boxes off a shelf, she heard a buzzing sound and backed away from the sooty, cobwebbed window. A wasp was crawling along the edge of the wood frame. Now and then it spread its wings and rose up to batter itself against the glass, then fall back down to the painted wood and begin the long climb up again. She was going to swat it with a rolled-up seed catalogue, but Ivy stopped her.

He placed his cupped hand on the screen next to the wasp, his movements slow, smooth, and deliberate. Zoe's breath caught as she watched the wasp crawl onto his hand and flex its tiny waist, wiggling its bottom and probing his skin with its antennae as it crawled toward the center of his palm.

Ivy stayed perfectly still. "Open the window," he said.

He stretched his hand out into the air carefully, as though he were holding something precious, and held it there until the wasp opened its wings and lifted into the sunlight. Zoe watched, not knowing what to make of his reckless courage, or, for that matter, the fact that he even cared.

It seemed to her that he was always walking the border between two worlds, and it made her uneasy knowing it would be possible for him to cross that border one day and never come back.

"Cooper's hawk." She heard the cry a minute after Ivy did. They were out on the prairie working the first week in July when Ivy called out to her. Zoe straightened up and looked at the sky, hand shading her face. Ivy pointed toward the woods. "Over there."

She felt a twinge of something dark, envy maybe, as they walked toward the woods, because he had seen it first: her hawk. Zoe's eyes scanned the trees until she saw a movement. It was big, probably the female, standing on a dead branch, head cocked, watching and waiting, her hunting pose. The babies back at the nest were all feathered out now, gangly and as big as crows. They spilled over the edge of the nest, flapping and shrieking, trying to get first crack at the sparrow wing or gopher leg their parents showed up with. It was a full-time job just to keep those babies fed.

The hawk looked at Ivy, whose eyes took in not only the hawk but the field around the bird, watching to see if some unlucky rodent or bird would stumble into her field of vision. He seemed as intent and excited by it as Zoe was.

"I could show you something," Zoe said.

They walked back to the nest together late that afternoon. Ollie saw Zoe leaving the house to meet Ivy and insisted on going with her. He was always tagging along. And she was already too late to talk him out of it.

They walked single file down the path with Ollie duckwalking ahead of them, feet spread wide, wearing white socks and an enormous pair of black basketball shoes that looked too big for him but weren't. He was all feet lately. It seemed to be the only thing on him that grew. His toothpick arms stuck out of a red T-shirt that was big enough to fit Garrett and most probably *was* his. And his skinny little legs filled up the small gap between the end of his navy shorts and the beginning of his white socks and black shoes.

"Do you see them, Ollie?"

"Yes. No."

Now that the trees were leafed out, the nest was well hidden. But Zoe could hear squawking as they approached. It looked and sounded like some prehistoric jungle. The ground under the nest was littered with an assortment of leftover bones and feathers, and there were spots of white dung all over the ferns and mosses that thrived in the moist, well-fertilized soil around the trunk.

"I see them!" Ollie began jumping up and down under the nest.

Zoe shushed him. "Be quiet. You'll frighten them." She looked up through the curtain of leaves. The babies were alone in the nest, and relatively quiet, as long as there was no prospect of food.

"One . . . three . . . There's one missing," Ollie said.

"You must have miscounted."

"I *know* how to count." Ollie pouted.

Ivy walked around to the other side of the nest. "He's right. There *are* only three."

"There are four baby hawks. I'm telling you," Zoe said. "I've been here every day since they hatched."

"Maybe one's hidden underneath." Ivy walked over to a neighboring tree, grabbed hold of a low-hanging branch, and boosted himself up with his arms until he could swing a leg over and climb up to get a better look.

"Look!" Ollie shouted. Zoe rushed to his side. She expected to see a bird lying on the ground, but instead she found Ollie standing in front of a young hawk, perched on a low bush. The sight of the bird close up stunned her. It was ruffled and downy, with yellow eyes staring out from sunken little sockets on either side of its head. It had an enormous curved beak, made for tearing, and talons like meat hooks wrapped around the branch.

Ollie took a step closer. The bird eyeballed him.

"Leave him alone, Ollie." Zoe looked up in the air, expecting that at any minute the parents would return and attack Ollie. Or maybe this so-called baby would suddenly lunge and peck Ollie's eyes out. The hawk gripped the branch she was perched on like a lifeline, blinking up every now and then at the nest.

Ivy dropped to the ground and walked over, making a

wide circle around the bush, while the bird's eyes followed nervously.

"Do you think she's hurt?"

"No, just learning to fly," Ivy said. "She'll be all right."

Zoe inched closer. The bird lost her balance, then spread her wings trying to recover. "We should stay with her."

"All night?"

"If we have to."

"That won't help. It will only keep the parents from feeding her."

"What about the foxes and coyotes?"

"She's strong," Ivy said. "She can take care of herself."

Out of the corner of her eye Zoe saw Ollie lunge toward the hawk. She put a hand down to block him. The bird's head darted forward, mouth gaping and wings wide open and flapping wildly. Ollie fell back, grabbing on to Zoe's leg so hard his fingernails sank into her flesh as he hid behind her.

"You see?" Ivy said.

Zoe bit her lip. The bird regarded Zoe with her fierce predator eyes.

"Come back tomorrow," Ivy said. "I'll come with you."

It was barely light out when Ivy came the next morning. Ollie was still asleep. Zoe was waiting at the mailbox at the end of their drive, watching the sunrise over a field where goldfinches rose up in the air like flowers with wings. A blaze of red and yellow was just beginning to appear behind the black line of trees.

They walked single file toward the woods. There was an early morning chill. Zoe rubbed her bare arms, wishing she'd brought the sweater she'd left lying on the kitchen chair. It was strangely quiet once they got to the woods: no birds chattering, no wind rustling the leaves.

But when they reached the hawks' tree, a great commotion broke out. Zoe raised the binoculars and searched the canopy of leaves until she spotted the nest. The female was standing above it, her head bobbing up and down, feeding her demanding chicks, their beaks clattering in the air like castanets. The male was off to the left, hunched over, watching them. It must have been a successful hunt.

Zoe looked everywhere, but there was no sign of the young hawk that had ventured out of the nest.

"She's gone," Zoe said.

"Let me have a look."

She handed the binoculars to Ivy. "Something's the matter. I knew this would happen."

Ivy surveyed the trees, the ground, and the bushes but saw nothing. He handed the binoculars back. "Keep watching. I'll go around the other side and see if I can stir her up."

"I told you," she said.

He turned, backpedaling, and threw his arms into the air. "She's probably just fine."

She watched Ivy disappear into the trees as she stood in the open, nervously shifting from foot to foot. Why hadn't she trusted herself? Maybe Ivy didn't know as much as she thought he did. Maybe—

There was a rustling in the trees.

"Wooooeeee!"

She heard Ivy's voice. A bird sputtered up out of the lower branches at the edge of some trees, sloppy, wavering, clearly a new driver. Ivy was underneath it, spinning around with his arms out straight, whooping and hollering and twirling. The hawk zigzagged from branch to branch and then suddenly took off flying directly at Zoe, wings pumping for all she was worth, climbing higher and higher.

And there was Ivy running along, shouting, "C'mon, bird. You can do it, bird." He was running full tilt, and when he reached Zoe, he threw his arms around her, spinning and twirling her, lifting her off her feet, shouting for all he was worth.

She looked at him and realized that she loved him, out of nowhere, pure and simple. She loved him: this boy who fit so naturally in the water, the wild, and in everything else. She loved him: this boy who seemed to grow up out of the ground itself. There was a part of her that had known this from the first time she had seen him. This was what love was: a landslide in your heart.

## CHAPTER 24

Cup plant, Indian grass, rattlesnake master, old man's whiskers; she knew them by name now. And the names alone called up pictures in her mind: prairie schooners and oxen, voyageurs in canoes, the endless ocean of grass. If she closed her eyes, she could imagine herself at the edge of this world.

She liked being around Hub because he taught her things about the plants and animals. Their names dropped from him like ripe apples. Ripgut: a grass with blades so sharp it slashed the bellies of the horses as they passed. Compass plant: the first leaves that sprout in the spring always point north and south. Prairie chicken: the bird that taught the Indians how to dance.

The names had stories locked up in them. It was almost as though the people who had created the names had known that this world was about to disappear and that they had to find words to describe all that they loved that would one day be lost.

Hub was the keeper of those stories. He was the center, the piece that kept the wheel rolling. But something about him made Zoe feel both hope and despair. There was the hope that somehow the bulldozer of progress could be routed around them. And there was the reality that most of what was beautiful and alive here for thousands of years was already gone.

That was why Hub expected so much from everyone. Pete had told Zoe this early on. What they were doing was important, and they were running out of time.

He was harder on Zoe than on anyone else. He worked her until her body ached and her head pounded with the heat. She would come home feeling older than Hub, and come back, joint-stiff and bone-sore, two days later. He snapped at her for dragging her feet, and hounded her over mistakes, until she shouted at him and told him he'd better lay off or she was going to walk.

"You can scream at me all you want," he said, his face like a stone. "But I'm not giving in, and I'm sure as hell not giving up."

She might have changed her mind about volunteering for extra days, except for the fact that Zoe was also the one that Hub took time out to teach. He showed her the map the surveyors had made of the area in the 1840s, and took pride in how easily she learned to read the landscape in it, the patches of woodlands like green clouds, the Indian trails and the settlements, the squiggly line of the creeks. He showed her soil maps and aerial photographs, and seemed pleased when she insisted on taking them outside with her, because you didn't know a place until you knew it with your feet.

He taught her too to see the stages in things. She learned how to recognize the sprouting leaves, then the bloom, then the seed head. And he taught her about the rhythm of the seasons, how each plant that appeared grew taller than the last.

The first two weeks of July had been hot and there'd been no rain. Just day after day of pale gray skies that finally broke down and drizzled. Pete was alone in the office, pounding nails into a table he was fixing, when Zoe walked in. "Where's Hub?"

He pointed his head in the direction of the prairie. "Crazy old coot. Can't stand to be cooped up."

Hub had made a tarp shelter out in the field. At noon Zoe brought him lunch—damp cheese and apples—and sat down with him while he ate.

"You don't have to stay," he said. "There's not much work we can do today."

"I don't mind. It reminds me of home. It always rained whenever we camped." She rubbed her face off with the back of her hand. "In fact, it always rained period."

There was the smell of wet earth, grass, and flowers in the air. She had come to love the scent of this place on her skin and how it changed as the weeks passed. The flowers were like fireworks that went off each month, lavender and blue exploding and then fading into a burst of yellow and fiery orange. The low-growing prairie violets and spiderwort in spring gave way to waist-high coneflowers, followed by cup plant that could grow ten feet tall. The feel of it changed from the soft furry stems of pasqueflowers to the rough sandpaper leaves of prairie dock.

But what she liked best was the perfume. The prairie was like a spice box, a mix of familiar and exotic. The minty leaves of bergamot, the citrus smell of New Jersey tea, and the scent of the grasses all blended together into a complicated whole that rubbed off on her as she brushed against seed heads and flowers, lopped off branches, and crushed leaves under her feet.

On the first day Zoe had come to work there, Hub had picked a dry seed head from one of last year's yellow coneflowers, crushed it in his hand, and held it out for her to sniff. It reminded her of the lavendar farms in Washington where they used to gather fistfuls of flowers each year to dry and sew into pillows. It was different, but the same.

Now Hub shifted position, stiff-limbed. His rheumatism was acting up. He was so charged with energy and so determined to outwork everyone else that Zoe sometimes forgot he was an old man.

"Glass, that's the trouble," he said from out of nowhere.

"What?"

"I was thinking. Everybody says it was the wheel or fire that changed the world."

"It wasn't?"

"It was glass. People sitting inside, looking out and thinking they know what's out there, without getting cold or hungry or wet. Life is messy. That's the thing. Nobody wants it that way. So they hide out inside. Now they're looking at a television or a computer screen and thinking it's a window. If they knew what they were losing, maybe they wouldn't be so quick to let it go."

Zoe looked up at the gray sky. "Did you ever feel like just giving up?"

"I did once, a long time ago. I lost some people I loved. Sold my business, got in my car, and started driving west. I had no idea what I was going to do when I got there. It wouldn't have much mattered to me if I'd kept driving until I landed in the Pacific."

"What happened?"

"I only made it as far as Chicago. It was a god-awful hot day. I got stuck on the expressway and sat there sweating a half hour, hardly moving an inch. I finally just blew up and turned off into a run-down neighborhood—nothing but abandoned buildings, yards full of glass and rubble, garbage cans overflowing, smashed cars. And then I crossed some old tracks and all up and down the railroad bed I saw spikes of yellow flowers: compass plant. Just like a lost tribe making its last stand.

"I turned the car around, right there in the street, with the guy behind me honking and swearing. I didn't know what my next step was. But it seemed to me that everything beautiful and important in my life was behind me, and I couldn't leave it without at least trying to bring it back. Course I didn't really believe I could do it. I'm not even sure I believe it now. The things I'm doing aren't going to bear fruit in my lifetime."

"So how do you know that what you're doing even matters?"

"I don't. Maybe we never do. Love and work; that's all we're given. No guarantees."

Hub stopped and looked at the haze that had settled over the waves of grass and flowers.

"In the meantime we can enjoy it. That's what we're here to do. Stop killing everything and stop trying to run the whole show. Enjoy the whole blasted thing and leave it alone."

He looked at her, straight on. "You're almost finished here. I'm turning in your last work sheet on Saturday. Your debt to Ms. Davidson is all paid up."

Zoe looked down at her feet and drew imperfect circles in the dirt with a stick. "I was thinking maybe I could work for you . . . like Ivy," she said quietly. "You wouldn't have to pay me much—not anything, really."

Hub smiled under the shadow of his hat. "Six fifty an hour sound good? Monday to Thursday?"

Zoe nodded. "Better than McDonald's."

"Yeah, well, there's no free lunch. And you have to put up with me."

❖

It turned out to be more than she'd bargained for. Zoe came home each night and fell into bed exhausted by nine o'clock, then dragged herself up the next morning and had to do the same thing all over again. One day she was waiting for Ivy, who was late getting to work, and she fell asleep under the bur oak.

"Zoe," Ivy whispered, shaking her.

She opened one eye to look at him.

"Lucky it was me who found you sleeping," he said.

The next time it was Hub who woke her up. And he didn't whisper. He yelled.

He was always ranting and prodding her. But all the while he did, she knew it was important to him that she be there.

Hub believed in her, though he would never say that out loud. He needed her. So did Ivy. And with every day that passed, she could feel herself growing stronger.

The first Monday in August, Billy announced that he and Garrett were going to start screwing plasterboard over the bare studs, then they were going to tape and paint. It was the last step they had to go through before the construction was finished and the house could open up as a bed-and-breakfast.

"Sort of the beginning of the end," Billy told them.

"Don't you mean the beginning of the beginning?" Zoe's mother asked.

"That depends on how you look at it," Billy said.

"And on what happens next," said Nelia, the voice of reality.

The house was barely recognizable now as the place they'd come to four months before. The outside had new siding, the porch no longer sagged, and with each day that passed more of the rough wood, exposed wires, and pipes inside the house were covered with walls that were smooth, white, and flat.

Still Zoe couldn't help feeling that something was disappearing inside those fresh, clean walls. When she needed to escape, she would go up to the attic, throwing the windows open and setting up an ancient fan so she could tolerate the heat while she sat and looked at curled-edge photographs and flipped through stacks of yellowed books. The attic was the one part of the house that hadn't changed.

And there was something else that drew her up there, something she had noticed the first time she'd opened the dormer window that looked out on her gradmother's garden. On the wall above the window there were penciled circles and lines, arranged in rows and patterns. At first she'd thought it was a sketch for a wall decoration that had never been finished. But as she'd looked past the figures, outside the window, she'd realized that what she was looking at was a sort of map.

Someone had once stood where she was standing now, looking down from the window, and imagined the garden as it was going to be: the arbor here, the fence there, lilac bushes in a row along the back. When she took a rag and wiped away the dust, she could see there was a legend on the window frame that told her what each circle stood for—Iceland poppy, garden peony, resurrection lily—though many of the flowers had long since disappeared or decided for themselves how and where they would grow.

Underneath the window there was something even more intriguing, a line of dates and notes on weather. When Zoe had first discovered this, she had taken her finger and traced the soft, round curves of what she'd assumed was her grandmother's handwriting. And she had started to write her own notes on either side of the window about the garden as *she* wanted it to be—the garden she would make if she could convince Hub to give her some of the seeds they gathered in the fall.

She'd been making drawings of the prairie flowers and grasses on the walls, so she would remember how tall they would be each month and when they would bloom. She added her own notes on the weather: May 1 high winds and thunder, June 15 soaking rain, July 5 hot and dry.

"Pay attention." She could hear her father saying this as she moved from the walls up to the ceiling, drawing the phases of the moon and positions of the stars each week, until the attic became a map of her world—the one she had come from, the one she was living in, and the one that was waiting for her up ahead.

Sometimes when she looked out the window she would see Nelia and Garrett nuzzled up together on the glider bench in the yard.

"You're not getting serious about him, are you?" Zoe had asked her one day.

"Maybe."

"That isn't like you, Nelia."

"Well, I'm not going to end up like Mom, if that's what you're referring to."

"What's that supposed to mean?"

"Getting married so young. Weezy thinks I ought to go to college. Maybe apply for some scholarships this fall. What do you think, Zoe?"

"Stranger things have happened."

"I knew I could count on your support."

Garrett was at their house even more than usual lately. Billy had him working overtime to help the crew install the last of the plasterboard. When all the walls were up, Zoe's mother decided to have a picnic and celebrate.

She set it up for Sunday so Zoe could invite Miranda. They'd barely had a chance to see each other all summer, since Zoe was working weekdays at the prairie and Miranda was often babysitting nights and weekends.

"Maybe you ought to invite Ivy, too," Miranda suggested.

Zoe thought about everyone sitting around the picnic table with Ivy in the center like the main course. "I think maybe not," Zoe said.

Garrett and Billy grilled the hamburgers and hot dogs, Nelia and Zoe made potato salad, Miranda brought a jug of lemonade, and Weezy made four kinds of pie.

"Sometimes I wish I'd had a family," Weezy said.

"I always thought you'd have a husband and a yard full of kids, the way you talked when we were young," Zoe's mother said.

"I had a chance or two. Ten, actually."

"Ten proposals?" Nelia said.

"More or less. There was the anchor salesman, the antique dealer, the stock car racer . . . Oh, I can't remember them all anymore."

Nelia leaned in closer. "Why didn't you take anyone up on it?"

"I did once. He was a barber from Philadelphia. We were going by train to Las Vegas to get married. My fiancé, Bob was his name, got to talking to some guy in the observation car about whether or not crew cuts were ever going to come back in style, so I went to the other car and fell asleep. Well, in the morning I woke up and went to find him, because I realized he'd left his shoes under the seat. And when I got to the last door, the conductor yelled at me to stop, because there was no more train.

"'What do you mean, there's no more train?' I said to him, standing there like a perfect fool, holding those wing tips in the air. Well, it turns out that in the middle of the night the first half of the train uncoupled and went on to Seattle, and the part I was in headed south to Nevada. I wanted him to stop that train and let me off, but all I could think to do was stand there shouting at him, 'But I still have his shoes.'"

"So what happened?"

"I went back to my seat, sobbing my eyes out, and this man from Cincinnati, whose name happened to be Bob, came from across the aisle to comfort me. He told me no man who'd be that careless deserved to have a woman like me. Then we got to talking and realized how much we had in common, and by the time I got to Las Vegas, he told me he wanted to marry me."

"So you just traded one Bob for another."

"No, I did not, Billy. If you would just sit there and listen for a minute and stop interrupting maybe I could get to the point of my story.

"I told him I wanted to get to know him better before making a big decision like that, and it was a good thing I did. We got right back on the next train going east, and when we got to Cincinnati, I found out he was already married. His wife and kids were there to meet him at the train. Wanted to surprise him I guess, and boy *was* he, surprised that is. I should have known someone that considerate about a woman's feelings had to have a wife somewhere."

"What happened to the shoes?" Billy asked her.

"I still have them. I'm saving them in case the real Bob shows up again."

"You ought to have them bronzed, Weezy."

"Shut your mouth, Billy. You know that fairy tale about the beautiful lady that kisses the frog and he turns into a prince?"

"Yup."

"Well, in my experience it's the other way around. It's been my misfortune to have kissed a whole lot of princes that turned into frogs. Some of them even turned out to be snakes. Now, if I could find a man like you: handsome, handy around the house . . . If you weren't my cousin, I'd marry you myself."

"Weezy!"

"Well, Annie, am I right or not?"

Zoe eyed her mother, afraid she might take the bait. "He's a catch all right," she said, "for the right person."

Billy just smiled.

"Guess I'd better get dessert ready," Zoe's mother said.

Ollie got off his mother's lap and went over and climbed up next to Miranda on the glider bench. He handed her a book to read: *Heroes of the Bible*. It was one of a stack of books Zoe had brought down from the attic for Ollie. But he especially liked this one because of all the stories with boats in them: Noah and the ark, Jonah and the whale, baby Moses in the bulrushes.

"Kind of a busman's holiday reading to Ollie, isn't it, Miranda?" Weezy asked. "I hear you've been babysitting all summer. How are those Cooper twins doing?"

"You mean the devil children?" Miranda rolled her eyes. "They're fine. I just wish I could say the same for myself. Yesterday they hosed the mailman, put shoe polish all over the phone, and locked themselves in the bathroom. And that was the good part of the day. If I ever have kids, they'll be in boarding school by the time they get to that age."

"How old are the little guys?" Garrett asked.

"Five," Miranda said. "And they're girls. Amy and Ella."

Garrett let out a long low whistle. "I thought I had it hard, working for Billy."

Zoe's mother walked out the back door carrying a big tray. "Sounds to me like you all need some pie therapy."

Weezy got up to help her pass out the plates.

"You know what I'm thinking, Weezy?" Zoe's mother said. "Maybe we should open up a side business selling baked goods along with the bed-and-breakfast. We could generate a little extra income that way. God knows we both need it. At least I hope He does."

Weezy smiled. "Good idea. What do you think we ought to call our business?"

"How about Pie in the Sky?" Nelia suggested.

Weezy reached down and took Nelia's plate back. "Just for that, I'm eating your piece too."

When everyone went home, Zoe got into the shower and soaped up, enjoying the moist heat that made her want to go to sleep right there, standing up. When she finally forced herself to step out and reached over the sink for a towel, she caught sight of someone that looked like her, but didn't, in the bathroom mirror. She moved in closer, wiping the steam from the mirror so she could get a better look. Breasts; she had two of them.

Ivy had asked Zoe to meet him Monday before work at the bank of the river, next to a maple tree with gnarled roots reaching out to the water. But when she got there, he was nowhere in sight. She edged down the rocky embankment with one hand held out for support, crab-walking part of the way and half-sliding on her bottom where it was steep, skinning her hands. She looked up and down the narrow shoreline and saw nothing but the upside-down world reflected in the water.

"Hello?" she called out. She waited for a response. There was none, only the murmur of the river and the patter of some ducks that were bobbing their tails up in the air farther up current, fishing for something to eat.

The tree was located at a bend in the river where there had once been a bridge. You could still see the broken remnants of a road that had led down to it, buried in the brush that had grown up through the cracks. She guessed that the road must have continued on the other side, although she'd never been across it to find out.

From where Zoe stood she could see the ruins of a stone structure that had held up the center of the bridge halfway out in the water. It squatted on its own private island, like a ruined castle.

She heard something fall behind her, a heavy thud, and turned to see Ivy drop from the tree, grinning at her, dusting off his knees.

"Don't you ever keep your feet on the ground?"

He smiled at her, a crooked grin that echoed in his eyes and went down her spine. "I have something to show you," he said.

She looked at his dusty bare feet and his empty hands.

"Oh?"

"Turn around."

"Why?"

"Just don't look."

She turned her back on him. Behind her she heard the sound

of the river gurgling and then a splash, as though Ivy had waded in. She turned her head slightly, but he caught her.

"Don't look yet."

The sound of something heavy dragging across the dirt, and another splash.

"What's going on?"

Silence.

"Okay, now you can look."

He was standing on the bank of the river, a broad smile on his face, and beside him there was a raft. She walked down to the bank to take a closer look at it, her breath shallow, heart beating like a bird's. It was made of tree limbs, cut so they were all the same length, then sanded down and tied together with rope.

"Did you make this?"

Ivy nodded. "A couple years ago. I keep it over there on the island."

It was not perfect—rough cut and ragged, clumsily done.

"It's beautiful," she said.

"Well?"

"Well what?"

"C'mon out and try it."

She balked. "I don't like to swim."

"Who said anything about swimming? I won't let you fall in. Anyway, it's not that deep."

He turned his tanned back and swished out to the center of the river until the water was nearly up to his chest, then he turned around and raised his arms in the air. "See?"

Zoe scowled and looked down at the water running past. "It might get deeper downriver."

"If you fall in, you can float."

"What about the current?"

"If you don't want to, just say so."

"I want to . . ." But her voice caught. "I'm afraid," she said.

Ivy waded back to her. "You don't have to be afraid." He held out a hand to her.

She walked in hesitantly up to her knees and stood there shivering. Ivy took hold of her hand and led her around the bend in the river to a quiet inlet where the water pooled. Then he held his hands out flat on the glistening surface. "Go ahead. Lie back. I'll hold you up."

Her heart jumped. She looked at him skeptically.

He put his arms under her back. Her knees buckled and she sank down in the water, still wearing her blouse and shorts. Her body curled and she held on to him, climbing up his bony shoulders as though he were a tree.

"Relax."

"I am relaxed."

"You're fighting the water."

She tried to keep her legs still but they kept thrashing the water into a foam, her arms jutting straight out into the air and hitting the water over and over with a sharp smack.

"It's okay," he told her. "I won't let go until you're ready."

She could feel his hands on her spine, the pressure of his skin on her bones. They were strong hands, as big as her face, and they seemed to fit in the spaces in her back as though they belonged there, an arch to hold her up. She let her body relax, and he sank down into the water next to her. She could feel the closeness of his body through the water.

"Put your head back," he whispered. "Let it fall."

She could hear the rush of the river in her ears, feel her hair drifting.

"Open your eyes," he said.

She hadn't even realized that they were tightly shut.

"What do you see?"

"Sky," she said. Clear blue and endless. A canopy of trees. And his face.

Water washed up over her nose. She started to panic.

"Look at me," Ivy said. "It's okay."

She let her body go again, stretched her neck and arched her back. She felt the release of his hands. Her body drifted a bit, and her arms floated straight out to the side like a bird in flight. Ivy smiled and flicked his dark hair out of his eyes. He held his hands up in the air; a magician. Water splashed down on his tanned chest and she watched as it rolled down, caressing each muscle and rib.

"What are you thinking?" he asked.

"Nothing."

But she heard a voice deep inside her. She was thinking this: Love will hold you up.

# CHAPTER 25

"What's it like?" Ivy asked her.

"What?"

"The ocean."

"You've never seen it?"

"No."

It was like someone telling you they'd never seen grass or daylight. As long as she could remember, the ocean had been the one thing that was always there—the sound of it, like music that was different each time you heard it, the pounding surf and the aching wail of the seagulls and the smell of salt in the air.

"It changes," she said. "That's the most important thing. Always moving, tides going in and out, weather passing over, waves rising and falling. Some mornings it's smooth and silver, like the back of a fish, and by afternoon it's howling up a storm."

She looked at Ivy and thought, strangely, that she could have been describing him. He had weather too. Some days he was happy, laughing, chasing her through grass that was tall enough now to close up over their heads. Other days he was moody, easily angered, hard to reach, for no reason that she could tell. He could be pushed to the flash point by anything Hub said.

It was late August, dog days. More than once the thermometer had topped out at one hundred. Ivy and Hub had been fighting a lot. For one thing, they were shorthanded. Hub was spending most of his time lately doing what he liked least, playing politics, trying to convince the zoning board to block a development that threatened to swallow up a big chunk of land adjacent to the prairie. He was holed up inside all day, writing letters, making phone calls, talking to anyone who would listen to him. When he came out, it was usually to bellow at them, and Ivy was there waiting for him with his back already up. Ivy and Hub were so much alike. Neither one of them had a clue how to back down.

On Friday, Ivy called and asked Zoe to meet him down by the river. He was already there when she arrived. But the raft wasn't. Ivy was pacing up and down the bank like a caged animal.

Zoe stared at the place where the raft was supposed to be. "Are you sure you left it here?"

He glared at her, as though it were somehow her fault. "Do you think I'm stupid?" He stalked back and forth. "I tied it up to that tree when we went out the last time. You were here. You saw me do it. I should have dragged it back up onto the island, where no one would have seen it."

"Maybe it came loose and drifted downstream."

"I *tied* it," he growled. "It didn't come loose. Things don't just happen."

They walked down the river together, searching the banks, hoping it had washed up somewhere or had gotten caught in the shallows. Zoe spotted it first and knew as soon as she saw it that Ivy had been right. It hadn't just drifted away. Someone had wrecked it. The raft was lying in pieces on a muddy spot under an overhanging branch.

She felt the familiar weariness of grief, looking at the shattered wood and the pain on Ivy's face. He kicked a broken piece of the raft into the water and watched it swirl in the current as it sailed out of reach.

"We can build another one," Zoe said.

He didn't answer her, just walked back and forth with his hands on his hips, staring at the tracks he was making in the mud. "I hate this place." He punched his own hand with his fist. "If I ever get half a chance, I'm leaving and not looking back."

"Where would you go?"

"I don't know . . . west . . ."

Zoe's face flamed.

He bent over to pick up a stone, wound up like a pitcher, and flung it at the opposite bank and did not look at her. "Maybe head for the coast."

There'd been a string of record-setting hot days; the little rain that fell was mostly drizzle. Even the trees looked thirsty and wilted. "A tinderbox," Hub said.

Lately there had been some threatening skies—black clouds sailing along the horizon like dark ships, racing before a hard wind. It was the kind of weather her father loved. It made him long to be on the sea.

Zoe always knew when her father was about to leave. She would catch him staring out at the ocean with his hand shading his eyes, as though he were looking for something he'd lost, something that had drifted out just beyond his reach, carried off on the outgoing tide. Sometimes he'd take Zoe and Oliver with him and head down to the docks, wandering from slip to slip, asking the returning skippers how the catch had been, making guesses on the weather and passing on advice to those who were getting ready to leave.

Sooner or later, his moods would drive him back out. If the season hadn't opened yet, he'd haul the tent and cooler down to the boat and take whoever was willing with him island hopping, camping in little deserted coves too small to be mentioned on the weekend boaters' maps. He'd come back to life again then, like a fish thrown back into the ocean, jarred awake by the slap of cold salt spray on his face.

When Zoe thought of his face now, he was always surrounded by darkness. The last time she had gone fishing with him, it was night by the time they put the boat back in its slip. There had been a full moon, lighting a path across the water so white it seemed you could get out and walk across it up to the sky. But during the whole day they had not caught anything worth keeping.

Her father had gone into a rant about it. "They're killing everything that's wild. The rivers are choked with dams so there's no place for the salmon to spawn. When I was young, these islands were all forests." He waved his hand at the black hulks of the headlands all around, with the glittering lights of houses scattered like stars across them "Look at them, will you?"

Zoe had not heard from her father in several weeks. There had been storms all up and down the coast, but it wouldn't have stopped him from going out. The fiercer the storm, the more energy it seemed to give him. Bad weather made Zoe uneasy, the waves breaking over the bow and the thud of the boat slamming into the whitecaps. But it seemed to make her father grow larger when he stood at the wheel, turning the boat full throttle into the wind, full of fire and angry grace.

They didn't know whether he was still on the *Kenai Lady*, had picked up a job harborside, or had headed back to Washington. But she knew this: A storm would never have kept him in port. That was why she had begun to get worried.

On Friday afternoon Zoe went out alone to check on the hawks. The young ones had all left the nest, but they were still hanging around their home tree and one another. They spent their days practicing dives; preening and sitting for hours, heads darting back and forth, *tsee-tsee*ing at anything that moved. They were as keen-eyed and watchful as their parents, but too noisy, reckless, and impatient to catch much of anything. Their mother was becoming distant, resting in a nearby tree, paying little attention to them, except when she occasionally fed them. The male hawk was hardly there at all.

When the baby hawks were just learning to fly, Zoe and Ivy had seen a squirrel climb straight up the trunk of their roost tree and make its way toward the nest. The hawk babies leered at it from their various perches. The squirrel climbed farther out onto the branch, moving straight toward them, stopping every now and then to scold them and whip its tail. The big female, the one that Zoe had come to think of as Nelia, started up an enraged squawking and leaped toward the squirrel, wings spread wide. Zoe was sure the squirrel would turn back, but it kept going recklessly forward, ready to take the hawk on.

"What's it doing?" Zoe asked Ivy. "Squirrels don't rob hawks' nests."

"No, but hawks eat baby squirrels. Maybe she doesn't like the new neighbors."

Today when Zoe arrived, the birds were in a circle in the lower branches of a maple. She took out her binoculars to see what was attracting them. The big female stood off to the side. She had something in her talons. Zoe saw a flash of yellow, a songbird probably. She reached down and picked up a rock, threw it at the hawk and missed.

She threw another rock, this time close enough to unnerve the hawk, which must have loosened its grip. The yellow bird broke away and made a rush for freedom, wings pumping. Zoe held her breath, hoping the bird would escape, but it dove headlong into a bush, where the hawks descended on it, jeering like a street gang, knocking it to the ground so the big female could capture it again. She stood there crushing it in her talons, until the bird stopped moving, then she bent to rip feathers off its back.

Zoe raised a stick into the air as if to strike the hawk, but stopped. She dropped the stick. The hawk rose up and retreated to a nearby branch.

It was just instinct, she told herself. That's how it was: Eat or be eaten. But it did not comfort her.

Zoe helped her mother move the furniture back into the dining room on Saturday morning. Billy had set a new land speed record getting the painting finished because of Weezy's nagging. She told him she didn't want his paint fumes mixing in with the smell of her good cooking. So she bribed him with the promise of ham and biscuits for Saturday lunch if he'd get it done.

Billy looked too comfortable sitting there, like someone who actually belonged, raving about the biscuits. Ollie was galloping in circles around the dining room, his meal nearly untouched.

"Makes me think of Scattershot," Billy said.

"Whose cat got shot?" Ollie looped past him, nearly knocking over Weezy, who was coming out of the kitchen carrying a cherry pie.

"*Scattershot*, my pony." He patted the empty chair next to him. "If you plant yourself down a minute, I'll tell you about him."

Ollie made a last loop before deciding that it was worth sitting still for.

"My dad picked him up down at the livestock auction when I was about your age—an old brown swaybacked thing about as high as this table, with a big lock of blond mane falling in his eyes. Spent the better part of his life working carnivals, tied to one of those wheels, so all he would do was walk round and round in circles. Never went much beyond a slow plod. But he loved to eat, that horse did. If someone yelled 'Scattershot,' he'd take off running straight for the barn. And if you happened to be on his back, you'd better just duck and hold on. My friends used to yell his name and make bets on whether or not he'd knock me off."

"I want to see him," Ollie said.

"Scattershot? He lived to be an old, old horse, but he's gone now. One night when I was in high school, he didn't come in for supper, and we knew that could only be bad news. Found him down by the river, just dropped over dead in the water. He was too big to move, so my dad told me to bury him where he lay. The thing was, he kept floating back up."

Weezy put the pie down on the table and interrupted him. "Billy, do you honestly believe this story qualifies as polite dinner table conversation?"

"Well, it's the truth, and you know it. We finally took his heart and buried it up by the barn. That was the only way we could put Scattershot to rest."

"He made that whole story up, Ollie," Zoe said.

"I'll show you the headstone, right outside the hay loft." Billy drew a line of invisible words in the air. "It says, 'Scattershot's Heart.' And underneath we wrote, 'You can't keep a good horse down.'"

Weezy had been asking Zoe to take her out to see the garden. Zoe had cleared out a patch of deadly nightshade, and uncovered a stone bench at the end of the flagstone path that led from the arbor. She had used old photos to locate a few remnants of the roses and a stone circle where the herb garden used to be. And she had cleared away the grasses and vines that had grown over them, to give them a chance to come back. "You have to discover the 'once was' if you want to put it back." That's how Hub put it. Land had stories too. They were written in the rocks, the soil, the pattern of plants, their wounds. There might even be seeds asleep in the darkness under the earth, waiting for the right combination of fire and water to wake them.

In the end she decided to leave the back half of the garden wild, at least for now. Next year—She stopped herself from going on with that particular line of thought because there was no point in looking very far down the road. Who knew what next year would bring.

Zoe finally gave in and brought Weezy out to see the garden after lunch on Saturday. They sat together on the stone bench, watching gray clouds race across the southern sky, threatening rain again.

"Did you know her very well?" Zoe asked.

"Your grandma? I knew her the way you know all the adults in your life when you're a kid—sort of like props. As long as you've got a roof over your head and the food appears on schedule, you don't really think much about them. It never occurs to you that they have a life that doesn't revolve around you.

"But your grandma, she was different. Even then there was a sadness about her. She used to take us on picnics down by the river. And while the kids were playing on inner tubes, she would just sit there for hours, staring out at the water. It was like she had seen her own future there and couldn't look away. She was very beautiful, dark like you."

Weezy fanned herself with her hand. "Lord, it's hot as blazes today." She stood up and walked to an overgrown corner of the garden, looking for something. "You know what used to be here? There was an apple tree, an ancient one, all bent over like an old widow. It was starting to die, and your grandfather wanted to cut it down, but your grandmother wouldn't let him. She planted a trumpet vine and it grew up and wound its way all around the old tree. It was the strangest thing to see the two of them wound together in the fall. It looked like a single tree that grew big orange trumpet flowers and green apples; one thing dying and another coming to life, all blended together so you couldn't tell which was which."

There was no trace now of either the tree or the vine. So many years had gone by, they had probably fallen and gone back to the earth. "What about my grandfather?" Zoe asked. "Did you know him?"

Weezy walked back and sat down on the bench. "Your grandma could have had any boy in town, but when your grandfather showed up, it was all over. He had a lot more charm than sense. Her father tried to stop them from getting married, but she just ran off to the county seat, lied about her age, and didn't tell anyone. By the time they broke the news to her dad, she was already pregnant. But you know, I shouldn't be telling you all this. Why don't you ask your mother to tell you these stories?"

Zoe shrugged. "She's got more sense than charm."

Weezy smiled and put an arm around her. "Oh, Zoe."

After the dishes were done, Weezy went home and Billy took Zoe's mother to the store to pick out paint for the living room. Zoe had offered to stay home with Ollie. They'd been walking in the fields trying to catch grasshoppers when the wind suddenly picked up and the sky darkened. This time it looked like more than just a threat.

The phone was ringing as they walked into the house, and Zoe picked it up.

Her mother's voice was crackling with static, and Zoe could pick out only a few words, something about a storm.

"Where's Nelia?" This time she came through loud and clear.

"She's still not back with the car from Garrett's."

There was silence on the other end of the line.

"Mom?"

". . . road's . . ."

"Mom? I can't hear you."

". . . when we can get through."

Zoe went out onto the porch and looked out across the fields. Lightning stabbed from the gray clouds off in the distance. She counted the time between the flash and the thunder. Three seconds. The storm was getting closer.

She went inside and helped Ollie put on his pajamas. It was still early in the evening, but the house was dark. They sat upstairs in his bed, leaning against the headboard, Ollie with his legs tucked up, trying to fold his whole body under her arm. He had piled the stack of books from the attic on the end table, and he made her read them over and over again, stalling so she wouldn't leave. He finally fell asleep with his mouth open like a fish. She eased her tingling arm out and threw the covers over him, then went down to the kitchen and sat at the table with a glass of milk and the last piece of cherry pie, which she ate right out of the tin.

When the rain started, it came down in sheets, thunder cracking so close Zoe could feel the floor rattle. She sat at the table and looked out through the water drops that glistened and quivered on the window glass. A flash of lightning lit up the world outside, followed hard by another.

Zoe put down her glass of milk.

Someone was out there. She had seen something: a vague shape moving toward the house in the driving rain.

Thunder surged and receded. Her throat tightened.

She waited, breathing heavily, pressed back against the chair, gripping the seat. Lightning flickered again. She could still see the pelting rain and the grasses whipped by the wind outside the window. But no car. Nothing human. Nothing else.

She went over to lock the back door, then she changed her mind. *Don't give in to your fears. That's what sinks you.* She flicked off the kitchen light, pulled back the curtain, and looked out into the night. Then she turned the knob and stepped outside onto the back porch.

She stood, back against the house, cold biting into her legs, and peered out at the darkness through the waterfall of rain falling over the porch roof. A shadow in the driveway caught her eye. Lightning lit up the sky again. The shadow resolved itself into the shape of a man, walking toward her, water flooding down his face.

"Zoe," he called out.

She had forgotten how it sounded when he spoke her name. She went down the stairs and out into the rain, water sweeping over her in waves, bare feet sinking into the cold mud. She opened her mouth to speak and water ran into her mouth.

"Zo." Her father reached out to her, opening his arms wide, holding her close. Rain came down all around them, soaking them to the bone.

"I thought you died," she said. "I thought you would never come back."

"I'm here, girl." He rubbed his open palm along her cheek.

She pressed her face to his chest, breathing in the familiar smell of salt and wind.

"I'm here," he said.

## CHAPTER 26

How big was he?" Ollie stretched his arms out to the side as far as they would go.

"Bigger," his father said.

"This big?" Ollie skipped over to touch Zoe with his outstretched fingertips. Then he side-skipped over and touched the wall with his other hand.

"At least," his father said. "Why, his pincers alone were as big as you, Liver. Of course, I didn't realize it till I'd already hauled that old crab in, or I would have let the net out. And then, when he told me about the wishes . . ."

"He could talk?" Ollie's eyes grew wide.

"Well, not in our language, of course. But I understood him well enough. Not to be bragging, but I do speak a bit of Crustacean. You're bound to pick up a bit of it in my line of work. Just a word or two, enough to get by in a pinch, if you know what I mean. I can't read a word of it to this day."

Zoe's mother pushed her chair back, folded her arms, and gave him one of her looks, but her father kept talking.

"As I was saying, I probably shouldn't have believed him

about the wishes, but he had honest eyes, all crabs do. So I bent myself down and started untangling him from the net, at which point he grabbed me with one of those pincers and told me to get off his boat."

"Crabs don't have boats," Ollie said.

"That's what I was thinking. But you don't argue with a giant crab. You've got to outwit them. So I said I'll get off your boat, just as soon as I get my three wishes. And that's exactly what I did."

"You got your wishes? All three of them?" Ollie held three fingers up.

"I did indeed." His father folded his fingers down as he counted them. "Nelia, Zoe, and Oliver. That makes three, doesn't it?"

Ollie thought awhile. "I would have wished for a treasure."

His father swept Ollie off his feet and slung him over his shoulder. "And isn't that just what I got?"

"Put me down."

"Not until you give me three wishes," his father said.

Ollie waved his arms and kicked his feet, giggling as his father spun him around. "You can only have one," Ollie said.

"He drives a hard bargain, that one." His father set him back down on the ground. "Fine. I wish Ollie would run upstairs and get dressed before I can say, 'Ready, set . . .'"

Ollie ran out of the room like a shot.

". . . go."

They listened to the pounding of his feet on the stairs, followed by a strange silence that settled on them as they sat around the table cluttered with the remains of breakfast. Nelia got up and cleared some dishes. Zoe studied her parents warily.

"You shouldn't lie to him like that, Daniel," her mother said finally.

"Telling stories isn't lying, Annie. Let him have some fun. Let him be a boy."

Her father folded his hands on the table and looked out at the dining room with its fresh coat of paint. His face softened. "You've done a fine job here. The place looks good. It must have been a lot of work."

"I've had a good bit of help," her mother said. "People have been good to us."

Her father's eyes narrowed.

Nelia came back to the table. "I'd better get to work." She put a hand on her father's shoulder and pecked him on the cheek. "I'm glad you're back, Dad," she said.

Her father grinned and hugged her back. "Dad. There's a word I haven't heard in a good long while."

Nelia looked at her watch. "I wonder what happened to Garrett. I thought Billy was sending out a crew to get the painting done in the living room."

Zoe looked up. "They called early this morning. I told them not to come."

Her mother snapped at her. "What?"

"I told them you didn't need them now that Dad's here."

Her mother scraped her chair back. "Zoe, it's not up to you to decide whether or not—"

Her father leaned back in his chair. "For the love of God, Annie, can't you just once leave these kids alone? Stop trying to run everything."

"I don't have any other choice, Daniel. I'm the only one who—"

"And whose fault is that, Annie?" Her father's eyes flashed as he rose to his feet. "Whose?"

Zoe was relieved when her mother turned to her chores after Nelia went to work, because it meant that Zoe, her father, and Ollie could go back to the fields, Ollie riding on his father's back monkey-style and Zoe in front, flattening a path through the tall grass, leading the way to the hawks. There was so much she wanted to show her father. So much she wanted to tell him. There was time now, time to share stories and talk. Things would be like they used to be. He would go places with them, do things.

Zoe spotted the hawk first, one of the young ones, preening on a low-hanging branch. She could hear screeching up in the leaves, which meant the others were up there somewhere too. She reached into her pack for the binoculars. Her father glanced down as she pulled them out.

"Nice glasses you've got there," he said.

Zoe felt his words drill into her. "They're Billy's," she said.

"Billy, huh?"

She nodded. "I'm just borrowing them."

"He comes in handy, that Billy."

Zoe shrugged.

Her father nodded toward her. "Can I have a look?"

She pointed at the branch and laid the binoculars in his open palm.

"It's one of the females," she said. "They're the biggest. The others are probably up there somewhere. They're too young to be alone yet."

He scanned the tree with the field glasses and lowered his voice. "You're a bit of an expert on these birds, eh, Zoe?"

"I've learned some."

He stopped moving and focused. "She's a beauty, all right."

"I wanna look." Oliver jumped up and down at his father's feet, until his father gave in and let him have the binoculars.

"You're aiming too high, Ollie." Zoe bent down and grabbed Ollie's shoulders so she could adjust his line of sight. She could feel her father's eyes on her.

"You've changed, Zoe." He looked at her closely, as though she were as strange a creature as the hawk.

"What do you mean?"

"Look at you. You're a young woman now."

Upstairs in the attic that night, just below August 12 new moon, Zoe wrote this: August 21 thunderstorm, Dad is home.

She wrote it down partly because she wanted to remember it, like everything else she had recorded on the dusty walls, and partly because it didn't feel real until she had written it down. As though that would somehow make it last.

There were times now when her father fit into their lives as if nothing had changed. She'd find him in the kitchen making apple pancakes like he often had when she woke up in the morning. The only thing that was different was the stage set.

But other times the fit wasn't quite right. Nelia got testy when her father commented on how late she came home. Ollie was clingy. And Zoe resented having to share her father with anyone else.

Her mother treated her father warily. Their conversations danced around each other's feelings, coming close, but not quite touching. And then there was Billy. Her father and Billy treated each other like two tomcats who'd both showed up on the same front porch.

Zoe went to work alone on Monday, Tuesday, and Wednesday,

but on Thursday she made up her mind to invite her father along. It was the last weekday she would spend at the prairie before school started up again. If she was going to do it, there'd never be a better time than now.

She was upstairs in her bedroom getting dressed when she saw Billy's truck pull up. Her father was already outside, standing next to the station wagon. He walked toward the truck, and Billy got out to talk to him. Then the talking turned into shouting. Ollie started whining from inside the station wagon. Her father went back to him and got in, slamming the car door and pulling out of the driveway so fast that his tires spit gravel as they left.

Zoe went downstairs. "Where did Dad go?"

Nelia shrugged. "He took Ollie and went somewhere. Said there was something he had to pick up."

Zoe frowned.

"What's the matter?" Nelia asked.

"I was going to ask him to go to work with me so I could show him around. Did he say when he'd be back?"

"No."

Zoe glanced up at the kitchen clock. "When he gets back, give him directions to the prairie, and have him ask for Hub. He'll know where I am." She started to walk out the door, but Nelia called out to her.

"Zoe?"

"What?"

"Don't get your hopes up too high," she said.

"What are you talking about?"

"I'm just saying. It's not good to expect too much."

Her father didn't turn up at the prairie. Zoe called home to let her family know she had some work to finish up and would be home late. Her father still hadn't come back.

"What time are you getting off?" her mother asked her.

"Around six thirty or seven."

"You'll be tired," she said. "I don't want you to have to walk. If Dad comes back with the car, I'll send him to get you. Otherwise I'll ask Nelia and Garrett."

It was her mother who showed up to get her, and she was in Weezy's car.

"I told her I'd run an errand for her. You don't mind, do you?" her mother asked. "I'll pick up something for you to eat along the way."

By the time they got back to the house, it was eight o'clock. Her mother dropped Zoe off in front, then put the car in the garage. It was getting dark and Zoe didn't see her father sitting on the porch steps until she'd nearly tripped over him. "Where's Ollie?" she asked.

"Asleep."

Her father's face was in the shadows. But there was something in his voice.

"Why are you out here?" she asked him. "Aren't you coming inside?"

He put his hand down on the stoop and pushed himself up to stand, wavering before her. She saw his face dead on, creased with lines and stubbled with a beard, looking out at her with those watery blue eyes.

Her mother came up behind her. "Is Ollie all right?"

Her father pulled himself up taller. "Why wouldn't he be?"

"You've been drinking," she said.

"You wouldn't deny a man a drink now and then, would you?"

She scowled at him. "You can do whatever you want, as

long as you don't do it here. I think it's time for you to leave, Daniel."

He stared at her, listing to the side, hands raised in a gesture of surrender. "You wouldn't throw me out on the street at this hour."

"Tomorrow morning, Daniel." Her mother pushed past him into the house. "Zoe?" She held the door open, waiting for her to follow.

Her father had one hand behind his back and he brought it out now, holding a matted bear out to Zoe. "Shhh," he said, finger to his lips. "Don't wake Booda."

She winced at the smell of him. "Did Ollie see you like this?"

Her father stepped back from her, swaying. "Like what?"

She felt like she was going to throw up.

"I'm not a bad man, Zoe."

She turned her back on him.

"Am I?" he called after her as she walked through the open door.

Upstairs in her room Zoe yanked open the bottom drawer of her dresser and shoved Booda in the back. Then she went down the hallway to Ollie's room.

He was sleeping soundly, unhurt and unafraid. She walked over to his bed and put her hand out to touch the soft skin of his face. She could feel his breath on her skin; baby's breath. He was still little more than a baby.

Her love for him was fierce. It made her believe that love was something she could do.

Ollie stirred. She reached out and pulled the blanket up over his shoulder.

"It's all right, Ollie. Everything's all right."

❖

Zoe tossed in her bed, memories gnawing at her. Even when she buried her face in the pillow, the image wouldn't go away: Ollie, his forehead ripped and bloody. It was when they were in Washington, the time he'd fallen over a bait box in their garage. He had his head thrown back and was howling. "Stop crying, Oliver." She said it over and over. A river of blood and tears ran down his face and snaked along his neck, staining the top of his T-shirt red.

She turned away and had an impulse just to run and keep on going. But instead she grabbed his hand and pulled him toward the house next door. Oliver dug in his heels and howled louder, pitching forward until she was holding him by the arm like a broken doll.

Zoe knocked on the screen door. Mrs. Kelly's face appeared in the shadowed hallway. She lifted Ollie's head to look at the gash. "Where's your mother?

"At work."

"What about your father?"

"I . . . don't know . . . He . . ."

Mrs. Kelly went back into the house and returned with her car keys, scooping Ollie up in her arms. "Tell your father to meet me at Island Hospital.

"Go find him, Zoe!" Mrs. Kelly shouted over her shoulder. Zoe heard the engine roar to life, and the shock of it made her feet start to move.

Zoe ran all the way down to the marina. A man she recognized stood at the counter, sorting bolts. "I'm looking for my father. . . . Daniel, my . . ."

"Daniel McKenna?" he said. "Try the Salty Dog, then."

The smell of beer and smoke hit her like a slap as she walked out of the bright light and into the damp and dark of the Salty Dog. Men she'd seen at the docks were hunched at the bar on stools, their weathered hands coiled around mugs of beer. She searched for her father's face among them.

He was at the end of the bar, shouting at a man who was shoving him, while the bartender tried to wedge his body between them. Her father's voice churned like rough water. The bartender struck him in the chest with the heel of his hand, and he reeled backward, upending several chairs before he fell to the floor, too drunk to get up.

Zoe ran over and reached out for his arm. The men at the bar stared at her. "You have to come with me. Oliver needs you. He's at the hospital."

Her father stumbled to his feet and shook her hands off his arm. "I don't need the likes of you to tell me what to do," he said. He staggered out the door, with Zoe following.

"I'm your father, you understand?" He held on to a parking meter, as though it were the only thing keeping him from drifting out beyond all hope of rescue.

"I hate you," she muttered.

He raised his hand in the air. Then he looked at her perplexed. The hand he had raised to strike her waved back and forth, a man with a question for which there was no answer.

Her father packed his bag up in the morning. They stood on the porch watching as he walked down the driveway, his sea bag slung over this shoulder, his body tilted, off balance, a man out of his element, unused to dry land.

He had almost made it to the road when Zoe took off running after him.

Her father set down his bag and put his arms around her.

"I want to go with you," she said.

"There's no place for you back there, girl."

His eyes were swimming with pain. He was going down and not even struggling to come back up. She *had* to go with him. He needed her.

"Your mother's right. I can't live here until I can be a real father to you."

"She told you that?"

He looked past her at the empty road. "I'm not the man you want me to be, Zoe."

She could feel the ground giving way beneath her, a gaping hole opening up, pulling her in.

"I shouldn't have come here."

He looked so tired and used up, a man thrown down and shattered. "Don't leave us again," she whispered.

"I love you," he said. "I've never wavered in that."

Her father let go of her and picked up his bag. "You can go on without me, Zoe."

She called to him again and again, but he didn't turn around. When he got to the crest of the hill, Zoe started back toward the house. She couldn't stand to watch him disappear.

# CHAPTER 27

September skies were full of lavender clouds at sunset, streaks of light raying out from a ball of fire. Mornings were dark. The days were so short now that the sun was just starting to rise through the haze as she walked down to catch the school bus each morning.

"You okay?" Miranda would ask her occasionally, as Zoe sat staring out the bus window at the fog covering the fields like a blanket.

"Mmmmhmmm."

"You're kind of quiet lately."

"I'm just tired."

Which was the truth, but not all of it. Since her father had left, there had been little time to think about him, and even less time to look back. Her life now was school and homework, followed by weekends working at the prairie.

From a distance the gentle slope of the prairie was like the back of a great golden animal. But up close you could see that the grasses were taking on colors from blue to bronze, the yellow flowers fading away, and the purple asters coming into bloom. The wind that always seemed to be blowing now whispered through the dry, brittle grasses and rattled the dead brown leaves of the prairie dock.

There was so much that had to be done before winter. Zoe and Ivy worked long hours each Saturday and Sunday harvesting the spent flowers and grasses, then sitting in the cellar, rubbing the plants over a screen to separate the chaff from the seeds.

Fridays after school they usually hung out with Miranda, but this Friday Ivy hadn't shown up at school. "He wasn't here all day," Miranda said. "At least he wasn't in first period math."

"Then why didn't he call last night to tell me?" Zoe said.

"I don't know. Call him."

Zoe did. But no one picked up.

He didn't come to work on Saturday either.

"What happened to Ivy?" she asked Pete as he was gathering up some tools to go out into the field and help her.

Pete shrugged. "He left a message up at the office. Some trouble he got into with his dad. I don't expect it's any picnic being Doug Walker's son."

"What's that supposed to mean?"

"You ever meet him?" Pete asked.

"No."

"Well, when you do, you'll know."

Ivy's house was on the far side of town, down a dirt road that ran alongside a row of run-down storage buildings with rusted cars abandoned in the weeds behind a barbed wire fence. "Holy Hill Road," Miranda had told her, when Zoe had called her after work Saturday to ask how to get there. "It looks more like 'Holy Hell.' Ivy's house is the last one on the right before it dead-ends."

It was a peeling white clapboard with a beaten-down fence in front that badly needed paint. Out back there was a swaybacked shed, a dog house with a broken chain but no dog, and an odd assortment of junk that included a pair of broken white lawn chairs, a propane tank, and a chipped pink toilet with plastic flowers sticking out of the tank.

She should have gone directly home after work, but instead her feet had pointed in the opposite direction, and she found herself halfway there before she even admitted to herself where she was going and why. All the while she trudged down the road, she recited an assortment of excuses to herself. She wanted to see if he was all right. She wanted to tell him they needed him back. But mostly she was angry that he hadn't at least called her to tell her what was wrong. If he didn't care about her, she wanted to know that now.

She walked up the tarred driveway with ripples of grass sprouting in the cracks, past an old camper with a hand-lettered sign in the window that said, MUST SELL, $500 OR B.O. It was dusk, but there didn't seem to be any lights on inside. She stepped up onto the porch, pushed the doorbell, and didn't hear anything. The stained curtains looked like they were permanently shut. There was a dead plant sitting on the windowsill.

Zoe raised her hand, hesitated a moment, then knocked. No answer. She was about to give up and leave when she heard voices coming from the back of the house, a man shouting, loud and angry, and another voice she recognized as Ivy's. She couldn't tell what they were saying. But the venom in their voices made her nervous.

The sound of breaking glass shattered the air. She thought of going around to the back, but what would she do? Kick the door in? She heard a car engine roar to life in the garage. She pressed her body back into the shadows. A car careened backward down the driveway, tires screeching. She couldn't see who was in the front seat. But as the car turned and sped down the road, and she stepped out of the shadows, she thought she saw someone looking back.

Her mother was sitting in the darkened living room when she came home "Zoe?" She called out to her when she walked in.

Zoe closed the door and stood in the hall, arms folded across her chest.

"I was worried about you."

"You don't have to be. I can take care of myself."

"Where were you?"

"Work."

"In the dark?"

"I went for a walk afterward."

"Alone?"

"What difference does it make?"

"It's not safe for you to be alone in the woods at night."

"I went to see a friend."

"Miranda?"

"Someone I work with." She could feel the hairs rise on her neck. "A boy. He needed help."

Her mother shifted in her seat. "I don't want you going places without telling me, Zoe."

"Why are you suddenly so interested in everything I do?"

"I just don't want you to make the same mistakes I made," her mother said.

"Is that what Dad is to you? A mistake?" She could see the torrent of feelings in her mother's eyes, but the words kept spilling out. "Who knows?" Zoe said. "Maybe you'll get lucky and he'll never come back."

An unbearable silence closed around them. Zoe stood still, waiting.

Her mother drew a deep breath. "The thing is," she said at last, "sometimes people can come back and still be lost."

Zoe stalked out of the living room and up the stairs. It didn't matter that her mother was upset. Nothing mattered.

Pete was telling her about some brush that needed cutting on Sunday afternoon when she spotted someone who looked like Ivy, far off in the fields. She craned her neck, trying to make sure it was really him, smiling the whole time so Pete would think she was paying attention.

"Are you listening to me, Zoe?"

"Mmmhmmm."

"What did I say, then?"

"Brush cutting . . . along the tree line."

"In *front* of the trees, Zoe. What's got you in such a state this morning?"

She was already on her way out before he finished the question.

"Zoe!"

"I will. I'll take care of it, promise."

When she finally reached him, Ivy had his back to her. She called his name, ready to throw her arms around him. But when he turned, she stopped. His eye was swollen and bruised and there was a red, raw slash across his face from his mouth to his jaw bone.

"Oh my God," Zoe said.

Ivy turned his face away. "I fell. Stupid, huh?"

"Ivy." Zoe tried to look into his eyes, but he avoided her gaze.

"What?"

"I was there," she said.

"What are you talking about?"

"I was at your house last night. I heard you and your father arguing."

She wanted him to deny it, to tell her he wasn't even home last night. But instead Ivy looked at her, his face unguarded, caught in his lie.

"You can't tell anyone, Zoe."

"What do you mean?"

"I don't want him to get in trouble."

"Why are you protecting him?" her voice was rising, thick with anger.

He looked away. "It's not that simple. You don't know."

She touched his face gently. Ivy pulled back.

"He was on a bender, told me if I gave him any more trouble, he'd flatten my ass."

"What are you going to do?"

"Hide out here for a few days. Give him a chance to cool off."

"You're going back there? After this?"

"He'll get over it, when he sobers up. He always does. I told Hub I was climbing and lost my grip. You can't tell him. Promise me. I'll figure this out on my own."

"Ivy, I don't—"

"*Please*, Zoe."

Sunday night Zoe sat at the kitchen table with Ollie and Nelia. They were supposed to be helping Weezy make bread, but Ollie kept getting up and going to the refrigerator.

"What's that behind your back, Ollie?" Nelia asked.

"Nothing." Ollie pulled his lips back like a little chimp and gave her a toothy grin.

Nelia walked over to him and closed the refrigerator door. "Show me those hands, little man."

Ollie pulled his arms from behind his back and held his hands up in front of her, fingers spread wide. There was a green olive on each fingertip.

Nelia opened the refrigerator door and took out a jar with a few lone strands of pimentos swimming in a sea of olive juice. "Ollie, for pity's sake."

"I love them," he said, thinking apparently that she might forgive a crime of passion. He managed to pop one more into his mouth before Nelia plucked the rest of them off his fingers.

"Did you know that kids can't tell lies until they're four years old?" she said.

"And why would that be?" Weezy asked. She was pouring flour from a bag into the mixing bowl, a white cloud rising in the air above it.

"Because before that they think we know everything they do." She emptied the jar into the sink. "As though we'd want to. Welcome to the grown-up world of trickery and deceit, Ollie."

"Oliver olive," he said, for no apparent reason.

"Maybe you should be a psychologist, Nelia," Weezy mused.

"It's too depressing," Nelia said. "Everyone is sick."

"Well, you've got another year before college. You'll think of something good to study, right, Zoe?"

"Hmmmm." She had her hands elbow deep in a pile of sticky dough that Weezy had given her to knead, and she wasn't listening to them.

Weezy worked away at her bowl with a wooden spoon until she had the flour all mixed in. "Why don't you help knead too, Nelia? It's actually a lot of fun, gets your aggressions out."

Nelia looked sideways at her. "Don't try to manipulate me," she said. "You're not dealing with some simpleton who is innocent of the ways of human behavior, you know."

"Sorry, I forgot. You're not just anyone. Knead it anyway." She scraped the dough out of the bowl onto the table in front of her.

"Knead, Nelia," Ollie commanded, pointing a finger at her.

"Stick a pimento in it, Ollie." Nelia picked up a stray olive that had escaped her attention and popped it into his mouth.

"This isn't just any bread, you know," Weezy said. "My aunt Muriel gave me the sourdough starter, and she got it from your grandma. I've carried it with me wherever I've lived."

"Through all ten proposals?" Nelia asked.

"As a matter of fact, I believe this bread may have been responsible for one or two. And now I'm handing it on to you."

Nelia went over to wash her hands and coat them with flour. "All right, if you put it that way. You must have really loved your aunt Muriel, Weezy," she said.

"Frankly, she was a big pain in the patootie. She didn't have a good word to say about anyone. And when she died, she left her house to Malvolio."

"Malvolio?"

"Her cat. But she could cook, there was no doubt about that: fried chicken, pork pies, biscuits and gravy. The kind of things you're not supposed to eat. Now that I think about it, maybe she was trying to kill us; death by saturated fat."

"Zoe?" Weezy stopped, her voice suddenly serious. Zoe looked down. Her hands were buried in yeasty glop. There were tears dripping down onto them. She swiped at her eye and got a big smear of liquid bread on her face.

"Is something wrong, angel?" Weezy asked quietly. She reached over and wiped Zoe's face off with the dish towel.

Nelia turned. She stood across the room, her powdery white hands held aloft, like a rubber-gloved doctor beginning surgery. Ollie pouted. He stuck his thumb into his mouth and chewed on the place where an olive was supposed to be.

"You know what let's do?" Weezy said to Zoe. "Let's let this bread rise and Nelia can take over so you and I can go out."

Weezy chattered all the way, pointing out the houses of people her family knew and Zoe didn't, as they drove through the dimly lit streets.

"That's where the new vet lives—young woman, just out of school. And see that tan one with the wraparound porch? That's Hank Pearson's. He's kind of gone downhill since he's had to use that walker. He used to work for your great-grandpa, you know."

At the crossroads Weezy turned right and drove down a dark road until they reached a small white wooden church, placed at an angle to the street, with a bell tower rising above it. She pulled the car into the deserted gravel parking lot, turned out the lights, and sat quietly for a minute.

"We're a little late, aren't we?" Zoe said. "It's Sunday night."

"I don't much like crowds, do you?" Weezy asked.

She got out of the car and walked up the concrete steps. Zoe followed, not knowing what else to do with herself. Weezy took out a key and twisted it in the lock, and the door yawned open. The only thing Zoe could see in the darkness was a red vigil light hanging down from the ceiling near the altar and the red exit lights glowing on both sides. It was unbearably lonely. She stopped in the doorway, unable to move forward or back.

"Well, come on in, angel," Weezy said. "God won't bite." She struck a match and lit a white candle in a tall brass holder near the altar, then she skimmed down the aisle, her hand cupped around the flame, lighting the candles at the end of each pew.

"Aren't you going to get in trouble for this?" Zoe said. She took a few steps inside.

"The caretaker's a friend of mine. He gave me the key so I can let myself in whenever I want."

"Is he one of the ten?"

"Apostles?"

"Proposals."

The church echoed with Weezy's big-hearted laugh. Zoe looked over her shoulder, waiting for the wrath of God to come down and smite them.

"Maybe I'll make old Charlie number eleven," Weezy said. "He still has a lot of life left in him, even if he is ninety-five."

"I didn't think you were supposed to do that."

"What? Marry an old man?" Weezy lit the last candle.

"No, laugh in church."

"Well, sure you are. Laugh, sob, worry, ask questions, get pissed off when you don't get an answer—and give up, when it looks like everything you've done is nothing but spit in the wind. Where else would you go with a heart like that?"

She walked over, sat on the hard wooden pew, and patted the spot beside her. Zoe sat down.

"I used to come on Sunday mornings like Billy," Weezy said. "But there was just too much noise. All that singing and sermonizing. You couldn't hear God if He used a megaphone. So I figured, old sinner that I am, it would be best for all concerned if I just sat here alone on Sunday nights instead."

Zoe straightened her back, crossed her feet under the pew, and folded her hands in her lap. It was so quiet, you could hear the wood creak if you moved. The walls on both sides of them had stained-glass windows with Bible scenes: winged men and children, shepherds and kings. They were dark and colorless, waiting for the sun to come up again and bring them to life.

Weezy leaned back and closed her eyes, her breathing soft and even. She might have fallen asleep. They sat together in the silence for a long time.

"Am I supposed to be praying?" Zoe asked finally.

Weezy didn't open her eyes. "Listening," she said.

"For what?"

"In case God has something to tell you."

"Don't you ask for anything?"

"Mostly I just say, 'Surprise me.' That's what He's going to do anyway."

Zoe looked up at the altar in its mute and shadowed beauty. There was a dove descending in the window above it, caged in by lines of lead. "Did you ever feel like there was something you needed to do, and if you didn't do it, awful things might happen?" She felt suddenly embarrassed when Weezy opened her eyes and turned to look at her. She'd forgotten that she wasn't alone.

"Is that how you feel?" Weezy asked.

Zoe didn't answer. She was crying.

Weezy reached out and covered Zoe's hand with hers. "It's

all right," Weezy said. "It's just holy water." She closed her eyes again. "People are mostly just doing the best they can, angel—even when it's not good enough."

Zoe got out of the car at the end of the driveway when Weezy dropped her off, so she could walk the long slope up to the house alone. She stood in the moonlight, under the evergreens that towered protectively over the house, and she breathed in the pine-scented air. There was a haze out in the fields. The night air was cold. Ivy had probably hauled a sleeping bag out onto the prairie to keep warm. He'd be asleep, under the bur oak, by now. She told herself she'd go there very early in the morning, bring him some graham crackers for breakfast and try to talk him into going for help. And if he still wouldn't talk to anyone, well, maybe she'd have to tell Hub.

# CHAPTER 28

It was the screaming that woke her: the sirens. Zoe bolted up and shoved back the curtain. In the distance she could see a huge cloud of gray smoke rising in the direction of the prairie. The flash of emergency vehicles glittered on the road, and there were more coming, wailing in the black night.

Zoe got out of bed, still in fleece pants and a T-shirt, stopping only to kick her feet into her shoes, and went down the hall.

"Zoe?" Nelia appeared in the door of her room, half-asleep. "What's the matter?"

"I have to get to the prairie."

"It's four in the morning."

"I know."

"Zoe!" Nelia called after her. But she didn't stop.

She took off running across open country toward the road. Firestorm: The word swept through her mind, dragging behind it all that she had heard from Hub about prairie fire. Flames as tall as buildings . . . faster than a horse . . . the dry grass . . . and if it gets out of control . . . if it gets out of control . . .

She was barely able to see where she was going, stumbling

over the uneven ground, falling then pushing herself back up to her feet and bulling her way forward, the taste of blood in her mouth. She was running toward the flames. Stupid. That was a stupid thing to do. She knew it. And only one thought in her mind: She had to get to Ivy.

She took the road instead of the path through the dark woods, running full out, even though her body ached with effort and her breath came in short gasps, her chest heaving. And still she felt like she wouldn't get there in time.

Now she was close enough to hear the roar. Heat rising, smoke stinging her eyes, choking her throat. No safety, she remembered that. No safety if the wind changes and the fire turns back. She should be watching for that. Watch the winds. Be ready to run the other way. Run toward water. But what if you're trapped?

There were two clusters of pulsing lights. One on the prairie, where a stand of old evergreens on a hill had gone up in a blaze, and one near the edge where firemen were arcing streams of water over the scattering of houses that could catch fire if the blaze got away from them.

She veered off toward the woods, where Hub would be. She would find him. He would know what to do. She ran as close as she could to the edge of the fire, but the heat kept beating her back. How quickly fire traveled, devouring everything: a dragon, all flaming tongue and teeth. If it gets out of control . . . if it turns back . . .

"Get the girl out of here!" someone shouted behind her. She felt like the hair was being singed off her arms. She was stupid, so stupid. She tried to get her thoughts to focus, but they bolted like frightened animals.

She ran behind the line of men, the yellow reflector jackets and hoses, searching their faces, looking for Hub. One after another, the wrong face.

"Where'd that kid come from?"

Someone reached out to grab her and she fought back, wrestling her way loose, running a few more steps before a pair of arms closed around her in a bear hug. From out of nowhere Hub appeared. Face black with ashes.

"Zoe," he said. The bear-hug man released her and she buried her face in Hub's barrel chest.

"You can't stay here," he said.

She could hear voices behind her, calling out orders, warning people off.

Hub looked her in the eye. "Go up to the house," he said. "You hear me? Call your mother. Let her know you're safe."

There was only one hope she could hold on to now. Ivy must have run. He would be hiding somewhere.

There must have been a power line down, because there were no lights when she reached the house. She picked her way across the yard in the moonlight and went down to the cellar, where Hub's office was, and pushed open the door.

The house was weeping. There was water dripping down from the ceiling and puddled on the floors. It must have come in through the cracks and crevices of the old frame when the firemen hosed it down. She put her hand on the damp stone wall, feeling her way along in the darkness.

"Ivy?" she called out. There was a musty smell, the scent of damp earth and hay. She walked over and pushed open the door to Hub's office. She had to shove hard and kick it before it opened because it was swollen shut. Soggy papers and books were scattered across the room. There was no sound except the water coming down through the light fixture, dripping onto Hub's desk.

"Ivy, are you here?"

There was no answer.

She pulled the door to Hub's office closed and turned to leave. Ivy stepped out of the darkness in front of her. He put his hand up to her mouth.

"You alone?" he whispered.

She nodded her head, breathing hard.

Ivy took his hand away.

"What's going on out there?" he asked.

"Firemen, police; they're everywhere."

"Did they put it out?"

"Not yet. It's dying down. They saved the houses."

Ivy exhaled. "Do they know I was the one?"

"The one what? What happened?"

"I lit a fire, fell asleep."

"Ivy . . ."

"I need help. I've got to get out of here."

"You have to tell them."

"And let them put me in juvie?" He was nervous, pacing. He looked like he was ready to bolt.

"It was an accident, Ivy. They'll understand that."

"I've been in trouble before. They're just looking for something to lock me up for." He stared at the ground.

"But you didn't mean to do it."

"No one will believe me."

"Hub will. They'll listen to him."

"I'm not taking the chance," Ivy said. "I know what it's like in juvie. I'd die in there." He glanced at the door, as though he might take off at any minute.

"Where will you go?"

"I don't know. I don't *know*. Hop a freight, maybe." He reached out and held her to him, heart pounding against her chest. "Come with me, Zoe."

She found Hub standing alone out on the prairie, just as the sun broke above the trees. The fire was out. The trucks were gone. The pungent smell of smoke hung in the air, biting at her nostrils and seeping into her clothes. Pete and a few sooty volunteers were scattered out on the ruined field with water packs on their backs, walking through the ashes, looking for still smoldering embers to put out. Hub stood off by himself, eyes sunken from a night without sleep.

"It will come back," Zoe said.

He looked out over the wasteland the fire had left: the blackened grass and the ruined flowers and seeds. "If people want it to. We're just lucky those houses didn't catch."

Zoe took a deep breath. "Do they know what happened?"

"The police think it was a campfire. Someone saw smoke earlier in the evening." Hub turned and faced her. "Ivy's dad said he didn't come home last night."

Hub looked out at the prairie. "You know where he is, don't you, Zoe?"

She could not lie to him. He would see right through her.

"I'll have enough problems convincing the zoning board that we need this prairie. It's not going to help if it turns out that someone I hired set fire to it and took off."

"It was an accident," Zoe said.

"That's why he needs to turn himself in. So people will believe him."

"All you care about is the prairie," Zoe said. "Who's going to protect Ivy?"

"You think I haven't tried before? His father told him he'd whip him if he opened his mouth, and Ivy backed down. I can't help him unless he turns his father in. He has to tell the truth."

Hub picked a cocoon that had somehow escaped the flames off a burned branch. He handed it to her. "Cecropia moth," he said. "They're easy pickings for the birds after a fire. Take it down to the river and put it on a willow tree so the caterpillars have something to eat when they hatch."

Zoe started to walk away, and Hub called out to her. "The best thing Ivy can do for himself right now is to come back. Tell him that, would you?"

Zoe didn't break down until her mother got out of the car and put her arms around her.

"My God, Zoe. I was so afraid."

"I tried to call you. The phone was out."

"Nelia told me she saw you leave."

"I'm sorry," Zoe said, "I know I shouldn't have—"

Her mother stopped her. She put her fingertips over Zoe's lips. "You're safe," she said. "That's the only thing that matters."

When they got home, Zoe's mother sent her upstairs to shower off the soot. Then she took the phone off the hook so she wouldn't have to answer any more worried phone calls.

Her mother made Ollie and Nelia breakfast, and sent them off to school. But she let Zoe stay home so they could both get some rest. "Sleep," her mother told her.

But she didn't.

Zoe waited until her mother went back to bed. Then she got up and went downstairs. If she was going to meet Ivy the following night at the edge of town, the way she'd promised, she was going to have to get ready now.

❖

What do you take with you when you leave? Take only what you can carry on your back. Nothing that isn't essential, nothing that will weigh you down. This is what her father had taught her, in all the leaving they had done. Let your boat be light. Turn the bow into the wind. And don't look back.

Take what you've learned: your memories, your stories. Take your daring, your strength. Take your courage. You will need them. But not your grief and pain, your fear and confusion. Throw them away. Abandon them. They will sink you if you let them. Lock them up and throw them over. Leave them behind. And don't look back. Whatever you do, don't look back.

Zoe closed the door to her room, took her backpack out of the closet, and spread the things she had gathered up from the kitchen on the bed: nuts and raisins, a few candy bars for emergencies, soap, water bottle. She added a towel, a few clothes, a compass. Maps, remember the maps. The tent; they would need shelter. She took the money she'd made from the prairie out of her bottom drawer. The prairie: ashes, smoke, stench of death. What had it looked like before, when it had been green and growing, alive with flowers, insects, birds? She had already forgotten.

*Don't look back.*

In the back of the drawer she saw Booda and pulled him out. She took a piece of paper and pencil out of her desk and wrote. "Dear Ollie, I have had many adventures, but there is no one I want to be with but you. I am home to stay. Love, Booda." She tucked the note under the ribbon around his neck and put him in Ollie's closet, where he would find the bear after she was gone.

❖

She considered taking the binoculars along but finally decided to leave them in her closet with a note that said they were Billy's.

*Take nothing with you that will weigh you down.*

Even though it was difficult for her, she wrote a note that said, simply, "Thank you."

She had been unfair to him. That was the truth.

There wasn't much she could give Nelia. She had everything. So Zoe took a photograph of the two of them out of her album. It was from when Nelia was eight and she was five. They were down on the waterfront, searching for beach glass. On the back she wrote, "You really are a good sister." She also wrapped up her set of Natural Wonder Bust Pads and wrote a note that said, "Give these to Miranda. I won't need them."

*Don't take the pain with you. Leave it behind.*

To Weezy she wrote a note that said, "Please take care of everyone."

And to her mother she wrote: "I'm sorry for not being what you wanted."

*Throw away your grief. It will sink you.*

When she was done, she put everything into her backpack and crammed it into the back of her closet, along with the notes she planned to put on her end table when she left.

She had told Ivy she'd meet him the following evening near the railroad tracks. There was nothing to do now but wait and pretend that everything was all right.

# CHAPTER 29

In the morning Zoe slipped out the back door and walked the path through the high grass at the edge of the field one last time. A group of sandhill cranes passed over her, headed home.

Not like her. She was homeless. Zoe had only thought of this word in connection with other people. But now it settled on her like dust. All she'd ever had were resting places. And it would be possible, she realized with a sudden wince of pain, to go her whole life and never find a place where she belonged.

She kept on walking until she reached the hawks' nest tree. It had been spared by the fire, but the hawks themselves were nowhere to be seen. They might have found a safe tree somewhere. Or they might be gone for good. There was no way of telling.

On the way back she walked down to the river and stopped, remembering with sudden clarity the trip her family had made to the area around Desolation Sound, north of Vancouver, just before her father had left for Alaska. It was a beautiful place, hemmed in on all sides by snowcapped mountains that rose up right from the water's edge. And there were endless islands where you could tie up and fish in secret inlets. But this trip had been nothing but trouble. The boat had been taking on water from a crack in the hull that should have been tended to before they left. Just past Queen's Reach the engine broke down. Her father wired it together, but he didn't trust it to hold.

They limped to shelter at Princess Louisa Inlet. The sun was going down behind the black mountains and the mooring buoys were already full of weekend boaters. One of them, a ruddy-faced man in a captain's hat, called out to them from the deck of a hulking cabin cruiser with the name *Roamin' Holiday* in curving gold letters across the stern. It was brand-new, glittering white fiberglass and polished chrome, at least twice the size of their boat, the *Cordelia*.

"There's a howler coming," he called from the upper deck. "We've been battling it all the way up from Halfmoon Bay. Better stay here until it's gone past."

"I don't mind a good storm!" her father shouted back over the sputtering of the engine.

"There's nothing good about this one." The man took his hat off and wiped his balding head with a clean white handkerchief. "Might be tough to weather in an old tug like that."

Her father put a hand on the faded white wheelhouse roof like you would pat the head of a child. "She's been through worse."

They had searched for an anchorage near Chatterbox Falls and hadn't found one that was solid enough. In the end they had settled for tying a stern line to the rock wall.

Zoe was handing her father tools as he bent over the engine, tinkering with his patch job, when her mother came up out of the galley.

"How does it look?" she asked.

He sat back and wiped his greasy hands on a rag. "It won't

get us home. But we should be all right until we get to the boatyard."

"Maybe we should stay here and wait the storm out. You'd have more time to work on it. At least here we know we're safe."

Her father glanced at the sheer cliffs rising up around them. "That depends," he said.

"What do you mean?"

"It depends on which way the storm comes. We're protected on three sides. But if the storm comes from the fourth direction, that way," he said, pointing at the way they'd come in, "we'll be smashed right up against those rocks."

"What will we do?" Zoe asked.

"There's nothing to worry about," her mother said. "It's not going to happen, Zoe."

Her father picked up his wrench and screwdriver and opened the toolbox to put them away. "If it comes from the fourth direction," he said calmly, "we'll cut anchor. Sail into the storm. Sometimes it's the safest place."

After breakfast Zoe went to school because she couldn't think of a good enough excuse not to. When the bus pulled up, she got on and sat down next to Miranda.

"Why didn't you call me, Zoe?" Miranda said, her voice concerned. "Your mom told me you were okay—when I finally got through to your house, that is. But when you didn't call back, I wasn't so sure."

Zoe shrugged. "I couldn't talk to anyone."

"What about the fire? Do you know what happened?" Miranda lowered her voice. "Everyone says it was Ivy."

"It was an accident." Zoe looked out the window. "That's all I know."

Zoe thought about just getting off the bus and walking away so she wouldn't have to face everyone. But the attendance office would call if she didn't show up.

Instead she went from class to class feeling numb, not listening. Her body kept moving through the day, answering questions, explaining, but her heart was so deep inside that nothing could touch it.

When she got home after school, Zoe went up to the attic to retrieve Virginia's flora and fauna book. She had decided to go see Hub, tell him she was quitting, and give him the book as a gift.

She had to search for the book, because she hadn't used it in a while and had forgotten where she'd put it. Zoe finally located it on top of a box of old photographs. When she lifted it up, something caught her eye. It was an old, yellowed newspaper article, tucked in between the stacks of curled and faded photos.

FOUR DEAD IN HEAD-ON COLLISION ON INTERSTATE 47. There were pictures under the headline: head shots of her grandparents, Annelise and William Lawson, and beneath them a photograph of a woman, Ellen Grunewald, holding her infant daughter, Karen.

She scanned the story: ". . . crossed the center line and ran head-on into a car driven by Grunewald . . . Lawson died several hours later . . . tests showed blood alcohol levels . . ."

*Grunewald.* She swallowed hard, and ran her eyes back to the beginning. "Hubert Grunewald, thirty-five, in critical but stable condition . . . wife and daughter killed instantly."

"Oh God," Zoe whispered.

*Throw away your grief. It will sink you.*

*Don't take the pain. Leave it behind.*

❖

Her mother was outside sweeping leaves out of the garage, her hair tied back with a blue bandana, when Zoe found her.

"Why didn't you tell me?"

"Tell you what?"

"Who else died in that crash besides your parents." Zoe held the newspaper article out, and her mother glanced at it, her face tight with pain.

"Why didn't you tell me who Hub was?"

"It wasn't anything you could fix, Zoe. What good would it do?"

"You let me go there day after day, working right alongside him, not even knowing?"

"Zoe, I'm sorry."

"Why did you do this to me?" She searched her mother's face for an answer, and saw that she had none. "Why couldn't you just tell me the truth?"

Hub wasn't there when Zoe went up to the prairie late in the afternoon. She went down to the cellar and called out but no one answered, so she went back outside and waited.

She saw Hub's car pull into the driveway and went over to meet him.

"Where've you been?" she asked, as he got out of the car.

"The zoning board decided to move up their hearing."

"And?"

"We lost the first round."

"So, what? They can just come in and bulldoze it?"

"Not yet. Not right away."

"What are you going to do?"

He shrugged. "The same things we've always done. Send out

letters. Raise money. Try to muster some support downstate. Maybe even take them to court. It's never forever. You have to keep fighting."

She turned her face away. "What's the point?"

Hub slammed the car door and turned toward her. "There are worse things to do with your life than fighting a losing battle."

"Like what?"

He caught her eyes, flushing her out.

"Like giving up."

Zoe looked away. There was nothing to say, nothing to do, nothing that would make things better for him. "I came to tell you I'm not coming to work anymore."

He looked at her, his brow furrowing. "Any particular reason?"

She shrugged. "You don't need me. And anyway, I've caused enough trouble." She held the book out to him. "I want you to have this."

Hub took the book and read the title on the spine. "You sure you can part with it?"

Zoe shrugged.

He opened the front cover and flipped through the pages. She saw, too late to repair it, that she had made one final mistake.

Zoe watched Hub reading the name inside the cover, Annelise Lawson, written in her grandmother's own handwriting. Hub looked at Zoe's despairing eyes. He was silent a long time.

"Is this why you're leaving?"

She clenched her teeth.

"I know who you are," he said. "I've known all along."

"I'm sorry," she said.

"You don't owe me an apology."

"You hate me, don't you?"

"No, I don't. I don't feel anything but grateful to you for what you've tried to do. I don't hate your grandfather, either." Hub looked out at the afternoon light gathering in the trees and the burned field in the distance, then turned back and met her gaze. "You can't hold on, Zoe. Not to hate. Not even to love. You kill things that way. There's only one freedom. Forgiveness. And sometimes the hardest thing to do is to forgive yourself."

She met Ivy that night at the railroad bridge, a massive skeleton of rusted iron that spanned the river outside of town. They had often seen freight trains slow down and sit on the sidetrack there, waiting for a commuter to pass through before lumbering on their way west. On warm summer days they would lie on the slope near the river and watch the trains go by, counting the cars, guessing what was in them, reading the names painted on the side: Burlington Northern, Rail Canada, Union Pacific. A game for dreamers, she thought. But now she saw that for Ivy it was different. He must have been dreaming of escape.

He was sitting on the ground, his back against a tree, and pushed himself up to his feet when he saw her approaching.

"What took you so long?" he asked. "I thought maybe you weren't coming."

He looked down at the tent bag she had under her arm. "Where's the rest of your stuff?"

"Back home."

A shield went up inside his eyes.

"I can't leave, Ivy. And I can't stand to lose you."

He turned away from her. "I don't know why I expected you to be different."

"Hub will help you if you turn yourself in. He told me so."

Ivy turned back toward her and his eyes flashed. "You talked to him about me?"

"He won't let them send you to juvie. And he won't let your dad hurt you. He'll back you up, Ivy."

"No one's going to believe me, Zoe. Hub can't change that."

"We'll get someone to help you—a lawyer."

"And while they figure it out, I'll be in the detention center. You think my dad would pay the bond—even if he had it?" He paced back and forth in the hulking shadow of the boxcars alongside him. "No, I'm not going to let them lock me up. I'd rather be dead." There was the keen grating noise of metal scraping metal as the train suddenly shuddered and lurched forward. His eyes shifted to a flat car that was moving toward them from down the line.

Zoe bit her lip. The smell of diesel and grease clawed at her nostrils. She reached into her pocket and held out a crumpled wad of bills.

"I don't want your money."

"Take it." She reached up to him, and he wrapped her in his arms, his lips pressed against hers, tears hot against her face, and she didn't know if they were his or her own.

He took the tent and stuffed it into his backpack, and hiked the pack up to his shoulder. Then he stumbled backward away from her, toward the tracks. Ivy hefted his pack up and pitched it onto the flat car, feet pedaling to keep up with the moving train. He turned back toward her one last time, then took a run at the flat car and grabbed for it, pushing himself up and dangling, half-on and half-off, for a minute before he could get a knee up and push his way up to his feet. He stood facing her as the train picked up speed, rumbling forward, as relentless as fate.

Zoe held her arms out, holding the empty space where he had

been. She thought until the last moment that he would change his mind, jump off the train and run back to her. But instead the night swallowed him up.

She woke the next morning to a thick frost: each blade of grass coated in white and the ache of change hanging in the air like mist. Ollie hung around the table while she picked at breakfast, begging her to take him back to the fields before they left for school. He followed her, simpering and hanging on to her arm when she got up to scrape cold oatmeal into the garbage. She finally told him she'd go. But it was only so she would be left alone later on to bury herself in her room and escape his endless sucking need.

He ran ahead of her, kicking at the leaves, which crackled to dust under their feet as they scuffed across them. Ollie had a red knit hat on, pulled low over his ears, and a heavy blue jacket. A flock of red-winged blackbirds rose up as they walked toward them, twenty at least, taking flight into the clear light of September. The trees, grasses, and shrubs were starting to take on their own brilliant reds and yellows. It was beautiful. She could see that. But she couldn't feel it. The beauty did not seep into her skin like it once had. It was like the weather in a distant city, something that didn't have any effect on your life.

She walked back toward the woods, calling for Ollie, who had managed to get out of sight. He didn't answer. "Ollie?" She walked faster. "Ollie!" She broke into a run, wishing she had paid more attention.

She found him sitting cross-legged, head down. He had taken off his jacket and wrapped it around something he was holding in his lap.

"What is it, Ollie?"

"He's cold," he said. "I'm warming him up so he'll come back to life."

Zoe reached out and pulled back a corner of the jacket and saw what Ollie was holding. It was a hawk, one of the young males. He was so perfect that at first she didn't realize he was dead—his beautiful white and tawny patterned feathers, the curve of his hooked beak, and his dull unseeing eyes. There was only a single drop of dried blood on the bridge of his beak and the strange angle of his neck to tell you there was something wrong. He must have collided with something, confused perhaps by the smoke.

"We ought to bury him," she said.

"You can't put him in the ground. What if he's afraid and there's no one to help him?"

"He's dead, Ollie. There's nothing we can do for him."

Ollie scowled at her. "He's going to come back to life."

They carried him home and put him in an old glass aquarium they found in the attic. Ollie spread sawdust on the bottom, and cut a blanket out of red felt with his dull yellow school scissors, his tongue sticking up over his lip to help him concentrate. Zoe laid the bird down gently, head hanging limply over the side of her hand, surprised at how light it felt. Ollie covered it with the blanket so that only the hawk's vacant eyes and once fierce beak stuck out at the top.

He insisted on keeping the glass coffin in his room, near his bed. He would lie on the floor next to it, his chin propped up on his hands, staring through the glass, as though he expected at any moment to see the bird fling off the blanket and rise up into the air. It was only the cold snap that convinced Ollie not to leave the window open all day so the bird could fly out while he was at school.

He was whiny and didn't want to leave the house in the mornings. Whenever his mother tried to broach the subject of a funeral, he would shout her down.

"No*ooo*. He's asleep," he would say. "Like sleeping beauty."

"You mean in a coma?"

"A *sleep*," he'd say, louder this time, as if she were deaf and possibly dumb.

"He's starting to smell, Ollie," Nelia finally said.

"People in comas can smell too," he muttered at her.

He was moody and wouldn't eat. He had gone back to sucking his thumb, and when Zoe took him outside, he would wander listlessly under the tree instead of playing. On Friday he got off the bus excitedly and ran to the backyard. Zoe thought he'd finally given up and forgotten all about the hawk. But his class had made wishing kites that day, writing three wishes down on yellow index cards and tying them to the kite's tail. Every one of Ollie's cards said the same thing: "I wish my hawk would come back to life." He spent all afternoon outside, dragging the kite across the lawn trying to launch it, even though there was no wind.

"Just how long are you going to let this go on?" Nelia asked her mother. They were sitting at the kitchen table, peeling apples for sauce that Weezy was going to put up.

Her mother shrugged.

"We could have him stuffed," Nelia said.

"Don't you have any feelings at all?" Zoe shouted.

"Well, we can't go on like this forever. What are we going to do when we start having guests? Tell them, 'Your room is at the end of the hall—next to the dead animal'?"

"I hope to God you grow a heart someday, Nelia."

"It's not a kindness to let him believe that bird is going to come back to life again, Zoe. Dead is dead. You know that as well as I do. And sooner or later, Ollie . . ."

Miranda came over on Saturday and went up to Ollie's room to sit vigil with him.

"He was a good hawk, Ollie," Miranda said. "A hero."

Ollie's somber face bobbed up and down.

"Remember when that whole flock of crows showed up, squawking their heads off, and he flew right into them and chased them off?"

"I loved him," Ollie said.

Miranda nodded. "A bird like that deserves a hero's funeral. Like the Vikings. They put dead warriors in a boat with all their treasures and launched them on the ocean, so they could sail to the afterlife."

Ollie's face softened. "Can you drive me to the ocean?"

Miranda looked at Zoe, in over her head.

"Can you?"

Zoe remembered the leaf. "The river will take him there, Ollie," she said.

Ollie put his head close to the glass and listened. "I think he wants to go."

They stood together near the bank of the river, Billy and their mother, Nelia, Zoe, Miranda, and Weezy in a tight circle. Ollie had made a boat for the hawk; Billy had helped him nail an old shoe box to a piece of wood. He lay the bird down in the boat under his red blanket, with a chicken leg for a snack and a rabbit's foot key chain for good luck.

Then he set the boat in the water and gave it a shove. The

boat drifted out into the center of the river as Ollie ran down the bank after it, waving good-bye. It bobbed on the current, tilting and listing, headed, Zoe realized suddenly, toward a willow tree that hung over the bank near the bridge. Her throat tightened. There was nothing she could do.

The boat crashed into the branches that dragged in the water and capsized. Zoe ran down to the bank. She could see the tawny body of the hawk and the red blanket caught in a web of sticks and leaves just beneath the surface of the water.

Her feet started moving and she plunged into the river, cold biting at her legs. She wasn't thinking, just pushing forward against the current. She held on to a branch with one hand and leaned out over the river, shoving her other hand beneath the icy water and reaching down, untangling the feathered hump from the branches and setting it free.

Her mother waited on the bank, her arms open. Zoe waded back to her. She shut her eyes and pressed her icy face to her mother's neck, her body overcome with violent shaking from the cold mixed with sobs. "I don't ever want to love anything again," she said. "It hurts so much."

"I know, Zoe." Her mother pulled her close. "I know."

Zoe remembered now what had happened on the last trip they'd taken to Desolation Sound. And why it was important, why she had to remember it.

All night the boat had tugged on her moorings, torn between the anchor and the stern line that held her to the shore. Zoe had been huddled in the bed up front, lulled to sleep by the creaking and groaning of the boat against the ropes, when the storm broke. Someone was shouting for help, a sound like a wailing train bearing down on them.

The boat lurched side to side as Zoe crawled through the darkness toward the stairs that led up to the deck, bumping her head on the table as she dodged silverware, cups, and cushions that were tumbling from the cabinets where they had been stowed. She could hear the sound of Nelia retching, and looked back to see her leaning over the toilet, pulling her hair back from her face as the door banged back and forth wildly, open and shut.

Zoe struggled up the stairs, gripping the sides of the portal to steady herself, following the sound of scraping up on deck. A curtain of rain hit her in the face, stinging her skin as she threw herself forward. Sheets of salt spray were pounding down onto the deck as the boat strained in the howling wind. Trees waved violently back and forth on the cliffs. She could just barely make out the shape of a boat—the one they had seen the day before—battered against the rocks by enormous waves.

Her mother was holding on to her father's arm, pleading with him not to set out, while he struggled to bring the anchor back on board. He must have gotten it up, because the boat careened wildly on its stern line.

Her father turned and shouldered past her mother, reaching for the line, hacking at it with a knife when he couldn't untie it. Zoe leaned out over the back of the boat, waves breaking over her, grabbing in both hands the rope that held them to shore, just as it was about to break loose. Her father dropped the knife and threw his arms around her waist, straining to pull her back to the safety of the deck.

"Let go, Zo," he shouted at her. *"Let go!"*

# CHAPTER 30

Let me do one," Oliver begged. Nelia and Zoe were sitting at the table in the dining room, stringing cranberries for the two spruce trees at the end of the driveway. It was Weezy's idea to get the decorations started, even though it was early November, because their first guests were arriving the day before Thanskgiving.

Oliver orbited noisily around them, snatching up any cranberries that rolled near the edge of the table and hoarding them in his pocket. He made a pass at Nelia's pile, but she wrapped her spare arm around them protectively.

"Where's your Christmas spirit, Nelia?" Weezy got up and went to the window, where the light was better to thread a needle.

"I like to keep it packed away until *after* Thanksgiving," Nelia said. "I don't wish to associate myself with the crass commercialism of our consumer culture. Unlike *you*, I might add."

"Come over here, Ollie," Zoe said.

He careened toward her, his face beaming with the pleasure

of having been summoned for once instead of nudged away.

"Thumbs up."

He thrust both of them into the air, and Zoe slipped her thimble onto one. Then she steadied a berry on the table while Ollie, wearing a look of fierce determination, managed to poke Zoe's needle through it.

"Nice work," Zoe said. "You even missed my fingers."

"Let me try again," Ollie said.

"Maybe you should quit while you're ahead."

"You can't stop with one," Nelia said. "One is not a string."

Zoe glared at Nelia. She held another berry on the table between two fingers and braced herself as Ollie jabbed at it with the needle.

"Push! Push!" he encouraged himself.

Zoe opened her eyes when she heard him grunt in triumph. She pulled the thread all the way through until the second cranberry nestled against the first one.

"My string is going to be bigger than yours," Ollie told Nelia. He fumbled in his chipmunk cheek pockets, pulled out a fistful of berries, then a second fistful, and smacked them onto the table.

"Let's let Nelia have a turn at holding the berry," Zoe said, pushing Ollie's string in her direction.

"Weezy's right," her mother said. "Handmade decorations are best. They feel homey." She was sitting in the wingback chair by the fireplace, digging through a dusty box of decorations she'd found in the attic.

"And that's another thing I have a problem with," Nelia said. "False advertising. We're not exactly the sort of family you'd expect at a bed-and-breakfast. The kind you'd pay good money to stay with. If people want to hear squabbling and fighting all day long, they can just stay home."

"Ahhh, but here they can have all that, *plus* the evergreen swags on the mantel. That's the beauty of it." Her mother dug in the box and pulled out a white plastic reindeer with one raised hoof. His black painted eyeballs and nose had nearly worn off. "Remember Miss Lavergne, Weezy? Something about Christmas always makes me think of her."

"Maybe because that was when we ruined her life," Weezy said.

"Who was Miss Lavergne?" Zoe asked.

"Our Sunday school teacher. Anyway, she was until Weezy and I spoiled the Christmas pageant. After that I think she gave up and decided to let us wallow in our original sin. Although she actually brought the whole thing on herself, if you ask me, giving us those parts in the Christmas play."

"What part did she give you?" Zoe asked her mother.

"Mary, the mother of God."

"Talk about miscasting," Nelia said.

"Actually, your mother made a wonderful Mary," Weezy said. "She looked downright holy, sitting up there in her long robes with Joseph, gazing down at baby Jesus in the manger. You'd never know it was really her."

"Was it the real Jesus?" Ollie asked.

"Oh, no, it was one of your mother's dolls."

"And it wasn't the real Joseph, either," Weezy said. "It was this little troublemaker named Ralph Waldo Duffy. Ralph Waldo is the one who really ruined the pageant. He picked up the baby Jesus by the feet, and your mother stood up in front of God and everybody and yelled, 'Joseph, put Jesus down before I smack you.' Even then she had the makings of a good mother." Weezy sucked on the thread one more time and finally managed to thrust it through the eye of the needle.

"That wasn't what made Miss Lavergne give up her Sunday school career, Weezy. You were the one who finished her off."

"What did Weezy play?"

"She was an angel of the Lord. You know, the one who comes upon the shepherds who were abiding with their flocks? It was a great part, because every year they lowered the angel of the Lord down from the rafters on a pulley. Weezy begged for that part."

"I did not. Miss Lavergne begged me to take it. I was the only one who wasn't afraid to fly."

"Well, either way, it was a disaster."

"And not my fault."

"What happened?" Zoe asked.

"Weezy had to sit there in the rafters through most of the performance, waiting in her halo, gauzy sleeves, and big golden wings. You were so proud of that halo, Weezy."

"Pride goeth before a fall," Weezy said.

"But when it was time for them to lower her from the rafters, the rope got stuck. She was dangling there at the top of the stage, and all you could see were those skinny legs of hers, bicycling in the air. And to make it worse, she was wearing a pair of dirty tennis shoes, because her feet got cold in sandals. The shepherds just stood there with their mouths open, gaping, while Weezy's feet swung back and forth over their heads, and all the while she was saying "Fear not. Fear not" over and over, because she was so upset that she had forgotten the rest of her lines.

"What happened then?"

"I don't remember," Weezy said. "It's a repressed memory at this point."

"I remember," their mother said. "Miss Lavergne gathered

up the heavenly host, which had scattered in confusion, screaming, and hurried them onstage and started them singing 'Glory to God in the highest, and on earth peace, good will toward men.' But she couldn't hold their attention because every so often Weezy's kicking feet would go by, about an inch from their halos. Then they brought down the curtain. And you could hear Miss Lavergne behind it, yelling at Weezy—who was still dangling from the rafters—telling her, 'This is the word of the Lord, Louisa Miller. You do not edit the word of the Lord.' And then you could hear Mr. Redler, the Sunday school superintendent, calling out, 'Somebody cut her down, for God's sake.' And Miss Lavergne told him not to take the name of the Lord in vain, especially with little ears all around. And he yelled, 'Judge not that you be not judged,' and they started this kind of Bible war, flinging scripture back and forth at each other like hand grenades."

Weezy spread her cranberry string out on the table and looked at it with deep satisfaction. "That part, I do remember," she said. "Mr. Redler and his judge not. And I remember the part about not messing with the word of the Lord, which, by the way, I think Miss Lavergne was completely wrong about. If you had to edit the whole lot of it down to two words, 'fear not' would do nicely."

Zoe had spent the last few weekends helping Hub process seeds, spreading them out on long plywood tables to dry. It was so cold down underground that Zoe's fingers went numb, even when she wore a sweatshirt, a wool hat, and thick cotton gloves.

But still, it was a comfort to see the rows of seeds in bags piling up on the shelves in the storage room, with the names of each plant written on the labels in Zoe's own large block print.

It would all come back. She knew this now. The burned fields looked like death itself. But by April the singed earth would be dotted with tender green shoots, springing back from the living roots.

It will come back. She told herself this, whenever the gray skies, cold wind, and brittle brown fields weighed too heavily on her. Death won't win out. The seeds will be scattered. The roots are deep. Life will come back.

The days were getting shorter. By the time Zoe finished up at four, the sun was already sinking toward the horizon.

"Need a lift?" Hub asked her as she was getting ready to leave.

"I'm fine."

She watched him get into his car, turn out of the driveway, pass the row of ancient oak trees, and disappear over the hill, then she walked across the road from the house and set off on foot across the prairie.

Zoe zipped her jacket up all the way to her chin, plunged her hands into her pockets, and hunched her shoulders against the wind as she walked down the hill toward the path that led through the woods. It looked as though all the life had been sucked from the world. The sky over her head was like a storm at sea: billowy gray and full of foreboding. Everything else—the trees, the grasses that had been battered by the wind on the prairie, even the animals—had faded to a dull brown, like the raw, scraped dirt of a newly plowed field. The color of earth and the color of water: That was all that was left.

Zoe trudged across the frozen dirt, watching the birds flail into the wind. The travelers would all be gone soon. Everything was either leaving or retreating underground to wait for better times, leaving a lonely silence behind. What if they didn't come back? It was a harsh thought, and she pushed it out of her mind as fast as it had dropped in. But what if there was nothing to come back to? It could happen.

Once the sky had been dark with passenger pigeons. Once you could walk across the rivers on the salmons' backs.

The path curved off to the right, and when she rounded it, a dark shape passed in front of her. Her heart speeded up. A word slunk through her mind. Something she'd heard from Billy, when she'd asked him why he had a shotgun in the cab of his truck. "Coyotes. Lotta them been seen around here lately."

She had seen coyotes before. Edge species, her father called them—things that lived in the borderlands, not really in one world or another. That's why they survived when other things didn't.

Her first impulse was to run, but she was stopped by the thought that the coyote might chase her. She could have backed down the path the way she had come, but it was already late, and she resented having to give way when this was, after all, her place as much as his. And there was something in her that was drawn to him, something that wanted to know him.

She stood her ground, watching, listening to her own breathing. Was he still there, looking at her? She was sure she could smell him. A mix of pity and terror filled her. He was, after all, alone like her, a wanderer, out of place, just looking for a way to get by.

She took a tentative step forward and caught a glimpse of him, standing in among the trees, perfectly still, dark eyes glistening and focused on her. He had a matted winter coat that looked just like the prairie this time of year, a mottle of brown and beige, the color of seed heads and dead leaves. He was not beautiful. But there was a strangeness about him that made her heart race. What was it like to see with those eyes? She was so close to him, close enough to see the thin hairs on the back of his head and the way his nostrils flared when he breathed. She took another step toward him, but he bolted into the woods and disappeared.

"What do you see in the prairie?" she had asked Hub that day when they stood on the hill above the prairie.

"An orphan," he had said.

Like her. Like the coyote. Like everything wild.

She had come to love it. This unbeautiful place, this orphan, needed her.

She was a seed that had landed and sunk roots into the black earth, something blown there on the wind. She was an edge species with a foot in both worlds. She might not stay there forever. Maybe things wouldn't work out. Maybe one day she would have to—or want to—leave. Things were uncertain.

She didn't go home right away. Instead she turned out onto the road and didn't stop until she got to the top of the hill. "If you're ever lost," her father had told her, "go to the highest place you can find. Then look down and see if you can tell where you've come from and where you should go next."

From the hilltop, now, she could see all the things that mattered to her. To the west and north there was the darkness of the woods and the prairie, dead on the surface but alive underneath, waiting to come back. To the south, off in the distance, she could see her house. And she noticed something else. There was a line that led from her house through the pond and the woods to the prairie. Her grandmother's garden was the middle ground, the gate.

The lights had come on in her house. She could imagine Weezy and her mother working in the kitchen, Nelia and

Oliver setting the dining room table. She loved them, and one day she would lose them. Love and loss were two faces of one coin. When you found that coin and reached out to pick it up, to make it your own, you had to take both sides.

Zoe put her arms out wide. It had begun to snow. She turned her face up to catch the flakes as they fell, and she saw in the gray sky above her a lone bird, a heron, like a great ship circling, legs dangling, wings stroking the air. It made a few passes over her head, and then it slipped into the misted clouds. She felt like she was melting into the air around her.

Improbable things happen. Things die and return. People who are lost can still help you find your way in the world. And life comes back from the roots.

Those were some of the things she'd learned. But she also knew this: There are some questions you carry with you your whole life, holding them close and dying without ever finding the answers for them. And maybe you learned to love them, too.

Zoe walked back down the hill that stretched before her, eyes focused on the road ahead. When she reached the edge of town and saw her house, Zoe stopped. There was someone waiting on her porch, half hidden by the trees. Even through the shadows, even at a distance, she knew it was him. And she started running for home.